THE
FORGOTTEN
GIRLS

A.J. RIVERS

The Forgotten Girls
Copyright © 2025 by A.J. Rivers

All rights reserved. Without limiting the rights under copyright reserved above, no part of this publication may be reproduced, stored in or introduced into retrieval system, or transmitted, in any form, or by any means (electronic, mechanical, photocopying, recording, or otherwise) without the prior written permission of both the copyright owner and the above publisher of this book.

This is a work of fiction. Names, characters, places, brands, media, and incidents are either the products of the author's imagination or are used fictitiously. The author acknowledges the trademarked status and trademark owners of various products referenced in this work of fiction, which have been used without permission. The publication/use of these trademarks is not authorized, associated with, or sponsored by the trademark owners.

PROLOGUE

Ava's pulse echoed the thud of her footfalls against the wet pavement. Rain fell in sheets and showed no signs of letting up anytime soon. The pavement was slippery and under the heavy rainfall, the already dim alleyways turned into a treacherous labyrinth of shadow broken only by the occasional, brief illumination from distant streetlights.

Detective Reinhold kept up admirably even though his breath came in short bursts as the rugged terrain of the city's underbelly played havoc on his aging knees and stressed his smoker's lungs. As they turned the corner into the third dark alley, he motioned for Ava to take the lead. "Don't let him out of your sight," he panted as she pulled ahead of him, nodding to preserve her own breath.

The suspect, merely a dark figure ahead of her, darted with a suddenness that left Ava struggling to keep him in her view.

The rain pelted against her face and melted her clothes to her body as she ran harder. The city revealed itself in slices as they passed openings too narrow to traverse with speed. If he escaped, they might never find him again.

Reinhold caught up as Ava slipped on something and crashed her right side into the ragged brick wall. Rebounding, she nearly hit Reinhold taking the lead again. It was only a matter of seconds before she passed him, and the suspect was taking another alley.

In the longer alley, the suspect darted ahead and disappeared behind a row of overflowing dumpsters that reeked of filth and rot.

"Left!" Reinhold shouted.

Ava veered sharply to the left. She splashed through puddles and the water shot up all around her feet in plumes that soaked her legs even more. As soon as the chase was over, she was going to take the longest, hottest shower of her life. The wail of sirens was closing in, but not fast enough. She wanted to yell for the man to stop, but that had not worked for her or Reinhold before, and she needed to preserve energy and air. There was no way the man would go down without a fight, and Reinhold was falling farther behind. She would have to deal with the suspect.

The man glanced over his shoulder, and in the quick flash of light as he passed a low window, Ava saw that his eyes were wide with panic. The game was nearly up. She was closing in, and he was running out of places to go. The expansive maw of the city neared, and it could either swallow him whole, or chew him up and spit him out on the pavement. Traffic grumbled and revved, horns blared sporadically, and the police sirens that had been closing in became distant again.

The man vaulted over a low fence with the ease of a cat, but Ava was on his heels, scaling it with a desperate leap. They landed in a courtyard. The narrow space amplified the sound of their breaths and the staccato pounding of the rain.

Reinhold stumbled through a side gate, cursing loudly and gasping for breath. "Corner him!" he shouted, sounding stronger than he looked.

The man sprinted toward a fire escape. Ava lunged. Her fingers grazed the back of his jacket. She tightened her grip and yanked him back just as he reached for the ladder. He twisted and swung wildly at her face, but she ducked, countering with a swift, hard jab to the ribs. The breath whooshed out of him as he doubled into the pain and simultaneously threw a fist up toward her chin. She flung her head to the side and jabbed again, that time aiming for his solar plexus.

"Enough!" Reinhold's voice boomed and bounced off the walls as he closed the distance. The handcuffs in his left hand dangled and glinted under the sparse streetlight.

Panting for breath, the suspect looked at Reinhold and then at Ava. His eyes flicked back and forth as if he were watching the world's fastest game of tennis. It was a calculating look, and Ava turned to fully face him.

"Don't do it," she warned, reaching for her gun.

He flashed a quicksilver grin and in a flurry of movement, he turned, lunged, kicked off the wall, using the narrow alley to propel himself upward, slipping out of reach.

Reinhold cursed, leaping for the suspect, but the man's agility was unmatched by either of them. He scrambled up the fire escape, disappearing into the night.

Ava stood panting beside Reinhold, his anger eking from him in waves. Rain mingled with sweat on her forehead and ran into her eyes, stinging as the echo of footfalls overhead faded into the vastness of New York City's noise.

"Damn it," Reinhold said through gritted teeth. "We lost him."

It was true that the man had disappeared leaving only the rain and their frustration behind, but she could still be optimistic, even if it was only for Reinhold's sake. "We'll catch him. We'll get him, Reinhold."

"You sound so damn sure." Irritably, he flicked water from his face and turned with his arms wide, looking down. "Damn mess. Damn man. Damn case," he muttered as he trekked back through the puddles. He slammed the gate wide and continued grumbling.

Ava caught up with him. "We need to go back to the scene. What was he doing there, anyway, you think?"

"Don't have a clue."

"He had his hand under a loose floorboard under the radiator."

"And his little parkour escape back there shows me how he got into Archer Vale's artist loft without being captured on any of the security cameras."

"Or being seen by anyone inside the building," Ava said, dodging a sketchy pile of refuse. "I want to go by there and see what he was searching for and then I want to go take a shower."

"I second that," he said. "You leave in the morning, right?"

"I do. My flight is at seven. Sal wouldn't even try to get me approved for more than three days."

Reinhold looked at his watch. "You might get a shower before you have to leave."

Ava jerked out her phone in a near panic. "Two in the morning?" she exclaimed. "We best get a move on. I'm not missing that shower or my flight."

Not finding anything that yielded any answers to Reinhold's case, Ava would leave the city with more questions than answers. The only thing she knew was that the culprit of the Art Murders was still around and was still active. Who, what, and why were unanswered. All they had were wild theories that would not hold up under scrutiny, but Reinhold was tenacious. If anyone could dig up a viable lead, or come up with a workable theory, it would be him.

CHAPTER ONE

Sal stepped out of her office, pecked on the glass beside Ava's door, and motioned her out.

"What's up?" Ava asked, gladly stepping away from the paperwork and out the door.

"The whole team needs to hear this. Come on." Sal went through the doorway to the bullpen. "Listen up, people. We got an important one here."

Always up for fieldwork over paperwork, Ava had a sinking feeling in her gut about the forthcoming announcement. She had only been back in Fairhaven two days, and already something important enough to get Sal upset had landed in their laps.

"The Baltimore Chief of Police, Thomas Panko, called. A federal employee has been murdered, and he's asked us to step in and help with the case. Customs and Border Protection Agent Ethan Holt was found murdered in his home this morning. You need to get there ASAP."

"Customs and Border Protection?" Santos asked with a bewildered expression.

"He lives at 436 Fells Point Place in Baltimore." Sal turned and handed Ava the file. "Take who you need. The whole team, if you think you need to. Holt is a federal agent; treat this as you would if he were one of our own."

Ava took the file and nodded grimly. "We'll leave right away. Is the chief holding the crime scene?"

"He is, but he can't hold it for long."

"Got it."

Ava and the team rushed to Fells Point Place, making the hour drive in just a little over twenty-five minutes.

Fells Point Place was an affluent neighborhood near the water at the end of South Gay Street. Federal employees and low-level, local politicians seemed to make up the brunt of the locality.

Ashton closed his laptop as Ava parked and unbuckled her seatbelt. "There are two city council members, the Assessor, and one municipal judge all living in Fells Point Place," he said. "The other sixty seem to be federal employees and family members of the politicians living here."

"Did you find anything on our Ethan Holt?" Ava asked, getting out.

Ashton and Metford got out, both turning to watch as Dane pulled in behind them. "Not much. What's already in the file. He works for CBP overseeing the inspection of imports at Patapsco Bay Terminal. He's worked there for twelve years. No problems at work or with police. No priors that I saw in the prelim search. I can dig deeper, if you want." He made ready to open the laptop again.

"No, that's fine for now. Thank you," Ava said. She waited for Santos and Dane to join them, and they all made their way to the door of the single-family, single-level home, where cops, forensic agents, and others hurried back and forth as they worked the scene.

Chief Panko stood by the front door with a man. They spoke animatedly, and Ava figured they were still trying to hash out the scene together in a way that made sense to them.

She held up her badge as she stepped closer. "Special Agent James," she said. Tilting her head toward her team, she said. "My team. What do you have?"

Panko thanked them for arriving so quickly, and then Detective Coffey ushered them inside to the scene as he spouted every fact he knew about the crime, which weren't many.

At the bedroom door, he held up a hand to halt Ava and the team. He motioned inside for the cop to step out. The lanky man nodded as he passed the team. "Can we get the room?" Coffey asked the forensic unit.

"We're not finished, Detective," a severe-looking woman replied as she stopped her crew from exiting. "We'll be finished in a while. I'll let you know." She turned back to her work.

"Well, I need the room now. Why don't you haul your asses out and stand in the hall for a minute?"

The woman spun, glaring. Before she could retaliate, Coffey pointed to Ava. "Got a whole team of FBI here, and they need to see the scene. Without you all standing in their way." He smiled, but it looked like a predator's grin. There was nothing friendly about it.

The woman didn't bother smiling. She shifted her gaze from Coffey to Ava. "I trust you know how to navigate a scene to preserve its integrity." She pulled off her gloves.

"Part of the training," Ava said without expression.

"Lots of things are, and lots of things aren't put into practice once the teacher isn't looking over your shoulder." The woman's eyebrows inched up a fraction. It was the closest thing to a genuine expression, other than annoyance, she had shown.

"Jesus, Mary, and Joseph, Blaire," Coffey said. He motioned once, hard, toward the hallway. "Now?" It wasn't really a question even though he delivered it as such.

Blaire frowned at him as she motioned her team out of the room. She walked out last, holding Coffey's scowl without flinching.

"Sorry about that," Coffey said. "She was never properly socialized as a child." He chuckled nervously.

"Thank you," Ava said. "I think we have it from here, Detective Coffey."

For a moment, confusion registered on his face. After a few blinks, the fog must have cleared and he realized Ava was dismissing him. Clearing his throat and trying to hide an angry expression, he stepped out into the hall with forensics. The sound of his muttered cursing diminished as he made his way in the other direction.

Ethan had been a handsome man. Even death had not taken that from him. "Probably asleep when the attack happened," she said.

Dane, leaning very close to the victim's hand, agreed. "Looks like only light superficial wounds." She pointed to the thin cuts on his hand and wrist.

Metford pointed to Ethan's center mass, namely his chest area. "Looks like a good-sized blade. If the attacker got that in his heart with the first or second blow, Ethan probably couldn't fight back much."

"That's why he's still almost in the center of the bed," Ashton said. "Instinct would have driven him away from the pain, and if the attack was prolonged, he would have gone off this side of the bed."

"But he didn't," Santos said. "What did you get into, Ethan?" she asked the corpse.

Ava wanted to smile. Finally, her team was working together, and at least one of them seemed to process parts of the scene the same way she did. Ava often asked the dead victim at a scene what had happened, what they had gotten themselves into, and who would have a reason to kill them. She never expected a corpse to answer, naturally, but it was her way of slipping into the POV of the victim, even if just a little. Sometimes, that little slip was all she needed to see something in a whole new light, and that often led to new and better leads that solved cases.

"There's no broken window, no forced entry," Ava said. "He's sleeping in his bed, which indicates he didn't suspect anything like this was in the works. How did the attacker gain entry?"

"Maybe he left a door unlocked," Metford suggested. "It's a nice neighborhood, low crime rate; you heard Ashton in the car."

Ava shook her head. "I don't think a federal employee would leave a door or a window unlocked, no matter how good their neighborhood is."

"He worked for CBP, not the FBI or CIA," Metford countered.

"If there was no forced entry, and he didn't leave a door unlocked, maybe he had someone spending the night," Santos said.

"The report says there was no door unlocked when they arrived. They had to break the front lock to get in, and there's nothing to suggest anyone was spending the night. Besides, this doesn't look like the work of a jealous girlfriend," Ava said.

Dane turned and grinned at her. "Maybe it wasn't his girlfriend. Gotta cover every angle, remember?"

"Doesn't matter; there's nothing here that seems to belong to anyone else."

"Won't know for sure until the DNA testing is complete," Ashton said.

Ava sighed. "From all appearances, Ethan Holt had a good job, was financially secure, was handsome, single, owned a very nice home and vehicle. Employment was stable." She walked the length of the room and looked out the window toward the road. "And was surrounded by nosy neighbors," she said, letting her voice trail. "Let's finish in here and get out there before they decide to call it a night." She pointed to the street where twenty or more neighbors and looky-loos had gathered and were giving the cops a hard time.

"Yeah, they're nosy neighbors when they see the flashing lights and hear the sirens," Metford said, heading for the door. "But when you ask them, they saw nothing, heard nothing."

"And that's just the way it goes, sometimes," Ava said. "Doesn't mean we get out of interviewing them."

Dane snickered and thumped Metford's shoulder as he walked past. "Gotta cover every angle, remember?"

"How could I forget?" He smirked as he reached for the door.

CHAPTER TWO

"Hold up, Metford," Ava said. "Dane, Santos, Ashton, you three go out and question the neighbors. Metford, stay in here and help me sweep the rest of the house."

Three faces dropped. Metford, smirking only slightly, let go of the door and walked back across the front room. Santos was the last one out the door. She looked back glumly. Metford smiled and gave her a little wave. Ava thumped his arm and motioned for him to follow.

"What exactly are we looking for? I think forensics probably did a thorough job."

She shook her head. "I don't doubt that, but I think there must be something in here that would give us the reason someone came in."

"To kill Ethan Holt, obviously," Metford said.

"But why? Why would someone want to kill him?"

"Maybe he was a jerk." Metford walked toward the bathroom.

"You better hope that's not the only reason someone would kill a person."

"Oh, and she made a funny. Or was that a threat?"

"Just an observation. Get searching. We don't have all day."

"We might be here that long. Questioning those neighbors might take forever. Most of them look really self-important."

"There are a few low-level local politicians and city council members among others living here, but I doubt we'll have to question all of them. When we're done in here, we'll help the rest of the team with questioning. I want this case to move quickly."

After finishing the deep dive into Ethan's entire house, Ava and Metford tallied their finds.

"An hour-and-a-half of searching, and I can tell you that I didn't find Ethan's ID, his swipe badges for work, his clearance badges, cellphone, work laptop and tablet, or his wallet," Metford said. "But I did find a planner that might bear more investigation." He produced the planner with a plain grey cover and spiral binding.

"That's odd because I found one, too. Where did you find that one?"

"It was in the top of the linen closet under a stack of bath towels. And even though it was hidden and not easy to access, it's up to date." He flipped it open to the current date. "He marked off the days with an X."

"And he marked yesterday off," Ava said, opening the planner she had found. "This one was in the back of the file drawer on his desk in the bedroom."

"So, it was hidden, too?"

"Looks that way. The last day marked off in this one was yesterday, too." She pointed to the page where the X marks stopped. "Are any of the appointments in that one labeled?"

"Only with times. There aren't any names or places written on them."

"Same here," Ava said. "What's that about, you think? Why would you just write down the time?"

"Because you have a super memory and never have to worry about forgetting who or where the appointment is," Metford quipped.

"But then why would you make a reminder at all?"

Metford flipped through a few pages of the plain grey planner and shrugged. "Maybe it's the same place or person he was seeing every time?"

Ava flipped through the plain blue planner in her hands. "Maybe you're onto something. What does he have written on last Monday in your planner?"

"Nothing."

"What about today?"

"Nothing," Metford said.

"Tomorrow?" she continued.

"And again, nothing. What are we doing?"

"I bet there's also nothing on Saturday, day after tomorrow," she said, not answering his question.

"And you would be correct. There is nothing on Saturday. That proves nothing except that these two planners were probably being used to keep up with more than one thing."

"Exactly. But why keep two separate planners for multiple events? Wouldn't it be simpler to keep up with everything in one planner?"

He closed the book. "I don't use planners, but if I did, I think it would be way easier to make all appointments in one book. That must have taken a lot of work to keep up with two planners like this."

"And who does that?"

"Well, I don't know. Like I said, I don't use planners."

"What do you use to keep up with appointments? Because if you tell me that you have a super memory that never slips, I'll be forced to remind you of at least three times in the past month that I know it has."

He pulled out his phone. "My phone's calendar app, of course. I can have it give me notifications before an appointment so I'm sure not to miss any. I thought most people used their phones for this sort of thing now. Except you. I've seen your planners and calendars, and come to think of it, you have multiple."

"But they all have the same things written on the same days. I also use my phone. I have planners and calendars at work, at home, and in the car. That way, no matter where I'm at, I can see if I have an appointment that day."

"So, your calendars are backups of your planner, and your phone is your backup of the backup?"

"Pretty much." She reached for the planner in his hand. "But this? This is too much. We'll take them for evidence and have someone go over the dates and times. Maybe we can make some kind of sense out of it and figure out where he's been. He has an eight o'clock this evening, nine tomorrow night, and eleven on Saturday night."

"He's not going to make them. Someone will be upset," Metford said, opening a bag for the planners.

Ava dropped them in. "That's not all I found." She produced a poker chip and a small, laminated card.

"Where did you find those?" Metford took them. "That's not a regular poker chip."

"What gave it away, the double-lined square on one side?"

"That's a boxing ring," he said. "And it was the picture and the colors. What casino has baby green and pink chips?"

Ava chuckled. "Teal. It's teal, not baby green. And I'm hoping we can find out." She took the chip. "A boxing ring, huh?"

"Yeah. It's obvious enough. Maybe you didn't recognize it because you're a—"

"Don't even go there. Being a woman has nothing to do with it. I'm not a boxing fan. That's why I don't see a ring when I look at it. Do they hand out chips like this at the big boxing matches?"

"Not that I'm aware of. Prestige," he said, turning the card over. "The man had style and money."

"Do CBP agents really make enough money to become members of Prestige, though?" She took back the card and dropped it into a bag.

"Probably not," Metford admitted. "Where was that?"

"I'll show you." Ava took him to an apothecary cabinet in the hallway, opened a drawer, and pushed down on the front part its bottom. The back end of the drawer bottom flipped up. She pulled the false bottom out to reveal a stash area that was about two inches deep that ran the width and length of the drawer.

"Did you check the rest of them?"

"Yeah, this is the only one with a false bottom."

They got Detective Coffey and brought him back into the room. Ava showed him what they had discovered.

"I want prints from this cabinet and every drawer front in the house. If something here is what the perp was looking for, hopefully they left prints."

Coffey nodded. "I'll have my people pull prints from everything in the bedroom and bathroom since they're already working on the scene there."

Ava agreed, thanked him, and left.

CHAPTER THREE

Ava and Metford joined Santos, Dane, and Ashton outside. Questioning took less than thirty minutes.

Trevor Green, one of the two city council members who lived in the neighborhood, seemed almost angry that Ava would even ask him about Ethan Holt.

"Mr. Green, I'm not asking hard questions here," Ava said. "I even followed you all the way back to your house because you said you didn't want to speak out there where your fellow neighbors could hear you. What was Ethan Holt like? Not a hard question to answer, I would think."

"I knew the man. He was my neighbor. That's about it. How well do you know your neighbors?" Green turned a fiery look to her.

"Well, I don't know them all that well, but I don't get pissed when someone asks what I think of them."

"So, you know them well enough to form an opinion worth giving at a time like this?" He turned away from her and walked to the cold fireplace to lean against the side of the mantel.

"I'd like to think I do. And yes, I would definitely give my opinion of them at a time like this. Especially at a time like this. He's been murdered, Mr. Green. Murdered. The smallest details could help us with the investigation."

"I'm very sorry that I do not have an opinion about him, and I wish you would leave now. I'm late for a council meeting. I don't have time to stand here and ponder the personality of my recently murdered neighbor whom I barely knew. I wish I did, but I do not. I have a city to help run." His self-importance shone through blindingly as he straightened his tie and jacket. He looked expectantly at Ava for a moment, and then he gestured to the door. "Please, let me show you out. That's something else I don't have time for today, but what the heck, right?"

She handed him a card at the door. "If you change your mind, Mr. Green."

He snagged the card between thumb and forefinger as if it might be dirty. "I won't, but thank you. Bye now." He swung the door shut.

Metford stopped on the sidewalk. "Did you just get a door shut in your face?" he asked.

Ava walked toward him. "It would seem that way. Councilman Green didn't have time to speak with me this morning. He's late for a city council meeting." She walked past him.

"Did he give you anything?"

"Yeah, a massive cold shoulder and unwarranted anger at being asked anything about Ethan Holt."

"And you're just walking away from that?"

"I am. And we're going to the CBP building. I want to speak with Chief Director Sterling."

"Does he know what's happened?"

"If he does, he hasn't called anyone about the investigation." Ava met the others at the curb and informed them of her intentions.

In the car, Metford shared what he had learned about Ethan from the neighbors he questioned. "The consensus among Ethan's civilian neighbors seems to be that he was sneaky, shady, and that he had rough friends. Dane, Santos, and Ashton got about the same information with a few more people who seemed to like Ethan. Granted, most of them didn't know him well, but they said he kept to himself and didn't disturb the peace."

"That doesn't necessarily make him a saint, just a decent neighbor," Ava said.

"And doesn't point to any reason someone would want him dead."

"Especially in such a personal and violent way."

They arrived at CBP and were led to Chief Director Sterling's office. A tall, thin, scowling man met them.

"Chief Director Sterling, I presume," Ava said, showing her badge.

"Uh, no. I'm Deputy Commissioner Jasper Halloway. Sterling isn't available at the moment, but I can help you with whatever you need. I understand this is about one of our Patapsco Bay Terminal agents." He glanced at a paper on the desk. "Ethan Holt, correct?"

"It is. Do you know what's happened to him?"

"The message says he was murdered sometime last night or early this morning. Tragic. What can I help you with?"

"We need to see the files you have on him."

Halloway shook his head and removed his glasses slowly as he turned to sit in the chair behind the big desk. "I'm sorry, that's not possible. You understand. The privacy of our employees' information is of the utmost importance."

"Your employee is dead, Mr. Halloway. Murdered. I need the files you have on him for the investigation so, no, I don't understand. Maybe you didn't understand that we're not with Baltimore PD, we're FBI." She showed her badge again. "Special Agents James and Metford."

The man rested his elbows on the arms of the cushy chair, steepled his fingers, and leaned back. "I'm sorry, but I cannot and will not give you free access to an agent's files. You have no warrant, no paperwork at all, and I'm just supposed to trust you on your word about why you need the files. You see my dilemma."

"No, again, I do not."

"Nevertheless, I won't do it without paperwork."

Ava inhaled deeply and sat back against her chair. She glanced at Metford and wondered if he was judging her actions, or if he was predicting how she would react.

"Okay, Mr. Halloway. That can be remedied, and it will be soon enough. What can you tell us about Agent Holt?"

"Are you investigating Agent Holt or his murder? He was a solid federal employee, and that's all you need to know. It's also all you will get unless you produce a warrant. Employee files are not public property." He stood and smiled congenially as he motioned toward the door. "I'm really very sorry that I couldn't be of more help to you, agents."

Ava stood. Her spine felt like a steel rod in her back, and her hands clenched into fists. "We'll be back with the warrant. You'll help us plenty then, Mr. Halloway." She headed for the door. "In the meantime, we'll see what we can get at Patapsco Bay."

"No, you won't. I don't see the necessity in going out there to harass Mr. Holt's coworkers. They are already behind on their tasks, and your intrusion won't reveal anything useful to the investigation. It will only hinder their work further and cause upset where there should not be any."

"How do you know it won't reveal anything useful to the investigation? This is a murder. I don't think you realize the gravity of the situation," Ava shot back.

"He does realize. He just doesn't care about anything but the bottom line," Metford said, giving the man a distasteful look.

"That's untrue, Agent. Mr. Holt was murdered at home, was he not?"

"Yes, he was," Ava said.

"Then, why would you think his coworkers would have useful insights into that murder? It is my understanding that there is very little fraternizing among them. They do their jobs, share their shifts with other agents, and then are happy to leave it all behind at the end of said shift. Much like you and your fellow agents in the FBI, I would suspect."

Biting back on a retaliatory comment, Ava forced a smile. "Nevertheless, we have an obligation to cover all our bases. It's the next step in the investigation, and I would think you would be glad that we're doing all we can to bring justice for one of your employees. And whether you like it or not, I have every right to go search Ethan's office and speak with whomever I please."

Halloway's cheeks reddened. "Obviously, I'm not a homicide detective, Agent James. If you would?" He motioned to the door again. "Just until you have the proper documentation."

Ava stepped out the door, and Halloway shut it quickly, almost catching her heel.

"That's twice in as many hours," Metford said, looking back at the door. "You're on a roll here."

Ava didn't react to the comment. She just wanted out of the building and far away from the enraging Deputy Commissioner Jasper Halloway.

CHAPTER FOUR

Patapsco Bay Terminal seemed to be a small city in and of itself. The skyscrapers consisted of stacked shipping containers. There were dirty streets on which dirty little port vehicles drove; buildings scattered over the area where people milled in and out carrying paperwork and items; workers in uniform and wearing hardhats like it was a construction zone, and then there was the persistent clattering and shouting and bustle of activity. The level of noise was higher than comfortable but not quite drive-you-mad loud. Farther from where Ava and Metford parked, the distant sound of ships' horns mingled with the hum of motors, clanging of metal shipping containers, and a staticky voice over a PA system.

"How long before Santos and the others get here?" Metford asked, looking at his watch.

"Dane said another ten minutes. They got stuck in traffic."

"It's past lunch."

"Seriously? You don't have to eat right at twelve every single day. You won't die, I promise."

"Did you just call me fat on the down-low?"

She laughed despite an effort not to. "No, I didn't just call you fat. What are you now, a girl about your weight?"

"That's sexist, and I resent it. Women aren't the only ones who worry about their weight, you know."

"And neither do you," she said, turning to see Santos pulling up beside them. "They're here."

"Great. Now we get to wade into the chaos down there, probably get dirty, and then go to lunch looking like that." He pointed to a man walking toward a truck. The man's jeans were grungy all the way up to his knees.

"And you prefer drive-thrus to sit-down restaurants any day of the week."

Tilting his head to the right, he opened the door. "You're right. No argument there."

They got out.

"Any idea who we gotta talk to here?" Santos asked, eyeing Patapsco Bay with something akin to disgust.

"We need to speak with the port director first," Ava said, flipping open her notepad. "Nathaniel Chambers. Then we'll find Ethan's direct supervisor, Cody Stillwell. You three do the same here as you did at Ethan's house: question everyone you can. Coworkers, supervisors, friends, anyone who might have known Ethan. I'll take Chambers. Metford will take Stillwell. We'll cut our time down if we split up. I'll search through Ethan's office before we leave."

The team nodded in unison, and Ava set off to find Chambers' office.

Port Director Nathaniel Chambers and Ethan's direct supervisor, Cody Stillwell, were in the same room. Ava liked the two birds with one stone feel of it.

"Can you two tell me what you know about Ethan Holt? What kind of employee and person was he? Did he have any enemies that you know of?"

Chambers ran a hand through his hair. "I never had any trouble out of him, if that's what you're asking." He glanced at Stillwell and then out the open door.

"Yes, that's what I'm asking. Was he punctual, thorough at his job, attend to the details of his duties every time?"

"Oh, yeah, yeah. All of that. Good guy. Really." He ran a hand through his hair again and leaned against the cheap metal desk.

"Are you sure that's all you have to tell me, Mr. Chambers?"

"Yeah, yeah. What else can I tell you? It's not like we chummed around socially. I knew him from work here. He was a good employee, and from what I knew of him, a good guy. Good work ethic. Disciplined."

"Right. You know, you can tell me anything that might help with the investigation to solve his murder. Anything at all, really. Even the tiniest thing that's going through your mind might help get justice for your friend."

"Friend? Did I say he was a friend?" Chambers chuckled and glanced several times at Stillwell. "Work acquaintances. That's it," he enunciated as if to a deaf person.

"It sure seems like you're holding something back."

"No, it's nothing like that. You said he was murdered. In his own home. In his bed."

"That's right," Ava said.

"It's just damned unnerving, is all. Damned unnerving."

"So, there's nothing else you want to say?"

Chambers shook his head. "Just that I hope you catch the bastard and put him away for life." He sniffed loudly and plunked a hardhat on his head. "I need to get back." He motioned out the door. "If it's okay?"

"Of course. Thank you. I'll leave my card just in case you need to reach me."

He took it and headed out the door without another word.

Ava questioned Stillwell, who it seemed had not yet spoken to Metford, but got nothing of further use.

"Mr. Stillwell, I need to go to Ethan's office. Could you point me in the right direction?" Ava asked after finishing with the questions.

"I'll do you one better," Stillwell said. "Follow me." The large bundle of keys at his side jingled and jangled noisily with every step. He'd never sneak up on anyone at work. He led Ava to the door of Ethan's office. "It's locked. Want me to unlock it?"

"Do you have a key?"

"We have a master. Agents aren't allowed to make duplicates, and we can't afford to have anyone locked out of their office."

"Do you have the master on you?"

He lifted the keychain that hung at his side and smiled.

She moved to the side. When he finished, he pushed the door open and stepped away.

"Mr. Stillwell, before you go…" Ava said.

"Yes?" His gaze darted to the dark room behind her and he shifted from one foot to the other as he cleared his throat.

"What kind of relationship did Ethan and Port Director Chambers have at work?"

"W-What do you mean, relationship?" He stuffed his hands into his jean pockets.

"I mean, did they get along? Were they friendly? Did they take meals together?"

"Oh, no. Nobody took meals with Ethan. They were friendly, though, yeah. He told you that."

"Why didn't anyone take meals with Ethan? I thought you all liked him."

"Yeah, but Ethan didn't like to be bothered on his breaks. Can't blame a man for that." He flipped a hand toward the constant noisome chaos outside the office. "Some people just like to be left alone in a quiet spot on their breaks around here. Nobody takes it personal." He chuckled lightly.

"There's a quiet place to be alone around here?" Ava grinned and shook her head in disbelief.

"Right?" He stepped farther away. "Phone's right there, if you need anything just pick it up and dial seven-one-two. That's the extension in Nate's office where you just came from. One of us will be there to answer."

"Thanks," Ava said, watching him retreat until he was out of sight. She texted Metford where she was, and told him to join her with the others if they were finished with the questioning.

Was there more to Chambers' reaction? Was it really just because he was unnerved by the news of Ethan's murder? She wasn't sure, but she did note that no one seemed particularly grief-stricken by the news of his murder. She made a mental note to be on the lookout for any piece of evidence that might signal something deeper was going on with Chambers, and perhaps even Stillwell, whose nervous reaction had not gone unnoticed.

CHAPTER FIVE

M ETFORD AND THE OTHERS JOINED AVA IN ETHAN'S OFFICE A FEW minutes later.

"I never did find Stillwell," Metford said. "I must have walked two miles around this maze. No one seemed to know where he was. If you've got a number, I'll give him a call."

"No need. I already spoke with him," Ava said as she moved to a large map on the wall opposite the large window.

"What? I thought you wanted me to find him and question him. I didn't question anyone else while I was trying to track him down. Why didn't you let me know?"

Grinning to herself, Ava continued to inspect the map of Maryland. "I thought the walking might do you some good."

"I told you she called me fat earlier," Metford said.

"I think you have put on a few pounds around the middle," Santos said. "It's not real noticeable, but…"

"Thanks. Thanks a lot. And I thought you guys were my friends."

"We are," Ashton said, patting his shoulder. "We care, or we wouldn't say anything at all."

"He's right," Dane said through a small laugh.

"What did you find?" Dane asked Ava, moving to stand beside her and look at the map.

"This map reminds me of the one Mrs. Lewis had hanging in my third-grade classroom," Ava said. She put her finger on the red pushpin in Baltimore. "Except that hers didn't have this marker."

Dane squinted at the map. "Looks like there were others around the city at some point."

"Yep, and the holes are too close for them to have all been there at the same time." She tapped the red pin. "This one has been moved around, it seems."

"And what does that mean?" Santos asked.

"Not sure." Ava wrote down the approximate location on the map. "Maybe nothing."

"Maybe something," Ashton said.

"Look through everything. Look for anything that stands out as odd. Ethan Holt, by all accounts, was a good employee. He was meticulous about details, had good analytical and communication skills, he was physically fit and worked out regularly to stay in shape, and he always upheld high standards of integrity and ethical behavior in all dealings related to his work here."

"And check for false bottoms in the drawers," Metford added, glancing at Ava.

"And false backs," she said.

"So, if he was such an outstanding and upstanding guy, why would he have false bottoms or backs in drawers?" Santos asked.

"That's a mystery I would like to solve," Ava said. "I found one at his house. It stands to reason that there might be more."

"Ava found a weird poker chip and a membership card for Ethan. Guy is a member of Prestige," Metford said.

Ashton looked at him with a shocked expression. "Really? On his salary?"

Metford shrugged. "Maybe he had his priorities straight and saved up for the membership."

"You two think that's a good thing, huh?" Santos asked, hands going to hips. "A gentlemen's club where there are no doubt women being forced into positions that require them to lower their self-esteem and act like sex objects?" She shook her head and threw up a hand. "You know what? Never mind. I don't want to know."

"They might lower their self-esteem for a little while, but they are definitely boosting their bank accounts," Metford said.

"That's not—"

"Drop it," Ava said hotly. "We'll be looking into his membership there later, but right now, we're here. We need to concentrate on this and not on the moral points of the club membership." She removed a planner from the top right drawer of Ethan's desk and laid it on top. Flipping through it, she said, "Another planner with only times written in it."

Metford immediately went to see. "What was this guy's deal with these planners?"

"Another mystery I would like to solve. I wonder if any of these times correspond to the ones in the other planners?"

"I can't remember anything from the one except that there was nothing on today's date, or for the next two days."

She nodded. "Thanks." She flipped to the current month. "Nothing for today. Six in the morning tomorrow, and eight in the morning for Saturday."

"Does that match the one you found at his house?" Metford asked.

"I can't remember exactly, but I think there were PM times on all three days in that one."

"More appointments he won't be attending," Metford said.

Ava closed the planner and turned to the others. "Ashton, get some clear pictures of the map on the wall. Get a couple zoomed into the spot where the pin is. We're done here." She took the planner when they left.

"There are three close coworkers of Ethan's who aren't here today," Dane said.

"It's their scheduled day off," Ashton added. "I checked with the personnel office to verify."

"That's fine. We'll interview them later. Will they be here tomorrow?" Ava asked.

"No, it's their day off. They work the weekend shifts, and are given Thursdays and Fridays off," Ashton supplied.

"We'll call and visit them at home, then," Ava said.

"Not gonna let a minute slip by, are you?" Santos asked.

"Not if I can help it. An agent is an agent, in my opinion. Doesn't matter if he worked for FBI, CIA, or CBP, he was an agent enforcing the law in the name of the federal government. I want to find out who did this as fast as possible."

They walked back to the cars. Santos stopped Ava before they parted ways and pointed toward a building a little distance away. "That guy is watching us pretty closely."

Ava shaded her eyes and looked. "That's Nathaniel Chambers. He's the port director. I spoke with him. He seemed overly anxious, in my opinion. Said it was just that Ethan being murdered in his own bed was unnerving, but I'm not so sure."

The others stopped and looked down the hill toward Chambers, who was propped against the back wall of the office smoking a cigarette and watching them.

"Since when is there smoking allowed at work?" Metford asked.

"There's not," Dane said. "Doesn't seem to bother him, though."

"I'd say he doesn't stick to the rules and regs as well as our boy Ethan did," Santos noted.

Indeed, he did not. Ava continued to watch him as the others got into the vehicles. Chambers was undisturbed by the fact that they had all so obviously seen him, or that she was blatantly watching him. After several more seconds, he tossed the cigarette, ground it out with his boot, and walked away. She watched until he disappeared into the labyrinth of cargo containers and metal buildings.

CHAPTER SIX

The next morning, Ava and Metford went out with three addresses and names of Ethan's coworkers. Baltimore traffic wasn't as bad as New York City, but it was pretty close.

"You want me to drive?" Metford asked after Ava had to slam on the brakes to keep from hitting a car that darted in front of her from a side road.

She hit the horn, sending one short, sharp blare at the reckless driver before letting off the brake pedal. "No, I'm fine. It's fine. I'll manage."

"Yeah, but what about the poor brakes?" he quipped.

"I'm more worried about getting rear-ended than about the abuse to the brakes."

"There's a semi behind us now, so go easy. If that thing hits us, we're going to be feeling it for a few days."

"GPS shows that Bailey Macomber's house is the closest one," she said. "We'll go to each according to distance so we're not in this traffic longer than necessary."

"And find routes back that don't make us cross it except at traffic lights." He tensed and wobbled his cup of coffee as she hit the brakes again.

"Do I have a target on the side of the car this morning?" she nearly yelled.

"Makes walking seem like a good choice, doesn't it?"

Unable to resist, she said, "For someone needing to get in a few extra steps, yeah."

"Wow, you're still on that? I'll have you know that I weighed myself last night, and I have actually lost two pounds since my last regular weigh-in at the gym two weeks ago. So, there. I know you're just yanking my chain."

"You did not weigh yourself last night."

"I did."

"Where? There aren't any scales in the hotel," she countered, laughing.

"There are if you ask."

She laughed harder.

"I'm glad I could be your comedic relief yet again. That's it. Yuck it up at my expense. That's okay. I have a thick skin."

She glanced at him with a mischievous look and bit her lip.

"What? What now? Another joke?"

"No. I was just going to say that maybe that thickened skin is what makes you look like you've gained—" She slammed the brakes again, and behind them, the semi did the same. The driver of the semi laid on his horn. Metford's coffee sloshed onto the carpet between his feet. Ava let loose with a string of expletives and gripped the wheel tight enough that she was sure her fingerprints were permanently embedded in it.

"Language," Metford said. "Seriously, you want me to drive? I don't mind, really."

"No," she said firmly and loudly. *Maybe a little too loudly*, she thought. Taking a breath, she made an effort to relax her grip. "I'm fine."

The GPS announced their turn in two hundred feet. Ava caught Metford's relieved exhalation as she turned onto the empty side street. Tension leaked out of her muscles as the GPS announced her next turn onto another street devoid of traffic.

"There it is," Metford said, pointing.

Ava turned into the driveway and parked behind a Chevy S-10 that looked to be from the late '80s or early '90s. It was shiny black. The chrome accents sparked back the early morning sunlight in brilliant shards.

"That's a thing of beauty," Metford said as they walked by the truck. "And diamond-tucked interior to boot." He whistled low. "Bet that cost a pretty penny. Do CBP agents really make that much money?"

"No, they don't."

She looked in the driver's window. The gear shift was a chrome skull, the dash was matte black, and the diamond-tuck upholstery was black. The steering wheel was fashioned to look like a chrome logging chain. Metford was right. The truck probably cost a pretty penny for sure. Maybe several pretty pennies.

Metford went ahead to the front door and waited for Ava. She walked up and rang the doorbell, readying her badge. The door swung open almost immediately. A man in sweats and a t-shirt opened the door. Sweat had made rings under his arms, down the center of the front, and the back of the shirt. He huffed for breath.

"Mr. Macomber?" Ava asked doubtfully.

"Yeah, and you're the FBI agent I spoke to yesterday." He stepped away from the door. "Come on in. Overlook my appearance. I was in the middle of my workout. Thought I'd be done long before you arrived." He motioned to the seats in the living room. "What can I do for you?"

"We're here because of your coworker, Ethan Holt. He was murdered yesterday or sometime the night before."

"I heard," Macomber said, toweling his face and hair.

"You don't seem too torn up about it," Metford said.

Macomber tossed the towel over the arm of the sofa and flopped down. "Can't say that I am. I mean, I hate that the guy was murdered in his own house and all, but it's not like I'm going to lose sleep. We're in Baltimore. Shit happens. Murder happens."

"So, you didn't like Ethan?" Ava asked.

"Not really, no."

"Care to elaborate on why you didn't like him?"

He sniffed loudly and leaned forward to rest his elbows on his knees. "Don't mind at all. He liked to play a brown-nosing little Boy Scout at work, but really he was nothing like that. He was corrupt."

"Corrupt?" Metford asked.

"Yeah, corrupt. Dirty."

"In what ways?" Ava asked.

Macomber shifted and sat back again. "Well, I don't have any proof, so I guess I better not go into all my theories, but I know he's dirty. I can tell just by the way he acts. Shady as hell. I don't know if it's something illegal he's doing when he searches the imports, or if he's smoking dope, doing drugs, or if he's involved with smuggling illegal items, and I don't care. I just know he was dirty somehow."

"Did you ever see him doing anything that would suggest he was involved with smuggling, say, at work?" Ava asked.

Thumbing his nose, Macomber sniffed loudly again. "Nah. Not really, but you never know. He inspects the imports. That would be a prime position to have if one wanted to smuggle almost anything, wouldn't you agree?"

Ava and Metford exchanged a look. Macomber was right, but without proof, or even a straight accusation, they had nothing to look for; no reason to think Ethan was smuggling anything.

"What kind of person was Ethan at work?" Ava asked.

"Like I said, he was a brown-nosing Boy Scout. Or, that's how he acted in front of everybody."

"Why would you think he's acting?" Metford asked.

"Ever know a teacher's pet when you were in school?" Macomber asked.

"Yeah, we all did, right?" Metford asked.

Ava nodded agreement.

"That's what he was. All the bosses down at Patapsco favored Ethan over everybody else. They didn't make any bones over it either. He was their favorite, and everybody knew it."

"Which bosses favored him so much?" Ava asked. "Which ones do you know for sure, from personal experience, who showed him favor over everyone else?"

Macomber snorted laughter. "The port director for one. You know him. I'm sure you talked to him when you went there yesterday, right?"

"Nathaniel Chambers," Ava said.

"The one and only. And another one is Supervisory Officer Cody Stillwell. Did you meet him, too?"

"I did," Ava said.

"And I'm sure they gave you a glowing review of what a great worker Ethan was; how dedicated he was to the job; how he always did everything by the book and was such a stickler about details."

"Something like that. Maybe not a glowing review, but they seemed to think he was a superb CBP agent."

"He wasn't any better at his job than the rest of us. That's the truth. As much as it would pain Nate and Cody to admit it, that's the truth. I've worked there for eleven years, and I've never seen Ethan do anything that would make him any more deserving of their praise than the rest of us. But they were all buddy-buddy, you know."

"No, I don't know," Ava said. "What do you mean?"

"I mean that I have seen the camaraderie between the three of them with my own eyes. It's wrong. Bosses aren't supposed to fraternize with employees."

"You mean you saw them together outside of work?" Metford asked.

"Yeah. At work, too. They didn't try to hide it. If they were trying to hide it, they failed."

"Where did you see them together?" Ava asked. "Was it at a football game, a bar, eating at a restaurant, where?"

"What difference does that make?"

"If they were together at a football game, they might have simply run into each other at a large public event," she said. "If they were at a bar, maybe the same thing. See where I'm going with this?"

"So, anywhere in public and that's okay even though bosses aren't supposed to hang out with their employees. Right. Got it. Now, you're starting to sound just like them."

"Where did you see them together? Maybe I'll change my mind."

Macomber shook his head doubtfully. "A bar. A hotel lounge. Casino." He counted the places off with his fingers. "And even once, I saw Nate driving into Ethan's neighborhood at night."

"Okay, okay," Metford said.

"And he could have been visiting anyone in the neighborhood, not just Ethan," Ava said.

"Whatever you think. People got passed over for promotions that Ethan ended up with, too. A few, actually."

Ava and Metford glanced at each other again. Ava knew he was thinking the same thing as she was. "Mr. Macomber, did you get passed up for a promotion?"

"If I say I did, you're going to think all this about Ethan is just because I'm pissed over the promotion. I am pissed, don't get me wrong, but that's not why I think the man was dirty right along with the bosses. That happened before the promotion."

"Did Ethan get your promotion?" Metford asked.

"He did. Didn't even ask for it. They just gave it to him after I had busted my hump for a year trying to get it. Tell me it didn't have anything to do with him and Cody and Nate all being friends. If you can prove it, I'll have to eat crow, but I don't have to worry about that because you can't prove it. I know that's why he got the job and I didn't."

CHAPTER SEVEN

MARTY STAKHOVSKY'S HOUSE WAS SIX BLOCKS AWAY FROM Macomber's place. Ava drove there, but even on the side streets, she was having a hard time dealing with the unpredictable nature of the Baltimore drivers. Was it the fault of the drivers? Were they just more careless in Baltimore than other cities she had been in, or was it her? She had been edgy and nervy ever since she had gone to New York and joined Reinhold for the latest Art Murder case. Maybe her mother and father were right and she was pushing herself too hard. Dr. Bran had been sure she was doing too much, also. Bran called it burning the candle at both ends and warned that, eventually, both flames would meet in the middle leaving nothing of the candle behind but smoke to be whisked away by the breeze. Not a comforting thought, but not wrong either. Ava had just never thought of it from that angle.

As she pulled into Stakhovsky's driveway, she determined to let Metford drive them to the last address. No sense making herself more stressed and scaring the life out of Metford in the process of being stubborn.

"Marty Stakhovsky," Metford announced. "His car is more believable on his budget."

The old Mercury sedan sported a faded maroon paintjob, plain wheels, and a light coating of road dirt that proved Stakhovsky did not visit the carwash very often.

Stakhovsky was slower to answer the door than Macomber had been, and Ava was all but ready to leave when Metford put a hand on her arm.

"Somebody's coming," he said.

Ava sighed and pulled out her badge for the second time since walking onto the porch. "About time," she grumbled.

Stakhovsky was a wiry, bearded man dressed in jeans and a graphic tee that sported a Guns N' Roses album cover.

"Mr. Stakhovsky?" Ava asked, holding up her badge.

"Yeah." He looked at their badges and then at them distrustfully. "FBI, huh? What was old Ethan into?" He moved aside and motioned them in. "Sit wherever you like."

Ava and Metford sat in cushioned chairs facing a small, worn sofa. One cushion swagged deeply in the center, and Ava knew that's where Stakhovsky would sit.

Stakhovsky walked directly to the sofa and sat on the swagged cushion. Ava noted he was directly in front of the small flatscreen TV sitting on a cheap stand. Stakhovsky wasn't rich, but his belongings seemed to be well taken care of. Except that the car could have used a good washing.

"Well, here we are," he said, looking from one to the other expectantly. "What can I help you with? I got an appointment in a couple hours so, if we could…" He made a rolling gesture with one finger.

"Of course," Ava said. She put the same questions to him as she had put to Macomber.

"I didn't like Ethan because he played office politics too well."

"And what does that mean?" Ava asked.

"It means that he played office politics so that he could fly under the radar at work and with the government. I don't think he was doing anything illegal at work, but maybe he was taking part in something illegal away from work, like, in his personal life."

"Any ideas as to what illegal activity he might have been partaking in?" Ava asked.

He shook his head. "It's just a feeling. You can be around a person and feel if they're really a good person or not, and I don't believe Ethan was a good person. Maybe not totally evil, but he wasn't good."

"What was he like at work?" Metford asked.

Stakhovsky sighed and rested his left ankle on his right knee. Looking up at the ceiling, he seemed to consider the question longer than necessary. "Let's put it this way: I was promised a raise a few months ago. I didn't get the raise. Boss said funding was down, blah, blah, blah, and they couldn't give me the raise yet. He promised I was first in line for it when the funding was back up to par, though. That same week, Ethan received a great big bonus for work well done. I call bullshit. They don't give out those bonuses but once a year, and it's to the employee of the year. That's usually one of the office twerps, not one of us lower employees."

"That would make me pretty mad," Metford said.

"Yeah, it did make me mad, but what was I supposed to do about it? Later, I was promised time off. Time which I had put in for a month ahead. I didn't get it. At the last minute, the boss called me into the office and said they had to have me that week because they had lost two workers. Guess who got time off without having to put in ahead for it that week?"

"Ethan Holt," Ava said.

Stakhovsky nodded solemnly. "I didn't get my time off any of the last three times I requested it even though I put in a month ahead. Now, Ethan can go in today, verbally ask Cody or Nate for tomorrow and the next day off, and he gets it. Not only does he get it on the spur of the moment like that, he doesn't even have to go into the system and spend twenty minutes of his lunchbreak to fill out the proper forms for it. He snaps his fingers and gets what he wants. That's against policy. There's a required timeframe in which to request time off, and barring an emergency, that's how it has to be done. Ethan says it's crucial that he be off tomorrow, and they ignore all the rules and regulations and policies and just give it to him. Never seen the beat in my life."

"Sounds like a teacher's pet if I've ever seen one," Metford said.

"Other than being favored over you, what was he like at work?" Ava asked.

"You know, most people don't even catch on to his shady ways. I think some don't see it, and others just don't want to see it."

"Why wouldn't they want to see it?"

"Because as long as Ethan is there, the bosses have someone to shine the limelight on, someone to favor, their golden boy, and that leaves the others to drift along, only doing mediocre jobs, never going above or beyond expectations, and they simply aren't noticed because everyone's looking at Ethan."

Ava finished with the questions and thanked Stakhovsky again for his time.

At the car, Ava tossed Metford the keys.

"Really?" he asked with a sideways grin.

"Better get in before I change my mind," she teased.

He was in before she got her door open.

"The picture the coworkers are painting of Ethan isn't looking too good," he said.

"No, it's not, but there are his neighbors. Some of them thought he was a good guy."

"And they didn't spend five days a week working alongside him either."

Ava had already thought of that. The picture of Agent Ethan Holt was coming together, but it had unflattering shadows and sharp edges. "There's still one more interview today. Maybe Ms. Belinda Sanders will have something good to say about Ethan."

"Wouldn't hold my breath."

"I'm not."

CHAPTER EIGHT

BELINDA SANDERS DIDN'T LIVE IN A PRESTIGIOUS NEIGHBORHOOD with politicians for neighbors, and she didn't live in an expensive apartment building where the hallways were well-lit and the walls were graffiti-free. Instead, she lived in a small house that was probably sixty years old and hadn't had any updates since 1980.

Ava paused with her hand on the doorhandle as a skinny man of indeterminable age stumbled by arguing with someone that only he could see. His sallow skin, sunken cheeks, and the sores on his arms and face indicated heavily that he was out of his head on meth or something very much like it.

Three men, who looked to be in their late thirties, sat in chairs in a yard two houses up. They whooped and yelled at the stumbling stoner, who didn't know anyone else was around. He was in his own world, and that world didn't include them.

"Well, it doesn't seem that Ms. Sanders is doing as well as Ethan Holt or the coworkers we've interviewed so far," Metford said.

"Definitely not." Ava got out of the car, keeping her head on a swivel. The men in the yard up the street catcalled at her, but she ignored them and instructed Metford to do the same.

Ms. Sanders' house had faded and turned nicotine yellow from what had surely been a pristine white way back when. The Masonite siding needed some repairs, and the guttering was falling away in a couple of places. Despite the age and the bigger maintenance needs, the windows were spotless, the welcome rug looked new, and the drapes that were visible were clean and in good condition.

Ava pushed the button for the doorbell but there was no corresponding sound from inside the house. She pushed it again. Again, there was no sound.

"Broken," Metford said.

"Thanks, Sherlock," Ava said as she knocked. "Sorry. I'm on edge."

"No problem."

But the look on his face said otherwise. Ava couldn't blame him. She would have been annoyed if the tables had been turned and he had bit at her like that.

Someone coughed inside the house. Ava knocked again.

"Ms. Sanders?" she called.

The curtain on the door moved to one side. A thin, pale face glared out at them. "Whatever you're selling, I'm not buying. Move on." The curtain dropped.

"Ms. Sanders," Ava said. She held her badge to the glass and knocked again. "We're not selling anything."

The curtain moved back a little. "FBI?"

"Yes, ma'am. We need to—"

The door jerked inward, and the woman poked her head out to look at Metford and then around him as if expecting someone else to pop up out of the bushes at the side of the porch. "Come on in. I don't like it when the whole neighborhood knows my business," she said in a hushed, urgent voice.

Her fierce gaze settled on Ava as she and Metford stepped inside. The place was immaculately clean, but everything was in need of an update, including the 1970s shag carpeting. It was no wonder the woman's approach to the door had been silent save for the coughing.

Belinda Sanders crossed her arms. "Well, what's this about?"

"Have you heard about what happened to a coworker of yours?" Ava asked.

Belinda blew out a breath and ran a hand angrily over her hair, pushing the mouse-brown mop away from her face. "No, and I don't exactly care. I'm a little busy here, so, could we get to the damn point?" She shifted her stance slightly.

"Sure," Metford said. "Ethan Holt was murdered sometime yesterday morning or the previous night. In his bed. We're just out trying to find out what kind of person he was, who he might have been hanging around with, just the standard questions."

"And that has what to do with me?" Belinda shook her head and reached for a pack of cigarettes on the hallway table.

"You were his coworker, and you weren't at work yesterday," Ava said. "We're talking to all his coworkers."

"Gold stars for you." She pulled a cigarette from the pack and held it under her nose. Inhaling deeply, she made a satisfied sound as if she had tasted the world's most exquisite dessert, and then she slipped the smoke back into the pack and laid it on the table again. "I quit over a month ago, but I miss the smell. Not the smoke smell, but that rich, deep tobacco smell."

Ava and Metford stared at her. Ava wondered if Metford was as shocked as she was at the strange behavior. Was Belinda a tweaker? She didn't seem to be. Sure, she was thin and pale, but not in a sickly way; it was more in a tired way.

Belinda laughed. "Jeez, you don't have to stand there looking at me like I have leprosy." She stopped laughing and cleared her throat. "I know Ethan; or should I say I knew him? Whatever. I knew him. I didn't like him. He was an asshole. End of story."

"Wow, now tell us how you really feel about him," Metford said.

"That is how I really feel about him," Belinda shot back, her eyes turning fiery again. "If you had to deal with him, maybe you would feel the same way. Or maybe you're the kind of guy that would have knocked him down a notch or two like he deserved?"

"Ms. Sanders," Ava said. "Why didn't you like Mr. Holt?"

Belinda exhaled deeply and pushed her hair back again. "Might as well come in and have a seat. I don't know about you, but I don't feel like standing here. I need to sit." She turned and walked into the kitchen.

If not for the fact that it looked like Belinda couldn't afford anything else, the kitchen, with its vintage cookstove and cabinetry, would have been quaint. The mismatched flatware and cutlery in the sink, and the scratched, worn pots hanging from the wall rack were clean as a pin, but they also suggested that Belinda's money was going somewhere besides housewares.

"Listen, I don't know who all you've talked to so far, and I don't care. I don't like any of the pricks I work with. I tolerate them because I need my job. I need it probably worse than any of them will ever need a job. My daughter, Amanda. She's ten, and she has…has…*ongoing medical problems.* The bills are outrageous." She scoffed and tossed her hands up to indicate the house. "This is all I can afford, and I can barely afford this place. And Ethan? He seemed intent on making it even harder for me to keep my place and pay for Amanda's hospital and treatment bills." Her voice hitched and she looked down quickly. It took a moment, but she composed herself and looked at Ava. "What else do you want to know?"

All the anger, bravado, and the toughness were just an act to conceal how scared Belinda was. Deep down, she was terrified of losing what she had such a tenuous grip on, and if Ava was right, that included Amanda. Hospital bills and treatments were usually code for cancer. People who had it, and their loved ones, didn't like to say the word aloud, so they used key phrases and acted in somewhat predictable ways.

"You said he was a jerk. Can you tell me what he did that made you say that?"

"Yeah. I can give you several. I could give you a laundry list of reasons."

"Tell me as much as you can," Ava said.

"The first and foremost thing I have, or had, against Ethan Holt is that he purposefully stole extra shifts right out from under me. He knew good and well why I so desperately need those extra shifts, and he would take them anyway. Like he was trying to prove he could do whatever he wanted and get away with it. He knew I had to work around Amanda's treatment schedule, but did that stop him? No. It made him worse. He didn't do it to others; just to me. Well, maybe a couple of times he did it to someone else, but it was nowhere near as many times as he did it to me."

"How did he know you had to pick up shifts around your daughter's treatment schedules?" Metford asked.

"Because I told him."

"I thought you didn't like him," Metford said.

"I didn't. After the second time he took a week of shifts from under me, I confronted him. I explained the situation to him." Her gaze shifted to the table and then to her hands.

"Did it do any good at all?" Ava asked.

"No, no way. He grinned that stupid little sideways grin he had, patted my shoulder, and told me it was a dog-eat-dog world, and that if I wanted those shifts, I would just have to figure out a way to get them."

"What did you do?" Metford asked.

"What could I do? It's just like this last time extra shifts came up. I put in for it. It would run twice a month. That's two weeks out of the month. At night after my regular shift was over. It was supposed to run for three months. Do you have any idea how much that would have helped me pay down these medical bills?" She reached behind her to the counter, pulled open a drawer, and took a stack of papers out. She dropped them in front of her on the table. "I could have paid off almost every single one of these. Maybe all of them. It's been four years since I was square with the house. My paychecks are gone before I even get them these days, and I'm losing hope." She snatched the bills and crammed them back into the drawer and slammed it shut. "And it's because of that asshole, Ethan Holt."

"I'm sorry," Ava said, reminding herself to stay as neutral as possible. It was hard considering what Belinda was going through.

"Does anyone else act like that toward you?"

"Oh, it wasn't just me that Ethan was a jerk to. It was anyone and everyone. If you are lower on the totem pole than him, you're fair game."

"And you don't think that maybe he really needed those extra shifts?" Metford asked.

"No. Ethan always had extra money. He was always bragging about living the bachelor's life and how good it was." She scoffed and rolled her eyes to the side as if disgusted. "And that Cody Stillwell is just as much to blame as Ethan. When I put in the request for the crappy shift that hardly anyone ever wants to take, I did it as soon as the paper went up on the board. Like you're supposed to do. Ethan came in and put his name on the paper, and got the shifts immediately. There were five of us on the paper for that shift and different jobs. Ethan and I were the only ones competing for the same job, though. Cody Stillwell gave it to him without a second thought, and he didn't make Ethan wait until the end of the week to get the news. The rest of us, though? We had to wait until Friday afternoon, after our shifts were done, to be told yes or no."

"How do you know he found out immediately?" Ava asked.

"Because I was in the hallway outside Cody's office and heard it. Not like they bother to close the door. I heard and I saw how they acted. Laughing and acting like a couple of good ole boys."

Her chin quivered. She covered it quickly and fought to keep her composure. "I was mad, furious, really. And it cut me right down to my soul that they would do that to me again. Just about everyone else there is backstabbing and two-faced. I'm there to earn a paycheck. I try not to speak to any of them unless I have to. I just want my baby to be okay."

Ava nodded to Metford. They had all they needed.

As they went to the front door, Ava offered Belinda three business cards without saying anything. She walked out with Metford.

"Did you give someone else one of your cards and tell them to call you if they needed anything? You have got to stop doing that," Metford said as he opened the car door.

"That's my business. And it wasn't my card this time. I gave her the numbers for some organizations that might be able to help her and her daughter."

"You know she'll pay-scale out of most of those programs."

"Not those. There are people who will help with Amanda's treatments. They'll pay for a few treatments per year using the money that has been donated to their organization. If they can't do that, there are branches that will help with utility bills, mortgage payments, cars, whatever smaller expenses there are."

"You're a good person, Ava, but you get too invested in the struggles of strangers sometimes. It worries me."

"Can we drop it, please? This is how I am. This is me."

"And it's not a bad thing. For other people. I'm just afraid that, one day, it's going to come back to bite you somehow. I actually admire that you have so much empathy for people." His smile was softer than usual.

"You know it's because you lack any sort of empathy, right?" She chuckled.

After several awkward moments of silence, Metford smiled his usual roguish smile. "You might be right."

CHAPTER NINE

It was impossible to decide if Macomber, Stakhovsky, and Sanders were simply bitter toward Ethan for some slight, or some perception of him being treated with favoritism at work that made them all speak badly of the man even after his murder.

In a place as large as Patapsco Bay Terminal, there were always the bosses' favorites, and that always inspired bitterness and jealousy in a few of the other employees. No matter what policies were put into place to avoid such ugly situations, they always survived and reared their heads again. Like death and taxes; envy, anger, and rivalry in the workplace are certainties of life.

No one on the team could decide if Ethan was a bad person, or if his personality just clashed with certain others, and those people were more willing to speak out.

"So, what now?" Santos asked. "The divide isn't equal. There are more people who say Ethan was reliable, fair, hardworking, and a law-abiding citizen than say otherwise."

"We have to figure it out for ourselves. There's still a lot to learn about his personal and even his work life." Ava pointed to the bagged evidence on the table in front of her. "Planners, membership, and that odd poker chip are the main things I would like to unravel. I think our answer lies in this evidence. Somewhere. The answer to why Ethan was killed might be staring us right in the face, and we simply don't see it." She flipped over the planners.

"The planners aren't much help," Dane said. "There's nothing written in any of them that points to any place or person. We don't even know for sure that Ethan is the one who put those times in them."

"These two were hidden at his home," Ava said. "He lived alone. How likely is it that someone else brought their planners in there and hid them?"

"Since you put it like that… Not very," Dane answered. "Are any of the prints back from the scene?"

Ava shook her head. "It'll be after lunch before they're finished running them. Until then, we need to dig up all we can on Ethan Holt. Ashton, look for any social media or online trails and run his credit and debit cards. I want to know where he was and when. Santos, run him through the systems—"

"But he was a CBP agent; he was vetted through the systems. I won't find anything there."

"Unless he was vetted prior to being hired, and not since. Or, not recently. There are ways to get around the background checks for government agents. We all know there are and we have to assume that Ethan, or his bosses, also had that knowledge. Don't underestimate them because they aren't with one of the intelligence agencies. We don't have the monopoly on all the knowledge or there wouldn't be any criminals." She turned away. "Dane, go talk to Ethan's family and find out who his closest friends were and what they're like. Metford, you're with me."

"Great. Are we leaving right now?" He reached for his jacket.

"No."

His hand stopped two inches from the back of the chair where his suit jacket hung. "No?"

"No," Ava said. She picked up the planners, membership card, and poker chip. She held out two planners and the membership card. "You're going to help me sort out Ethan's movements as well as I can."

Metford's shoulders slumped forward as if the planners weighed a ton. "Really? Can't we have Ashton run these through one of his super-smart techy computer programs or whatever?" He held out the membership card. "This, this is something we could be looking into while the computer works on the planners."

"Ashton has his assignment. Besides, he'd probably have to make the program, and by then we could be done with the three months of dates I'm interested in." She dragged a desk chair to an empty table and dropped the planner and poker chip. She was glad the hotel hadn't made them use the folding chairs as most hotels did. It was nice to have a comfortable seat in which to work. "Grab the casefile and let's get this done. I don't like this part of it either, but it needs to be done right."

He got the file and pulled his chair behind him. "Like no one else could do this right? I don't even know what we're doing or how we're going to do it. How do you figure out anything with just a bunch of times on a calendar?" He placed the items on the table and thumped into the chair.

"That's why I wanted you to help me. I have a plan, but I'll need some help, or it will take me all day. We have his work schedule for the last six months. His boss sent me a copy earlier. We have the planner Ethan kept at work. If the times in that planner match with his shifts at work, it's likely that's where he was and what he was noting in that planner."

"And if not?"

"That's why we have the other two planners. Ashton will have Ethan's credit and debit card transactions soon. Maybe we can match them to the times in one or more of the planners to figure out where Ethan was on certain days and times that are noted here."

After a moment's hesitation, Metford smiled and nodded. "All right. I see where you're going with this. Dane will find out when the family saw him, and we can match those days, if they're in here."

"Right. And so on, and so forth. We'll unravel this. It might take a while, and it will take all of us working together, but we'll figure it out."

They worked for an hour-and-a-half constructing a timeline from only the dates and times in all three planners. With the information, Ava used a whiteboard to draw a line intersected with three months and divided each with smaller lines to indicate days. Metford filled in the times from the planners and noted Ethan's scheduled workdays for the three months.

Backing up, Ava looked at the timeline and smiled. "That's something we can work with, I think. His work schedule doesn't line up with any of the times, though."

"Nope. The times are either an hour before his scheduled shift, during the middle of it, or after."

"So, maybe whatever he was up to on those days had nothing to do with work."

"When Ashton gets the locations from the financials, we can add them straight to the timeline."

Ava nodded. "Same with Dane's information. But for now, we're at a dead end with the planners." She picked up the membership card. "But this, we can follow up on now."

"We're going to Prestige?"

"We are."

Santos came in holding a stack of printouts. She offered them to Ava. "Nothing out of the ordinary. He's clean."

"No sign of duplicate reports being run in the last year or two?" Ava asked, taking the papers.

"None at all. I thought of that, too. It all seems legit to me. Where are you going?"

"We're going to Prestige," Metford said. A small smile played at the corners of his mouth.

"You're such a dude," Santos said. "Just the thought of that place gives me the ick. Bunch of rich misogynistic men." She shook her head. "Am I going with?" she asked Ava.

"Since you finished with this, yeah. Check if Dane will be finished in time to join us."

"You got it, boss." Santos dialed Dane's number and put the phone to her ear.

"Great," Metford said. "A ride along with buzzkill."

"Don't start," Ava said. "Let's go."

They climbed into the SUV. "Dane said she'll meet us there. She was on her way back to the hotel and should arrive about the same time we do."

Ava was glad she would have the women on her crew with her at the club. It might irk any men there, but that was okay by her. They needed to see and understand that their way of looking at women was outdated and no longer acceptable.

CHAPTER TEN

Downtown Baltimore was far from Ava's favorite place, but the grand, historic building that housed Prestige was a sight to behold, and even she was impressed as she walked toward the double-door front entrance. Adorned with intricate architecture, it conjured thoughts of a bygone era of decadence. At night, with the dim lighting, regal columns, and wrought iron details over the doors, the Prestige's entryway would surely radiate an air of opulence and exclusivity that was missing in the present-day world of its members. Ava marveled that all of that was on the outside. The mood would be set for the wealthy male members to slip seamlessly from their possibly hectic workday into some 1920s, or earlier, fantasy in which men ruled the world without question or argument from their female counterparts.

Dane gave a shrill whistle and raised her hand. She had parked farther down the street and walked to join them.

"You made it just in time," Santos said.

"Get much from the family?" Ava asked.

"Not a lot, but I did learn who some of Ethan's friends were. The family didn't have phone numbers or addresses for them, but they're mostly coworkers so I figured we had that information with the casefile."

"At least you got some information. Anything is better than nothing, and who knows where it will lead?" Ava headed for the double doors.

For all its beauty, the building still sent a cold spike of malcontent and anger through Ava's midsection. She knew the truth of what happened in places like Prestige. The word 'gentlemen' did not apply once the members were ensconced safely behind the paywall where the public couldn't see.

Metford whistled low with appreciation. "What a beaut, right?"

"A beaut? Really?" Ava shook her head.

"What? What's wrong with stating the obvious? The place is—"

"Yeah, I know. It's beautiful," Ava said, enunciating the last word for emphasis on the pronunciation. "Just because your head swoons over the bygone misogynistic era doesn't mean you have to start talking like they did back then."

He chuckled. "The dame has a temper."

"Good thing none of us were alive back then," Santos said, indicating herself, Dane, and Ava.

Ava bit back any further rebuttal and rang the doorbell.

A neatly manicured man in a black tailored suit opened the door. His smile slowly faded as he realized there were three women standing there. "May I help you?"

"You may, indeed," Ava said, flashing her badge. "We need to come in and—"

"I'm sorry, but I can't let you in. You're not members. I'm sorry."

"Did you not see?" Ava shoved her badge and ID under his nose.

"I can't let you in, but I'll get my boss. You can take it up with him. I'm only a doorman doing his job." He shut the door before Ava could argue.

"What the hell was that?" Santos asked. "He can't just *not* let us in or even hear you out."

"Yes, he can," Ava said with a tight exhalation to keep the anger at bay. "We don't have a warrant; he doesn't have to let us in."

"His boss will let us in," Metford said.

"What makes you so sure?" Santos asked.

"I'll talk to him." Metford shrugged his jacket straighter and ran a hand over his hair looking smug and sure.

Ava scoffed. "He'll let us in because we're FBI and it's the right thing to do, not because you, as a man, have some unspoken connection with him."

"It might make it easier if I spoke with him," Metford urged.

"If I need you to talk us into any place, I'll let you know." The words came out clipped and tipped with heat.

"Just saying: *Mano y mano* ..."

The door opened and Ava shifted so that she was between it and Metford. A tall man with sharp features, red hair, and an athlete's build smiled out at them. Ava was not fooled. The precisely measured smile was for show and nothing more. The look in his eyes said it all. Women were not welcome in Prestige. Especially women in positions of authority and power, and he was having nothing to do with it.

"Good afternoon. I'm Finnian Drake, managing operator of Prestige Gentlemen's Club," he said. "May I be of some assistance?"

Ava showed him her badge and ID. "We need to talk to you and possibly some of the other members about one of your former members."

"I'm sorry. This is an exclusive club. Members only. Unless you have a warrant, I can't let you in and just give you permission to harass the paying members. You understand, I'm sure."

"No, actually I don't understand. We're here on official business," Ava said through a tight jaw.

"So, you have a warrant, I assume?" Finnian Drake smiled, and the expression reminded Ava of a dragon from some fantasy movie she'd seen years before. The dragon smiled like that just before devouring a villager who had come to plunder its gold.

The slight hesitation was all Finnian needed for confirmation of his suspicion. "Right then. Thanks for stopping by, and I wish you all the best with your case." He stepped back into the shadowy interior to shut the door.

Metford bumped Ava as he moved quickly around her and put a hand against the door to stop it from closing entirely. "Mr. Drake," he said and chortled. "Finnian, if I could just have a moment of your time to explain what my boss is trying to say?"

Finnian emerged from the dimness with a genuine, if small, smile on his face. "A man of reason, I see." Finnian stepped out and offered Metford his hand.

After a hearty handshake and shoulder slap, a passerby would be unaware that the two men had only just met. They looked like old friends, and Ava's anger boiled in her chest.

"I know this is an exclusive club, and I know you have a reputation to uphold. I respect that, and so does my boss. She's used to being in charge." Metford leaned closer as if in confidence. "You know how that goes, I'm sure."

The men both laughed. Afterward, Finnian nodded solemnly. "Straight to their heads, in my experience."

For a split-second, Metford said nothing and stood motionless. Ava imagined the 'reloading page' wheel spinning in his brain, and then suddenly, he guffawed and slapped Finnian's shoulder good-naturedly as he managed to move him farther away from the three women.

"You know how it goes," he said, still laughing as he pointed to his head. "Straight to their heads," they said in unison. Metford cleared his throat after a moment. "It does, apparently, but we have to feed their illusions of power. That's just how it is nowadays, am I right?"

"Unfortunately, you are. Not that I have anything against women. I love them. All shapes and sizes, makes and models."

Still able to hear the conversation, Ava fumed. Metford's stupid tactic was working. Then again, maybe it wasn't all tactic. Maybe that's why it was working so well. Metford wasn't an Oscar-winning actor by any stretch of the imagination, but he was sure as hell giving the performance of his life this time. Unless it was only partially a performance. How many skewed perspectives did Finnian Drake and Metford share? Deep down, was Metford that much of a male chauvinist? Had she misjudged him so badly?

Just like I misjudged Jason Ellis, she thought miserably.

"Finnian, it would be a great help to me on this case if you would just let us in and talk to us for a few minutes," Metford said as the men made their way back toward the doors.

"It would be my pleasure to help out a kindred soul in need, Agent Metford." Finnian's smile was still of the genuine type. He stepped into the doorway with Metford at his side. He turned and motioned Ava, Dane, and Santos in as if they were only afterthoughts.

Ava strode in full of anger and some lump in her gut that she could only call resentment. The resentment had a clear target: Metford.

With the door shut, Ava noted the interior quickly. It was secondary to her anger. The foyer was lavish with mahogany woodwork, plush velvet drapes that framed entrances and hung over majestic, tall windows, and the glistening, oversized chandeliers would have been perfect in some billionaire's European castle where movies were filmed.

Finnian turned right, beckoning Metford to follow him into one of the spacious lounges furnished with leather armchairs and marble-topped tables. The men chatted easily about the interior and the furnishings, and all the rich old men who had started the club back in the nineteenth century.

If she had to endure much more, Ava suspected she might need to stop by the bar on the way out. She saw there was an extensive selection of top-shelf spirits behind three impeccably dressed and handsome bartenders. Bartenders that she suspected acted a lot like Finnian Drake and other men of his ilk.

"Excuse me," Ava said, interrupting Metford and Finnian.

"Yes?" Finnian asked in a saccharine tone as if he had no idea about the business at hand.

"We were going to speak to you about the case."

"Yeah, did you hear what happened to Ethan Holt?" Metford asked. "I suppose my first question should be whether you even know him."

Ava bristled at Metford's attempt to take the wheel again.

"Of course, I know him. Just as I know all the members here at Prestige. I hope he's not in any trouble."

Metford opened his mouth to say something, but Ava cut him off. "He's not in any trouble. He's dead. Murdered in his bed."

Shock registered on Finnian's face for a moment, and then he cleared his throat. "He's dead."

"That's what murdered means in this reality," she said. "Well, in most people's reality." She looked around the room. "Maybe in your little fantasy land here, it means something different, but not in the real world."

"That's a shame, but not totally unexpected," Finnian said, choosing to ignore her jabs.

"What? You expected him to end up murdered in his bed?" she asked in surprise.

"No, no. Of course not. It's a sad part of every person's reality now, isn't it? Nowhere is really safe. Not even your bed in your own home."

"You don't seem particularly fazed by any of this. Why is that?"

Finnian sighed and gave Metford a look that said he was tired of having to indulge the silly female, to yet again explain something so simple to one of the fairer sex. "All you have to do is look around at the world we live in. Look at the city we are in."

She shrugged.

"Don't you see all the violence staring back at you? That should be answer enough as to why I'm not fazed or shocked by Mr. Holt's death. I don't like to admit it, but I am afraid that I have been somewhat desensitized to violence and brutality over the last decades here in Baltimore and other big cities. Large cities seem to breed violence and death. If one doesn't become desensitized, he will be consumed by an abysmal and dark depression." He smiled brightly. "Wouldn't be hard to lose oneself in such a state and languish there, uselessly, forever."

They remained in the lounge several more minutes discussing Ethan Holt with Finnian Drake. Finnian had nothing bad to say about Ethan at all. He only praised Ethan, saying he was the kind of man they wanted as members of Prestige.

Prestige did not collect any personal data on their members. At least, that's what Finnian said. It was just the usual contact information and payment of dues receipts, although he suspected they might be able to give the FBI a list of dates when Ethan had been there in the last thirty days. After thirty days, all the security footage automatically dumped from the servers.

When Ava requested the footage, she was met with the same tired line about not having a warrant.

As they made their way to the entryway, Finnian escorted them, regaling them with the history of Prestige. Ava reached for the door, meaning to exit without slowing even for his passionate speech. He stepped swiftly between her and the door.

"The Prestige and its members are not the horrible things you have in mind. I can quite assure you that everything happening here is legal."

"And I bet the women are treated just like queens instead of merely entertainment that was put on this earth for the sole purpose of pleasing men like you." She reached around him, but he leaned his back against the door.

Ava's heart kicked and bucked as memories of trying to get out Jason Ellis' door surfaced and triggered her fight or flight response. She took two steps back, hands clenched at sides, and felt her nostrils flare. Metford put a hand on her shoulder, which she jerked away from. It was enough to bring her back to the present enough that she curbed the panic.

"The Prestige is a haven of elegance and indulgence, where guests can escape the hustle and bustle of the city and immerse themselves in a world of luxury and refinement without persecution or guilt. And, just so you know, yes, we treat all our fabulous women with the utmost consideration and respect," Finnian said.

Ava moved forward, grabbed the door handle, and yanked the door and Finnian with it. As she stepped out, she spat, "I doubt a man like you knows how to respect any woman, and I doubly doubt you treat your entertainers with anything of the sort." She stepped to the sidewalk. "We'll be in touch if we need anything else. And don't fret, we will have a warrant next time." She stormed toward the car, her ears ringing and her chest thrumming with unspent adrenaline.

CHAPTER ELEVEN

Metford caught up and jumped in the passenger seat as Ava started the engine. "Where to now?"

"Is Santos coming?"

"No, she's riding back with Dane. Well?"

"Well, what?" She pulled into the traffic. Brakes squealed as the car she darted in front of slammed on their brakes.

Metford flinched against possible impact and then spun in his seat to face her. "Do you need me to drive? Are you okay?"

"No, I absolutely do not need you to drive. I think you've driven quite enough today, don't you?"

"What are you talking about? Are you seriously mad at me over that back there with Finnian?"

"What do you think? Of course I am," she nearly yelled. "That's probably why Santos rode with Dane—neither one of them want to be around you right now either."

"You're serious," he stated flatly.

"Wouldn't you be mad if the shoe was on the other foot? What if I had done something like that?"

"Like what?"

"Like just jumping in and taking over the questioning, buddying up to some man-hater, and chatting her up like you, because you're a man, were just the stupidest thing around, and then going along with it right in front of you. Like that, Metford."

"I don't understand—"

"And you wouldn't because I know you, and I know you're not that good of an actor. You really feel that way about women, don't you? Don't you? Wow, did I misjudge you or what?" She thumped the steering wheel angrily with one hand and then laid on the horn when the car in front of her came to a sudden stop to allow a jaywalking man to cross the lane.

"Ava, chill out. They couldn't run him down."

"Why not? You don't care to mow down women in your way, do you? Is it because the pedestrian, who was jaywalking in case you didn't notice, was a *man*?" She yelled the last word and immediately regretted the juvenile outburst. But her arms shook and her torso vibrated with anger and another adrenaline dump.

"I don't condescend to you. I never buck the system because my boss is a woman, or because two of my closest coworkers are women. And never have I ever mown a woman down who was in my way. I'm not sexist, and you know it."

"Oh, no? Well, it certainly seemed that way up until five minutes ago."

He was silent for a moment. Ava gripped the wheel and clamped her mouth shut. She had to get a grip on her anger, or she would lose herself in it; do something she would regret.

"Does this have anything to do with the Jason Ellis situation?" Metford asked, not mincing words.

Heat rose to Ava's face and burned there. Her ears rang. Her muscles sang. And every nerve thrummed. It was akin to the fight or flight, only more intense because she could not run, and there wasn't a clear nemesis to fight. She fought only her own feelings and urges and fears. Metford had no right to bring up Jason or what she had been through with him and because of him. No right at all.

The argument that followed was less of an argument and more of a tirade aimed at hurting Metford. When it was over, he was silent and never took his eyes from the road through the rest of the drive.

As she pulled into the Harborview Inn parking lot, he broke his silence in a quiet, measured voice.

"You know, you're overreacting. Even for you, being hotheaded and quick to tell a person off, this whole thing that just happened was overreacting of the highest level I've seen yet."

She remained silent until she managed to drive to the far side and park the car. "Sorry. Let's just forget it and move on." She opened the door to get out.

"Sure. I'll forget how you just reamed me out and tore me a new one over a ploy we use all the time in our work; one that got us in the door back there without an argument or threats being thrown around, without all the unnecessary upset. But it's fine. We'll just forget it and move on." He flung his door open, got out, and slammed it hard enough to rock the SUV on its frame.

"Good!" she said loudly, barely keeping her cool.

Although she said it was all good, and she had apologized, she meant neither one. She was still angry. So angry, in fact, that she thought she might be sick before she got back to her room. The logical thing would be to apologize again, and mean it. He was right. They had used that ploy so many times she couldn't count them all. It was a staple in an agent's toolkit.

But he didn't have to be so believable, and use me as the example, she thought.

That set her stomach to churning again. The thought of Metford being anything like Finnian and the men who were members at Prestige was sickening. That she had been so wrong about her partner was even worse, but the worst was the personal betrayal. Even if he said he didn't mean it, she knew, on some level very deep down, he had.

Dane and Santos parked beside Ava, and she hurried away before they could see how messed up she was. She needed time to get herself under control again. Like it or not, she would have to push aside her personal feelings and continue working side by side with Metford until they were back in Fairhaven.

Behind her, Santos and Dane laughed and talked about the historic buildings and all the things to do in Baltimore as if they weren't bothered in the least by what Metford had done. Either they were hiding their true feelings better than Ava was, or they were being purposefully obtuse about it.

Did it bother her because Metford acted so 'alpha male'? Was he right that her reaction was rooted in the recent situation with Jason Ellis? Jason had been a textbook alpha male, and that was one of the things she had found most attractive about him. When Metford started acting in the same way, had it triggered her?

She had made the mistake of thinking that Jason was harmless and that he was just the result of his childhood environment. She mistakenly believed that, deep down, there was no way he could be a bad person, and at one point, she even thought about giving up her career to play the role of doting homemaker to his alpha male role. It had been fleeting, but she couldn't ignore that it had crossed her mind and had given her something to think seriously about.

Jason had turned out to be the worst kind of bad, and she had nearly lost her life because of that one lapse in judgment. Or had it been several small lapses as she continued to push away that niggling, nagging feeling that something wasn't quite right with the relationship?

She shut and locked her room door. The case needed working, but she couldn't work until she got her mind right. The last thing she wanted to do was blow up on Metford in front of the whole team. Undermining her own ability and authority was the opposite of what she needed to do.

After an hour, she conceded to herself that it was highly possible that she was being too sensitive about the whole thing. Even though Jason would spend the rest of his life in prison, he still seemed to have more control over her than he had before. It wasn't right to take it out on Metford even if his actions had triggered her. She was stronger than all the new-era language around how to handle stress and how to handle yourself with kid gloves and lots of love. Those were crutches and made people weak. She had to overcome and get control, or risk ruining a friendship and possibly her career.

CHAPTER TWELVE

Ava and the team were going through all of the evidence from Patapsco Bay Terminal that pertained to Ethan Holt. Ava was sure there was some pattern to the seemingly random times and dates in the planners. Seeing that pattern was proving very difficult. The times did not match with his work schedule, and in fact, most of the mid-day times coincided with days that he worked. The appointment times fell on his lunch hour. Two days that Ethan had left early were the same days that had early appointment times. Other than those two, everyone was coming up empty on matching the times with anything.

Ava was glad for the distraction when her phone rang. She spoke with the lab and then went to her laptop.

"What's going on?" Santos asked. "Everything okay?"

Ava pulled up the file and hit 'print.' "We got a match on the fingerprints lifted from the faces of the drawers at Ethan's house."

THE FORGOTTEN GIRLS

The whole team stopped what they were doing and looked to her questioningly.

"Silas Grey." She worked at her laptop for a minute as the others talked. "I sent the new report to all of your devices." She picked up the printouts. "Silas Grey frequents..." She scanned down the sheet and smiled. "Porter Casino and Hotel. He is partial to the casino side."

"Where's that?" Dane asked.

"Close to Patapsco Bay Terminal," Ava answered.

"I have credit card records for Ethan that put him at the casino at least once every weekend," Ashton said.

"Why would someone from the casino be going through things at Ethan's house?" Santos asked. "Maybe Ethan and Silas were friends."

"Silas isn't on any of the lists of people we've spoken to so far, and no one has mentioned him to me," Ava said. "Anyone heard the name before?"

No one had.

"And his family didn't mention a Silas Grey?" Ava asked Dane.

"No."

"Then we need to find him. Run him, get me an address." Her phone rang again, and she answered. It was Chief Panko of the Baltimore police. There had been another murder. She got the pertinent information and hung up. "Everyone with me. There's been another murder, and we're needed at the scene immediately."

"Who was killed?" Ashton asked.

"Another CBP agent. Emily Harper." Her phone dinged with a notification, and she read it.

"Was she killed at her home, too?" Dane asked.

"Terrace View, apartment 3C," Ava said.

"Answers that question, I guess," Santos said.

"She's on the list of Ethan's coworkers," Ashton said, holding out a piece of paper to Ava.

"GPS says Terrace View is about thirty minutes from Patapsco Bay, but it's only twelve miles," Dane said.

Metford stood at the door, silently waiting for the rest of them to catch up. Ava noticed he had nothing to say unless someone asked him a direct question. Not making small talk with him was fine with her. She still had not made up her mind whether she was in the wrong, or if it had been him. That deep inner voice told her that she was the one in the wrong, but it was easy to ignore that voice when there was a new case to work.

Santos groaned. "That means the traffic is going to be three kinds of crazy on a cracker." She hefted her bag over one shoulder, leaned into the weight, and motioned for Dane to head for the door. "I'm riding with you again."

"Why riding? Why aren't you driving this time? I drove last time."

"Because you're the one with all the big city driving experience." Santos grinned as they walked past Metford and out the door.

"Do I ride with you or Dane?" Ashton asked.

Ava looked from him to Metford. She could send Metford with Dane and Santos and have Ashton as a riding partner. She could let Ashton ride with her and Metford, but she did neither. All things considered, she and Metford worked better as a team in the field, and Ashton worked better with Santos. "Ride with Dane and Santos. We'll meet you there."

Metford waited until Ava was almost to the door, and walked out it, leaving her to exit alone. He was in the elevator when she turned the corner, and for a moment, she thought he was going to let the doors shut with just him and Ashton inside. At the last moment, and with Ashton giving him a puzzled look, Metford stuck his hand between the doors and held it until she was there.

The ride to Terrace View was tense and quiet. Very quiet for a ride with Metford. Their argument had done a number on him, and regret began to gnaw at Ava. It wasn't their argument; it had been hers. If she had not jumped down his throat, there would never have been an argument.

Although she knew and understood it was probably her fault alone, she could not find an appropriate, or comfortable, way to open the conversation to issue any sort of apology. So, they arrived at Terrace View with the tension hanging between them.

Ava and Metford, without a word, plunged themselves into the pandemonium at Terrace View and started helping get the scene under tighter control. Dane, Santos, and Ashton worked from their side to do the same. Ava had to wonder if the scene was being protected better than the outside and the lobby were. Police officers, detectives, a forensic crew, and residents swarmed the place. It was apparent that most of Terrace View's residents were home and they were scared.

Working her way through the crowd, Ava picked up bits of information about the decedent. Emily Harper was liked by her neighbors, she had lived at Terrace View for almost a decade, and the young men thought she was hot.

When she and Metford reached the third-floor hallway, they were met with chaos again. The police had tried to clear away as many people as possible while the scene in 3C was being investigated, but the corridor was still packed with slow-moving people trying to get a glimpse beyond the open door. An officer warded off two young women with cameras on selfie-sticks as they tried to get a couple of candid shots inside.

Ava stepped past the officer, and Metford remained to wait for Dane, Santos, and Ashton. Just as she spotted the chief and the detective, Metford stepped up beside her.

"They're here," he said without looking at her.

"Thanks." Ava moved toward the chief, calling his name.

Chief Panko turned and a look of relief washed over his face. "Thank God you're finally here." He shook her hand. "Emily Harper. Forty-two. She was a CBP agent for twelve years. Record as clean as they come." He bumped a long table behind the sofa and looked over his shoulder. "The crew is almost finished processing the scene. If you can make your way to the end of the room, you can see for yourself. Damn shame what happened here. Looks like she was sleeping on the couch for the night when she was attacked. No sign of forced entry, and no sign that she had a boyfriend staying over, or anything like that."

Ava moved to the end of the room and stepped around a woman in gloves kneeling down taking photos.

The scene was bloody, violent, and gruesome.

And it looked a lot like the scene at Ethan's house.

CHAPTER THIRTEEN

"Santos," Ava said after they had a moment to take in the scene.

"Yeah?"

"Help the officer at the door. He's having a hard time keeping the rubberneckers out. Shut the door and clear that hallway. If anyone needs to get to or from their unit, move them along. If they give you trouble, get their name for questioning."

Turning back to face Emily Harper, Ava studied the scene more closely. It was likely that she had either been sleeping on the couch for the night, or at the very least napping there. The television was not playing, so it was unlikely that she fell asleep watching a movie unless she had set the timer to turn it off.

"Do you have a roundabout on the time of death?" she asked one of the forensic team.

"I would say around twelve hours. Rigor is at its peak, and her body temp is just above eighty."

Ava looked at her watch. Eleven o'clock. "Her time of death would have been around eleven last night?"

The man nodded. "Give or take an hour."

Ava turned to her team. "How many older people did you see on the way in?" she asked all of them.

"Maybe two that would be considered older," Ashton said. "Unless you mean retirement age and older."

"Old enough to be in bed and asleep between ten and twelve last night," Ava said.

They all shook their heads. Ava exhaled. "Normally, people who work dayshift jobs that start between six and eight in the morning would be in bed no later than midnight, right?"

"I would think so," Dane said.

"To get a good night's sleep, they should, preferably, be asleep by ten," Ashton said.

Metford and Dane gawked at him in disbelief.

"You're supposed to get between six and eight hours of sleep every night. That's what research shows…" He let his words trail off.

"And who gets enough sleep?" Dane asked. "Ever? I didn't sleep six hours a night even as a kid."

"Me neither," Ava said. She turned to the detective. "Did anybody hear anything last night?"

"Did you see that colossal cluster out there, or was it just me?" He scoffed and took a step toward her. "I questioned a few people, but nobody heard a thing."

"Was the television on when you got here?"

"I wasn't the first on the scene. Bobby was. Hey, Bobby, was the TV on when you got here?"

An officer in the kitchen answered, "Nope."

The detective turned to Ava. "Nope. Why is that important?"

"Just wondering if she fell asleep watching something. And, if she had the TV playing, it might have covered the noise of her attack."

"Unless the killer turned it off afterward, it was quiet when she was killed." He walked toward the bedroom where another man was asking for his assistance.

Emily was half on and half off the couch. Her upper half had slid almost to the bloodstained carpet while her lower half was flat on the sofa cushions.

"Is her body positioned oddly to you?" Ava asked the team.

They closed rank around her and studied the position. They agreed that it was odd.

"If she had been fighting off the attacker, her whole body would have ended up on the floor," Dane said.

"Yeah, if there was a struggle, looks like she'd be on the floor," Metford said.

"Unless the attacker straddled her," Ashton countered, motioning toward Emily's hips. "If the killer straddled the victim and stabbed and slashed until she was dead, the victim might have been only trying to get away towards the end of the struggle, resulting in the odd position."

"But if she was dead and the killer got off, wouldn't Emily's body have just tumbled to the floor?" Dane asked.

"The victim is very athletic. Her legs are heavy with muscle. The muscle mass in her upper body is much less than in her lower resulting in the lower half being much heavier in comparison. If the killer remained in place until the victim stopped struggling, then this would be the result. See how her elbow is caught on the edge of the coffee table? That probably helped keep her in place until rigor set in. Then the stiffening of the muscles kept it in place."

"How big would the killer have been?" Ava asked rhetorically as she leaned in to see the cushion behind Emily's hips better.

"Probably strong but not large," Ashton said. "Same size as the victim, give or take a few pounds."

"Her name is Emily Harper," Ava said. "And it was a rhetorical question, but since you seem to have an answer, tell me why you say that."

"Because if they had been larger, the struggle probably wouldn't have gone on long enough for Emily to sustain all the superficial defensive wounds. Besides, for my theory about the killer straddling the vic—Emily Harper—to work, they couldn't have been very big or they couldn't have straddled her on this couch. It's too narrow. And the attacker couldn't have been too small, or Emily likely would have bucked them off easily."

"You know, Ashton, you're pretty darn good at this, man," Metford said, grinning. "And here I was under the impression that you were just a tech nerd."

Ashton straightened his glasses and stared levelly at Metford. "I've had the same training as the rest of you, and more than some of you. Metford."

Metford held up his hands. "Hey, I didn't mean to offend. I was trying to compliment you, buddy."

Ashton looked flustered and uncertain. "Oh. In that case, thanks." There was a pause that made it seem Ashton was finished, and then, he added, "buddy."

The awkward exchange made Ava cringe and Dane step away from the men.

"I think Emily was probably sleeping pretty hard when she was attacked," Ava said. "The defensive wounds are not deep and there aren't many of them." She leaned closer, turning her head from side to side to get the best angle on the wounds.

Dane leaned forward and looked, too. "If she had been awake, there would be more of a mess here, too." She stood straight and looked at the furniture. "She would have been plenty strong enough to shove the coffee table around in a bid to get off the couch. Might have even been able to punch the attacker." She pointed out Emily's biceps. "I'm not saying she's a Rhonda Rousey, but she's packing some heat in those arms."

Ava turned to the local crew working the scene. "Be extra sure to get samples from her hands and fingernails. She might have hit or grabbed the perp." She turned back to the body. "If she grabbed the perp, that would explain the lack of deep defensive wounds. The attacker wouldn't have wanted to risk a self-inflicted injury with full power strikes at the victim's hands and arms."

"Mm," Metford said, shaking his head.

"What?" Ava asked.

"If she had grabbed the perp, I think there would be evidence of a more brutal struggle here."

"So, am I supposed to just ignore that Emily could have grabbed the attacker? Just not mention to be extra vigilant with her hands and nails because it looks like she didn't put up much of a fight?"

"You're still mad. Good to know." He turned to the doorway and then back to face the scene again.

"No, I'm not. Sorry, it's just that I'm trying to work out every scenario I can think of here so we know what we're looking for in the attacker. You and Dane both make very valid points, and they're noted." Feeling very put on the spot, Ava took a deep breath and forced herself not to look around to see if the local PD crew had heard their exchange. Dane and Ashton had, and that was bad enough. "Please, any other insights or suggestions, I would be glad to hear them." She looked pointedly at each team member in turn.

"Well, I do have another insight," Metford said. "I think it's important. If the killer, as Ashton suggested, straddled Emily to deliver the killing blows with a knife, he would have walked out of here covered in blood. I think that might have been noticed by someone. If not here, somewhere."

"You're right," Ava said, looking to Ashton and Dane. "Any ideas? If our killer walked out of here with blood spatter all over them, why didn't anyone report seeing a man covered in blood?"

"If the killer had a kill kit, he might have had a change of clothes. Could have even worn a poncho to protect his clothing," Dane said. "I've seen some things working in New York."

"If the poncho theory is right, there would be evidence of drips or even pooling across Emily's midsection." He clicked on a flashlight and pointed it to Emily's waist. A moment later, they all stood straight. "Well, I didn't see any such signs of pooling or dripping blood."

"We won't rule it out, though," Ava said. "We need to check for any drip marks on the floor and other furniture. If there are any, the killer might have discarded a bloody poncho somewhere within a five-block radius."

"Right," Dane said. "We can tell the trash pickup crews to be on alert."

"Let's do a search of the apartment for evidence. We need to question the residents and the manager before we leave, and we still need to speak with Silas Grey and ask why his fingerprints were all over Ethan Holt's house."

"No rest because of the wicked, eh?" Dane asked.

"Apparently not," Ava agreed.

"In our line of work, that's job security," Metford said, grinning.

After a search of the apartment, the team realized that Emily's ID, workplace badges, laptop, and cellphone were missing. Again, it looked like all the obvious missing items were related to her work at Patapsco Bay Terminal for Customs and Border Protection.

"I'm not sure why she has this," Dane said, pointing into the corner of a closet in the bedroom. "But I thought you should see it. It is hooked up, and looks like it has the material to actually print items."

Ava looked into the large closet and was shocked to see a desktop 3-D printer sitting on a table. Ashton stepped in to take a look. He started talking in his computer nerd lingo, and Ava stepped out.

"Definitely mark this for evidence," she said. "There's a reason it's sitting in a walk-in closet instead of out here in the open."

"Maybe there wasn't a good place to put it out here," Dane said. "It is gaudy and awkward looking, and the rest of Emily's stuff seems to be chosen and placed with taste."

Ava shook her head. "She didn't want people knowing she had it. That's the feeling I get."

"It is strange to have it in there," Metford said.

"Moving on to question the masses now. Spread out and talk to as many people as possible," Ava said.

CHAPTER FOURTEEN

While Dane and Aston began their rounds of questioning the residents, Santos remained with the officer at the apartment door and questioned residents from there. At the end of the hallway, Ava asked Metford to accompany her around the building to look for security cameras and speak with the building manager.

"Okay, there were cameras at all the entrance and exit doors, two in the lobby, and the ones on the elevators," Metford said. "That's a lot of footage. The killer must be on one of them, if not more."

"If all of them are real cameras," Ava said. "You know how that is. It's cheaper to put up the fake ones, and a lot of building owners use that tactic nowadays."

"Compromise safety to save a penny."

"Building manager's office is over here." Walking toward the back of the property, Ava pointed to a brick add-on room that looked better than an afterthought, but not like it had been part of the original plans. It was two floors high.

"What building manager has a two-story tiny home built at the back of the apartment building?" Metford asked.

Ava looked at her notepad. "One Mr. Brion Ambrose, apparently. Not such a bad gig if you get this all to yourself." On closer inspection, the add-on was larger than a small apartment unit; it was more like four. Probably two units on the bottom and two on top. Plenty of room to live in for one person, or even two.

Ava rang the doorbell.

A man in his early fifties with thinning hair and glasses opened the door. "Been expecting you. Come on in," he said affably.

"Mr. Ambrose?" Ava asked.

"That's me." He closed the door behind them.

The room was obviously not a living space. Mr. Ambrose had stored extra linens, lamps, side tables, and chairs. The items were wrapped in plastic and stacked higher than his head.

"I live upstairs in those rooms, so don't think I live in this rat-maze of clutter. This is stuff for the apartments. You'd be amazed how many tenants call me needing this stuff because they're having unexpected guests, or because their stuff is broken. We make 'em pay for it, and it's a lot more than what we pay, but they still depend on me to get it to them. Easiest way is to have some on hand."

"Mr. Ambrose, we need the security footage for the last twenty-four hours."

"Poor Miss Harper. Lovely woman. Never caused any trouble, never got any complaints about her, and she was never late with her rent. I'm just sick that something so horrible could happen right here in Terrace View. I hope you catch the bastard." He raised his eyebrows and moved close to speak in confidence. "And I hope you think twice about allowing the justice system to take care of him, if you know what I mean." He pushed his glasses up and cleared his throat as he stepped away. "I have the entrance and exits covered with cameras, but the rest of them are dummies. Never thought anything like this would come along that we might need them." He led them through the maze of stacked inventory to a large room at the back, which was a very large office.

"We figured at least some of them were fakes," Metford said.

"The ones in the elevators were until last summer. I watched a true crime documentary about a woman who was killed in her room and the killer hauled the body out in a piece of luggage. If there had been cameras in the elevator and hallway, he would have been seen adjusting her body several times, but there was enough evidence to convict him anyway. I just thought it would be best to put real ones in there. They're cheap as hell, but they do the job in such close quarters."

"We need all the footage from each camera," Ava said.

"Thumb drive do okay?" Mr. Ambrose asked.

"That'll be fine," Ava said.

"Good because I don't know how to do all that compression stuff to send it in an email. If you know how, feel free."

"Thumb drive is fine, Mr. Ambrose," Ava assured him.

It took thirty minutes to get the footage transferred, and each camera was a separate file on the drive. "It's all there. All I have for the last twenty-four hours."

"Great. Do you mind if we look through the footage on your computer before we go?" Ava asked.

Mr. Ambrose floundered for a moment, but agreed.

Metford took a seat beside Ava as they watched through each file, and at the end, neither had seen anything that would raise red flags.

"Well, did you find anything?" Mr. Ambrose asked when they stood to leave.

"Not a thing," Ava said. "Everyone on the footage looked like they belonged here."

"You mean, nobody looked like they'd just murdered a woman," he said flatly.

"Yeah, something like that. You said Emily Harper was a sweet woman. How well did you really know her?"

"I've known her since she moved here. She used to have people over quite often; she was kind of a social butterfly back then."

"What changed?" Metford asked.

Ambrose shrugged. "Don't know. She just grew out of it, I guess. Don't we all?"

"When did she stop being so social?" Ava asked.

"I don't know. Maybe a year or two back. Hard to keep up with things if you don't put them on a calendar."

"Thank you, Mr. Ambrose." Ava walked back through the narrow walkway and to the door.

"If you need anything else, you know where to find me. And remember what I said about catching the killer." He winked and put a finger to the side of his nose before shutting the door.

"I'm sorry, did he just insinuate that we should—"

"Don't say it, Metford," Ava said quickly. "But, yes, that's exactly what he did."

Metford chuckled. "He knows we're FBI, right?"

"We showed him our IDs, I don't know how he couldn't. Just a man giving his take on how the outcome should play out. That's why people like us are the ones with badges and guns, and not people like the mild grandfatherly Mr. Ambrose."

"He wouldn't do it even if he had the chance."

Ava wasn't so sure. "People can surprise you. I've learned that. Sometimes the hard way." Jason Ellis came immediately to mind.

Metford played it safe and didn't respond.

They met Ashton and Dane in the parking lot. Santos was just coming out of the building. The ME had just driven out of the parking lot with the body, and forensics were behind Santos and the local cops.

"Looks like we all finished up at the same time," Metford said.

"Santos and the cops and the ME were only waiting for forensics to finish with the scene," Ava said. She stopped at the SUV and waited for Ashton. She held out the thumb drive to him.

Taking the thumb drive, he asked, "Security footage?"

"Yep. I need you to match every person in the footage with tenants of Terrace View. We watched it, and everyone seemed to belong here."

"Maybe a tenant killed her, then."

"The scene was so similar to Ethan Holt's that I find that hard to believe. Not impossible, but unlikely. The tenants here are just regular people going about their lives. Emily was the only federal employee in the whole place, and her CBP items were missing just like with Ethan. I think it has something to do with the CBP."

"At the very least, Emily's and Ethan's murders are connected," Metford said.

Ava agreed. "Anyone you find who doesn't live here will be investigated and questioned by you three."

"Where are you going?" Santos asked.

"Metford and I are going back to the CBP building."

"For what?" Metford asked. "The deputy commissioner isn't going to let us into Emily's files any more than he let us into Ethan's. We don't have a warrant."

"We're already out this far," Ava said. "It won't hurt to stop there and ask. Now that two of his agents are dead, maybe he'll see reason."

Metford turned and got into the passenger seat.

CHAPTER FIFTEEN

AVA MADE SURE THE OTHERS KNEW THEIR ASSIGNMENT. "COMPILE the interviews as well."

She got into the driver's seat. "What now?" she bit.

"We're wasting time going back to the CBP. You know he's not going to let us see the files."

"No, I don't, and neither do you."

"We could be looking into Silas Grey instead. That feels more like the right direction. More like forward movement instead of treading water."

"And I don't understand why you're so upset about it. We're already out this far. It makes more sense than coming back at a later date with the warrant. We could get useful information from their files that would propel us even farther forward than talking to Silas Grey."

Metford shook his head. "You're just so set on being right, on getting your way, that you don't see we're wasting time. While we're doing this, the killer could be targeting his next victim."

"On getting my way? You think I'm only going back there to try and get my way?" Anger reared up, and she couldn't squash it.

"You've been like this forever as far as I can tell, but ever since you came back from the whole Jason Ellis situation, you've been like a rabid dog about it. You sacrifice forward momentum to prove that you can get others to do what you want in cases. It's like you're out to prove you're right no matter the cost to the case, to your team, or to yourself."

"You're wrong," she said sternly, her eyes stinging.

"Am I?"

"Yes."

"Prove it, then."

"How?" she asked through clenched teeth.

"Let's put in for the warrants, get the info on Silas Grey, and go find him. Leave the CBP until another time. If I'm wrong, you'll be able to do it."

Ava eased off the accelerator. The turn was just ahead. Go left to the CBP; go right to the Harborview Inn. Was Metford right? Had she been that much worse since Jason?

She sat at the intersection, palms sweating as she debated which turn to make. The traffic inched forward. At the last minute, she jerked the wheel and jumped into the left turn lane. A horn blared and brakes squawked indignantly behind them.

"Guess that's our answer," Metford said in a low, even voice. None of the irritation or anger from just moments earlier was there. He sounded almost defeated.

"Guess it's your answer. This just feels like the next logical step to me. We're already out here. Why not give it a try? If he says no, it was a half-hour out of our day."

The remainder of the ride was silent, which was no big surprise to Ava at this point. It was better if they were silent when they disagreed. At least for a while. Metford had hit on some valid points about her and the way she was after the incident with Jason versus the way she had been before. Some soul-searching needed to be done, but until she had time to do it, she would be quick to go on the defensive. She could admit that much to herself, but she didn't like any of it. Then again, who enjoys hearing about or admitting their own shortcomings?

The CBP building loomed in front of them as Ava parked. It was the same process to get in as before, and the closer they drew to the deputy commissioner's office, the more certain she was that the end result would also be the same as before. It was too late to turn back. All she could do was hope for a different outcome.

"Mr. Halloway, thank you for seeing us," Ava said, trying for cheery but not overly cheery as they entered the office.

Mr. Halloway's scowl lightened only a little. He stood and removed his glasses, dropped them on the desk, and motioned for Ava and Metford to take a seat. "I assume you are here to request more employee files."

"You would assume correctly, sir. Emily Harper. She was—"

Halloway held up a hand. "I'm well aware of the situation, Special Agent James. However, that does not change my decision about the warrants. I won't let you into the files without one." He sat, still holding up a hand. "For each employee." He put down his hand.

"Surely, you can understand how serious this situation has become," Ava said. "First Ethan Holt, and now Emily Harper. They both worked at Patapsco Bay Terminal. In both cases, their work-related items were taken from the scenes by the killer. They're probably linked, and by all that we've seen, that's the way we're going to be investigating this."

"But it is two separate crimes," Halloway stated.

"We are aware of that. We need those files to see if and how Emily and Ethan are connected other than working at Patapsco Bay Terminal. We need to know what they might have been investigating there. Were they working on similar cases? Did they both investigate the same person or business? If so, what did they find? What were the results of their investigations? Do you see my dilemma?"

"I do, and I still can't help with that. You can go back to Patapsco and search there again. Maybe one of them took notes on their cases. Other than that, I don't know what to tell you except that you should get the warrants and then come back."

"Your officers are being brutally murdered in their homes, while they're asleep, and you don't seem to care at all."

"I assure you that I do care. We all do. There are also procedures and policies that are in place for good reason. I can't, and I won't, break those rules. Not even for you. No matter how convincing you are, you are wasting your time. Return with the proper documentation, and then we will have something to discuss. I'll be more than happy to oblige at that time."

Ava didn't excuse herself. She didn't thank Halloway. She simply stood and walked out.

She and Metford got back into the SUV without a word. "Go ahead and say it," she said.

"Say what?"

"You were right. I was wrong. Are you happy now?" Why did she feel like a petulant child admitting that?

"No. I wasn't going to say anything about it."

"Liar." Even more like a whiny little kid who didn't get her way. Why couldn't she just shut up about it? Why couldn't she just let it go?

He exhaled deeply and shook his head. "I wasn't. Hell, I even had some hope there for about three-point-five."

"Really? You?"

"I know. Sounds ridiculous, but there it is. Sometimes, your stubborn optimism rubs off on me."

"Stubborn optimism is not what you called it before we got here."

"No, it wasn't, but doesn't it sound better than what I called it earlier?"

She laughed tightly despite her effort not to. "You're not wrong about that, but I still know what you called it before."

"Yeah, well…" He let it hang in the air unfinished.

"Yeah, well…" she imitated. "It's possible that you were right."

"Maybe, but probably not." He scoffed and waved it off with a grin.

She nodded and readjusted her grip on the wheel. "Yeah, probably not, but I didn't want to keep telling you that."

They both laughed. It wasn't the unencumbered laughter they had always shared before, but it was a step in the right direction. There was still the apology she needed to give for the way she had acted after being at Prestige.

"What are we doing now?"

"Not sure. I think we should look into Silas Grey. If he's been located."

"Sounds like a good idea to me."

CHAPTER SIXTEEN

"Can't say I'm thrilled to be back here," Metford said as he and Ava got out of the SUV.

"Yeah, me neither. It's not my favorite place to be," Ava said, walking. "I'd really like to know what's going on here that's cost two agents their lives in the last two days, though."

Santos, Dane, and Ashton joined them as they descended toward the port director's office.

"Is there a boss left to speak with who might give you more information about the two agents?" Dane asked.

"There are all kinds of bosses, but they all said basically the same thing about Ethan. He was a great employee, outstanding work ethics, by-the-book practices and procedures, and he was liked by most of his coworkers," Ava replied.

"Well, something has to be off in that evaluation, or Ethan wouldn't be dead," Santos said.

"We don't know that," Ashton said.

"No, we don't know that for sure, but come on," Santos said. "He and Emily wouldn't have been murdered in such a similar way if everything was kosher. That's what I'm saying."

"Agreed," Metford said. "And I don't think any of us can argue that the cases aren't linked."

The team agreed.

The port director told them Emily was a good worker, but that he didn't know her very well. She kept to herself and was quiet at work.

After a few more questions, Ava thanked him and asked that he point them in the direction of Emily's office.

"She didn't have an office," Chambers said, looking confused.

"I thought she did," Ava said.

Chambers shook his head. "Not for over a year now."

"What happened? Why did she have an office but doesn't now?"

"She wanted to be transferred over to the other department. Ethan Holt was already in that office, so she took the position under him. Came with a little pay cut, too. Shocked me; all of us, really. I tried to talk her out of it, but she was insistent that she wanted out of her area and that she was fine working under Ethan." He shrugged. "What was I going to do, force her to stay where she was and risk her quitting? No. She was too dependable and good at her job for that."

"Did she have any personal space at all here? A storage area, a locker, anything where she could store her things?"

The door opened and a woman walked in. "Sorry, didn't mean to interrupt. Should I come back?" she asked Chambers.

"No," he said, motioning for her to stay. "As a matter of fact, would you mind showing these agents where Emily Harper's locker is?"

"Is she okay? Is she in some kind of trouble?"

Ava and the team looked at her and then at Chambers.

"She's not in trouble," Ava said, seeing that Chambers deferred to her.

"You're FBI, though. I remember you from Ethan..." the woman's voice trailed off and her face paled. "Is she?"

"She was murdered last night in her home," Ava said. There was never an easy way to say that sort of thing, especially when she was unsure of the recipient's reaction.

"Alex, are you okay?" Chambers asked, standing and moving toward her.

She inhaled sharply and straightened her shoulders. "I'm fine." She waved him off. "I'll be okay. It's just... Two of our employees in two days?"

Chambers nodded. "I know. It's a tragedy to say the least."

"Were you two close?" Ava asked Alex.

"No. Not really. I mean, everyone knew her, and she was a great worker, but we weren't friends. Friendly, is the best way to put it. She kept to herself mostly." Alex got her emotions under control. "It's just such a shock. What did she ever do to anybody?"

"That's what we'd like to find out," Ava said. "If you could show us where her locker is located, that would help."

"Of course." Alex led them out. "Do you think it's the same person who killed Ethan?" She walked ahead of them down a narrow hallway that disallowed walking two abreast.

"What makes you think that?" Metford asked.

"I don't, I mean, I do, but…" She stopped and turned to them. "Don't you?" She waited for a split-second and then turned and started walking again.

"Is there any information you could give us about her?" Ava asked. "She ever tell you anything about her personal life? Family, friends, boyfriends, anything like that?"

The woman shrugged. "Not really. She didn't seem to be involved with anyone outside of work, as far as I knew. But again, I don't know her super well. Didn't."

They exited the building, entered another, followed another hallway, and finally entered into a locker room.

"Right here," Alex said, putting a hand on one of the lockers. She jerked her hand back as if burned. "Sorry. I shouldn't have touched it, right?"

"It's okay," Ava said. "Is it locked?"

"With a padlock, yes, and we don't have keys to them. They're personal lockers. Only the owners have the keys."

"What about bolt cutters?" Santos asked.

"We have those in the maintenance room. Should I get a pair?" Still clasping her hands together, Alex moved to the exit.

"Yes, thank you," Santos said.

"Be right back." Alex disappeared.

"Was she okay?" Santos asked.

Ava considered it. "Santos, you can break the lock. Dane, you take Alex into another room and question her while we go through the locker."

"What about the other interviews?" Ashton asked. "Unless you think we all need to be here to go through that." He tilted his head toward the locker.

"No, I think Metford and I can handle it. Santos, after you break the lock, you and Ashton can go speak with Emily's coworkers. It will make our time here shorter."

"And I'm all for that," Metford said. "It's claustrophobic in here."

Alex returned and gave Santos the bolt cutters. Dane immediately asked Alex to step into another room for an interview. The woman was nervous, but went without hesitation.

Santos broke the lock, handed the cutters to Metford, and she left with Ashton.

Ava opened the door, and was shocked to find more than she had thought she would. "How much stuff do most people keep in their work lockers?" she asked.

"It looks like she was living out of this thing," Metford said.

"Changes of clothes, shoes, even socks," Ava said.

Ava pulled out a few items. "Planner, checkbook, who even has one of these still? Get the bag. We're just going to take all of it."

"All of it? It won't all fit."

"You brought the large paper and all the plastic bags, right?" Ava caught herself before she assumed he had not and launched into a sermon.

"I did, but still." He took out the bags and set them on a stainless table beside the stand of lockers.

"It will fit, then."

Ava folded each item of clothing and put them into the paper bag. The clothes alone filled it to the top without the shoes. As she cleaned off the top she pulled a large catalog-type book slowly toward her. Something clattered to the metal shelf. She put her hand to the back and raked her fingers gently toward the edge of the shelf. A poker chip appeared.

"That's a chip like the one in Ethan's drawer," Metford said in a surprised tone.

Ava turned the chip over and over. "You think she was into gambling, too?"

Metford shrugged. "Anyone can gamble. The casinos are everywhere."

"That links Emily and Ethan in one way, at least." She dropped the chip into a small evidence bag and sealed it.

Ten minutes later, they lugged the bags from the building back to the SUV.

"The others should have had time to speak to many of the coworkers. Let's get this done," Ava said. "Let's split up and find out what we can about Emily."

They went back into the larger building and went into areas where people were working. Ava held her badge out to a woman who looked frustrated as she moved a box from one stack to another.

"Special Agent James, ma'am. I need to ask you a few questions about a coworker."

"I already talked to someone about Ethan Holt yesterday." The woman kept working.

"Emily Harper," Ava said.

The box hit the stack at an angle and toppled to the floor. "Dammit," the woman exclaimed as she bent to pick it up. "What about Emily?!" she yelled over a tow motor engine.

Ava moved closer, forcing the woman to stop working and speak with her. "She was murdered in her home last night."

"What? Murdered?"

The look of complete shock was a testament to her ignorance of the situation. It seemed that no one at Patapsco had been informed of the most recent murder.

"Yes, murdered."

The woman waved a man over, told him to take over, and turned back to Ava. "We can talk over there. It's a little quieter."

They moved away from the noise and movement. "I take it you knew Emily Harper."

"Yeah. Everybody knows Emily. Or I guess everybody did." Her eyes darted around as if she were avoiding making eye contact with Ava.

Ava took out her notepad. "What's your name?"

The woman hesitated. "Lydia."

Ava looked at her expectantly.

"Lydia Bruno."

Small beads of perspiration formed on Lydia's forehead.

"How old are you, Lydia?"

"Thirty-five. Why do you need all this information from me?"

"Don't worry. It's standard procedure." She finished with the basic questions and moved on. "How well did you know Emily?"

Lydia scoffed. "Well enough to know she was someone I didn't want to be around much."

"Really? Why do you say that?"

"I didn't like her, okay? Isn't that good enough? I hate to speak ill of the dead. She just wasn't a good person."

"That's quite a contrast to what I've heard so far. I was just wondering what she did that made you feel that way about her."

Lydia shook her head and looked back to her job. "I really should get back. He's going to screw something up. He's only been here a few months."

"What kind of worker was Emily?"

"How the hell should I know? I already told you that I didn't associate with her. We didn't get along. I really should get back. Isn't that enough?"

"No, actually, it isn't. I want to know why you say Emily was such a bad person that you didn't like her. It's part of the investigation, and you wouldn't want to obstruct the investigation, would you?"

"Jesus, okay. We had a falling out over money. I borrowed money from her, we set up a payment arrangement, and she was demanding that I pay her more than the agreed amount and early at that. I work here. It's not like I had that kind of money just laying around. Paycheck to paycheck, just like the rest of the world."

"So, it was a significant amount you borrowed?"

Lydia stammered. "Not really. Not to an FBI agent, I'm sure, but it kept me from losing my car and putting my mortgage behind more than once."

"If you didn't associate with her, and you didn't like her because you thought she was a bad person, what made you feel comfortable enough to ask her for a loan in the first place?"

Floundering again, Lydia shifted several times. "We weren't always on the outs. We got along for a while."

"Everyone here says she was pretty solitary, and that they never saw her associating with anyone here unless it had something to do with work."

"And?"

"And why did no one ever see you two chatting or walking or laughing together if you were friendly before the loan?"

"Why is the grass green? Why is the snow cold? How should I know? It's been months; maybe even a year. Maybe they just forgot."

"How much over the payment was she asking for?"

"She wanted double payments."

"And how long ago did you borrow the money?"

"A year, give or take."

"When did she start demanding the increased payments?"

"Just a couple months ago. Maybe three or four, now that I think about it."

"And in all that time before, she never asked you for extra payments?"

"No."

The sweat that had beaded earlier trickled down from her left temple, and she swiped it away.

"Why did she start demanding the money?"

"I'm not sure, but personally, I think she had a gambling problem." She nodded solemnly as if she had just solved the whole case on her own with that one sentence.

"What makes you think that?"

"Because. She would disappear for a few days a month and come back flashing money around like she hit the jackpot. That is, until she started demanding the money from me. She disappeared and returned acting real humble until she caught me going to the car after work one day, and that's when she hit me with the first attempt at getting more money out of me."

"Where would she have gone to gamble, do you think?" The logical answer was Porter Casino and Hotel that was so close to Patapsco Bay Terminal.

"I have no idea. Where do people go to gamble? I wouldn't know because I never had enough money to play with like that."

Ava finished questioning Lydia and then thanked her. The others had been interviewed by the team. Had Lydia purposefully avoided them, or had she simply been on a break when they were in that department? Ava wasn't sure, but it was strange that Lydia was the only one out of nine who had been missed by Santos, Dane, Metford, and Ashton.

CHAPTER SEVENTEEN

"Are we looking for anything specific?" Santos asked, putting aside more papers from Emily Harper's house.

"I want to know what kind of person Emily was. Who she hung out with, where she hung out, which restaurants she ate at, anything and everything that will give us a fuller picture of Emily Harper the everyday person," Ava said.

"That's not specific at all," Santos muttered.

"No, it's not. If you were a civilian who wanted to know what kind of person Dane was, but all you knew about her was that she was an FBI agent, would that give you a decent idea of her as a person?"

"It would tell me that she had to be doing something right but that she was probably a little mental, or she wouldn't have chosen to be an agent. She isn't a criminal…" Santos left the sentence hanging as she looked up at Ava with wide eyes.

"Right, okay. But that's only the highlights and stereotyping. That doesn't give you a good notion of what she is like as a person. It's only one facet of her life, and the many facets are what makes up the person."

"Right. So, everything about her."

"Exactly." Ava had ignored Santos' obvious distress at the mention of how she thought an FBI agent couldn't be a criminal. She wanted to dispute the statement, but refused to give Jason Ellis one more ounce of power over her life than he'd already exacted.

"I have Emily's planner," Metford said, holding it up. "It actually has descriptions on the dates and times."

Ava took the planner and scanned through the last few months. "Check the dates and times against Ethan's planners just to see what comes up."

"Want me to do that?" Ashton offered. "I've already gone through three boxes of items from her house and found not much."

"No. Why don't you get online and find out all you can about her from that angle. Social media, friends, contacts, emails, DMs, texts, anything interesting. If she didn't associate with coworkers, maybe she had online friends."

"On it." He rolled the chair to the other table and opened the laptop, seemingly more content than when he was going through boxes of a female's personal items.

Ava took over going through the items from the locker at Patapsco, and she came across the poker chip again. Holding up the baggie containing it, she turned it to see each side in turn and then dropped it into one hand. It wasn't very heavy and seemed to be standard size for a poker chip. She pulled her laptop closer and entered a description to see if there was any information on the design. The search came up empty. Using her phone, she took a picture of it and had the search engine do an image search. Again, no information.

"Find anything about it?" Dane asked.

"Nothing. Lydia said she thought Emily had a gambling problem." She bounced the chip in her hand again. "Maybe she got into some bad debt with a loan shark while trying to fund her bad habit."

"Maybe somebody down at Porter's can tell you something about the chip."

"Porter's is close to Patapsco Bay, too."

"Pretty close, yeah."

"And there's a hotel attached to it." Ava put the chip down.

"There is." Dane took a tote with plastic bags of evidence inside.

"You thinking of staying and trying your luck, boss?" Santos asked with a grin.

"I might if I had any luck, but I've never had luck with any game of chance."

"It's only partly a game of chance," Ashton said. "It depends on what you're playing. Blackjack, for example, can be won by implementing statistics and probabilities and—"

"Isn't that called counting cards, you cheater?" Santos asked.

"No, it's, well…"

"Right. Well said," Dane said with a laugh.

"And you can do this thing?" Metford asked.

"Anyone can. It's not difficult once you—"

"Do you have any plans for this weekend?" Metford asked teasingly.

"I don't know," Ashton stammered.

They all laughed.

"All right. Come on, guys and gals. Put all that wit and energy into helping solve these cases," Ava said. "Did you ever locate Silas Grey?"

All eyes turned to her with blank expressions.

"Anyone? Silas Grey? The guy who left fingerprints all over Ethan's place."

"Do you want me to work on that?" Dane asked sheepishly.

"If no one has yet, yes, I would very much like that information. I would have liked it this morning," she bit. Reining her temper in, Ava turned back to the poker chip. "Ashton, find out everything you can about Ethan while you're online. Wherever he was gambling, it's a safe bet that Emily was as well."

"Will do."

"ETA on any information?" she asked.

"Give me a couple of hours. Maybe three since I'm looking into both people, and I don't have all the equipment from the office to speed this up."

"Sounds good. I'm going to Porter's. I'm going to ask them about Ethan, Emily, and the chips."

"I'll go with you," Metford said.

"What about the planners and the dates?"

"So far, so good. The times are all different, and Emily had labels on all hers. Unless Ethan was accompanying her to Sylvan Yoga studio three times a week, I don't think we're going to find any matches."

"We still need to make sure," Ava stated.

"I'll do it as soon as we get back. Promise. I won't stop until it's done."

Ava scoffed and walked to the door.

"I wouldn't mind going with you," Santos said. "Never know when you might need someone with a few more street smarts than you."

"Is that what it's called?" Metford asked, stepping past Ava and out into the hallway.

"What about you, Dane? Ashton?" Ava asked.

They exchanged a look and Dane stood. "I'll go. I can help talk to the patrons. With all of us there, it shouldn't take very long."

"I'm going to stay here and complete these online profiles. They should be ready by the time you get back. Want me to pull full financial workups, too?"

"Yes, that would be great. Thank you for your dedication to the job, Ashton," Ava said, smiling.

The others looked at her with their mouths agape and their eyes wide. Immediately, the clamoring started. They were dedicated to their job; that's why they were volunteering to go to a place like Porter's in the first place. No way were they trying to shirk their present tasks, which they did not in any way find boring and useless.

Ava held up her hands. "All right. I got it. You're all very dedicated. I was just yanking your chains, and it looks like I did a good job. Such a sensitive lot." She laughed as she stepped out of the elevator.

"Sensitive?" Santos scoffed. "Not on your life."

"Told you she could be funny sometimes," Metford said.

Ava turned to him as she opened the driver's door. "You did, did you? Why would you tell them something like that?"

He spluttered and stuttered. "Because it's the truth. Sometimes, you're funny. It's not that you can't be, you just aren't most of the time. You're super serious and go around like you're in a pressure cooker that's about to blow all the time."

"I do not." She swung into the seat and closed the door.

Laughing, the others got in.

"I was just yanking your chain," Metford said. "I didn't know you were so sensitive about it, but hey, if it's a touchy subject, I'll leave it alone from now on."

"Okay, you got me. Ha ha. Head in the game now."

They all sobered.

"What do we have linking Ethan and Emily so far?"

"Just that they both had one of those distinct poker chips in their personal stuff," Metford said.

"And they obviously worked together at Patapsco," Dane said.

"Other than that, nothing," Metford said. "Unless Ashton finds something in his online research."

"It's Ashton we're talking about," Santos said. "He'll know what Ethan's favorite color was in the fifth grade and how many pairs of shoes Emily had in the sixth by the time we get back."

"And probably their family histories back to nineteen hundred," Dane added. "That's not a bad thing, though. The man's a genius with technology."

"Maybe he could help me untangle my online accounts," Santos said.

"Dating apps aren't his forte," Metford said, chuckling.

"Funny. My bank and card accounts. I've got them all snaggled, and I can't even access my cash card's online account. I forgot which password I used, and I didn't write down the answers to my security questions. It keeps locking me out."

The crew talked about bank accounts and the blessings and afflictions of online banking. Ava let them while she drove and mulled over what they said and the people they had interviewed. Somebody had a motive. Somebody had a crazy violent streak. Had they spoken to that person? Was it someone Emily and Ethan worked with? Or could it have been someone they had in common? The thing that bothered her was wondering what mistake they had both made, and if they had made it in tandem or separately. Something big enough to get them both killed would likely have drawn the attention of others, even if they weren't buddies and didn't associate much with them. Right?

Porter's Casino and Hotel was huge. It took up a chunk of the seaside real estate. Lit up the way it was, it brought to mind images of Las Vegas.

"It's not even dark yet, and look at how many cars are here," Metford said.

"It doesn't have to be dark for people to enjoy gambling," Santos said.

"But it seems like a late evening or nighttime activity, doesn't it?"

"I never really thought about it, but people who want to get away and have a little vacation don't typically care what time of day they hit the craps table, I guess," Dane said.

"Unless their work schedules only allow them to play their luck at certain times of the day," Ava suggested.

She parked and they got out as a group.

The rounded front of the casino with its Corinthian columns and two-story marquees that lit up the walkway would have been more at home in Las Vegas. On the Baltimore seaside, it was tacky.

Inside was everything one would expect from a high-end casino. The patrons were dressed to the nines, and there were drinks in every hand. Lots of laughing, loud music, and the noise of the slot machines turning every other sound into droning white noise.

"Okay, ask around and see if anyone recognizes our two victims," Ava said. "If Emily was disappearing for a few days and acting like she'd won the lottery when she returned, this could be the place."

"It would be easy for her to leave work, come here, and stay in the hotel while she was getting her gamble on," Santos said.

"If the hotel is as nice as the casino, it wouldn't be a bad place to spend two or three days a month to escape the grind of everyday life," Dane said.

Dane and Santos walked away in different directions.

"You think this is where Emily was getting the large sums of money?" Metford asked.

"Getting it here would be better than getting in most of the other ways I can think of. If it was here, at least she wasn't into anything illegal, right?"

He gave her a doubtful look.

"Right. Then what did she do to get murdered?" She headed toward the back of the casino where a guard stood outside a closed, glossy black door. She flipped her badge out.

"I need to speak to whoever's running the place today," she said.

"Which one?" the man asked.

"I don't know. Whichever one is in there will do. Just need to ask a few questions about a couple of people I think might have been patrons here recently."

The big man took out his phone and texted someone and then pressed the button on his Bluetooth earpiece. He turned away and spoke in a low voice to keep Ava and Metford from hearing him.

He turned to face them. "Miss Blackwell will see you for five minutes. Make them count. She's a busy woman." He opened the door and stepped aside.

"Thank you," Ava said, not liking the time limit put on their questioning.

They stepped inside. Five people stood staring at large monitors showing the gambling tables. A tall, thin woman who looked to be in her late forties and wearing a black pantsuit walked toward the agents with a smile.

"Miss Blackwell?" Ava asked.

The woman extended her hand. "Cassandra or Cassie, please. How may I help you?" She took a moment to look Metford up and down appreciatively instead of making eye contact with Ava. She extended a hand to him and brushed by Ava. "Pleased to meet you … Special Agent … ?"

"Metford," he said with a goofy little grin. "And this is Special Agent James." He gestured toward Ava and pulled his hand from her grasp.

Cassandra turned to Ava as if she had forgotten the other woman was there. "Yes, yes, Special Agent James." She exhaled deeply and clasped her hands. "Now, where were we?"

"You were about to tell me if you knew either of these two people." Ava held out a picture of Emily and one of Ethan. "We think they were coming here. Maybe regularly."

Cassandra seemed to study the pictures closely. She shook her head and gave back the pictures. "I'm sorry, I can't say that I recognize either of them. But I see a lot of people in here on a daily basis. It's possible they've been here and I just don't recognize them. Are they in some sort of trouble? Should we watch for them and contact you if they come in?"

"No. How long does your system keep security footage of the gambling floor?"

"Forty-eight hours unless we mark footage to save it longer." She smiled broader and pointed to the pictures in Ava's hand. "If they're a problem, I need to know. I wouldn't want any trouble here in the casino."

"No, they're dead."

Cassandra's face blanched, and for a split second, her expression was one of sick horror. Then she was poised again. Her smile was a little tighter, a little smaller, and her posture a little stiffer. "Oh. That's...that's terrible. I'm sorry to hear it."

"And you're sure you never saw them in here?"

"Yes, yes, I'm sure. When is the last time they were here?"

"We don't know, but I'd like to have a look at the last forty-eight hours of security footage." Ava put a hand in her pocket and curled her fingers around the poker chip.

The small, tight smile grew larger and Cassandra's shoulders relaxed a bit. "Do you have a warrant?"

"I thought you might say that," Ava said, bringing the chip from her pocket. She held it out. "Do you recognize this poker chip?"

Recognition didn't flash over Cassandra's face, but her eyes registered a jolt of panic when she took the chip into her hand and saw it. She cleared her throat lightly and shook her head. "Sorry, no. That's not one of ours." She snapped her fingers. "Joey, bring me a poker chip."

Joey, a big lug of a brute, scowled at Ava and Metford as he handed Cassandra two poker chips. Ava didn't take it personally. She was sure that was Joey's default expression.

Cassandra held up the typical-looking chips. One red, the other yellow. "These are ours." She gave back the odd one. "I don't know where that one came from. It's definitely unique."

Ava took it and put it back in her pocket. "That it is."

Cassandra palmed the two chips and beamed. "Well, Agents, if there's nothing else? I have a meeting to get to." She glanced at the slim gold watch on her wrist. "I'm already running late."

"Thanks for your time," Ava said, knowing the meeting was over and hoping Dane and Santos had better luck.

"Joey, show them out," Cassandra turned and walked away, giving the order with a flip of her hand.

"We can find our way," Ava said. "It's fifteen feet in a straight line." She walked at a good clip, not waiting for Metford or confirmation from Joey.

Away from the guard at the door, Ava looked around. "Let's have a look around, find Santos and Dane, and see what they found out."

***

"No one recognized either one of them," Santos said. "Or they were all good liars."

"Were you at the poker tables?" Metford asked.

"No. What's that got to do with it?"

"Good poker players make good liars. They can even hide the usual tells you pick up on when someone is lying."

"Did management know them?" Dane asked.

"No. At least, she said she didn't. There were a couple of times I could swear I saw fear in her eyes, though," Ava said.

"So, this was a bust, too?" Metford asked as they hit the parking lot.

"Maybe not," Ava said. She pointed to the hotel section. "Unless Cassandra Blackwell has already called and locked down the registry at the hotel, we can get a look at it maybe and see if Ethan or Emily's names are in it."

"We don't have a warrant," Dane said.

"I'm aware of that, but if there is anything that raises enough suspicion, I might be able to get one."

They went to the hotel and entered the grand façade. Ava half-expected the interior to be a let-down after the grandiose entrance, but it was not. The interior was luxurious and elegant. No false advertising there.

Ava spoke with the hotel manager, who searched the online registry for Ethan and Emily. Neither name came up as ever having been a guest. He also did not recognize their photos.

Ava left disappointed. Her gears were still grinding as they all loaded up and left the parking lot, though. There had to be some connection between the murders.

"If they weren't gambling here with those chips, then where?" Santos asked.

"Maybe nowhere," Metford said.

Ava glanced at him. "What do you mean?"

"Maybe they're membership tokens."

"To where?" Santos asked. "The boxing gym?"

"Maybe. Or a club like Prestige. Maybe whatever club they belonged to issues these chips instead of membership cards."

"That's some *John Wick* stuff, if I ever heard it," Santos said.

Metford shrugged. "Just a thought."

"And a smart one," Ava said. "I like the idea of that. It's something we need to check into."

Whatever the connection between Ethan, Emily, the murders, and the poker chips was, Ava had to uncover it. Her mind would not let it go and give her a minute's peace until she did.

CHAPTER EIGHTEEN

Two days later, there was no movement on the case. The team had investigated every angle that seemed promising, and a couple that had not seemed worth the trouble. The poker chip being a membership token had not panned out either. Ashton had delved into the 3-D printer at Emily's house and found the files to print them. There was no way to tell whether she had created both chips, or perhaps copied one from an original, or if they really were from a local casino and Emily was just trying to copy them. Either way, it was like there were only two of the chips in existence, and Ava had them both.

Ava tried for the warrants. One for the security footage from Porter Casino and Hotel, and two for Customs and Border Protection employee files for Ethan Holt and Emily Harper. She was denied right off the bat for the security footage warrant. There wasn't enough evidence to prove it was necessary. Porter Casino was not tied to the deaths even in theory. The two warrants for employee files, though not shot down immediately, didn't seem likely to go through unless there was irrefutable evidence showing the deaths were linked.

With her hopes dashed yet again, Ava returned to the hotel and joined the team in going over all the tedious minutiae of the cases.

"Has the ME called or sent anything over?" she asked the team.

A resounding no was the answer.

"Why? It's been long enough that he could have sent us at least the prelim results on Ethan, and he should be working on Emily's."

"They were backed up," Dane said. "That's what he said when he took Emily's body."

"Yeah, this is Baltimore, not Fairhaven," Santos reminded her.

Ava waved off the information and dialed the number for Dr. Morgan Blake. When the doctor answered, Ava asked him about the examinations.

"You'll have them before lunch today. I was finished with Mr. Holt's autopsy, just waiting on the tox screen, when Miss Harper came in. I figured I would send both reports at the same time. I'll be waiting on the tox screen and the DNA samples from her before I can finalize. That might take a while, you understand."

"I do. I would have appreciated having Ethan's as soon as it was finished. Please, send over anything you have immediately next time." She kept her tone even and as impartial as she could manage to keep from seeming like a total jerk, but that self-control didn't do much to quell the irritation and anger building in her.

"You got it. Just know that the information will be coming in bits and pieces."

"As expected. I'll be waiting for the reports. Thank you."

"You'll have them by eleven." Dr. Blake hung up.

It was impossible to tell if he was angry or insulted or unfazed when he disconnected the call. It was nearly impossible to read the man when he was standing right in front of her, and completely impossible to read over the phone. She decided it didn't much matter as long as she got the information as soon as possible. The sooner, the better. There was no way to solve a case if they didn't have important information.

"That sounded like it went well," Metford said.

"We'll have the reports for both victims by eleven," Ava announced. "Until then, we need to keep working. Have we interviewed all of the coworkers and bosses at Patapsco Bay Terminal?"

"We have," Dane said. "And we've compiled all the interviews, cross-referenced for similarities and differences, and put them in lists that should make it easier to glean the important points that were brought to light."

"Was there anything revealed that was unexpected for either of them?"

"No. Not really."

"What about the financials?" Ava looked at Ashton.

"Believe it or not, I'm still digging and working on those. I don't think either one of our victims had a single bank account, and they had multiple cash cards and credit cards. They were juggling money all over the place."

"Is that normal?"

"For the younger generations, yeah, but not very common in their age ranges. I haven't found anything that raises red flags. Yet."

"Let me know when you're finished with it. And what about Silas Grey?"

"I have his address, and the local PD assigned an officer from each shift to randomly go by and check if he was there throughout the day."

"What about his work address?"

"He's a remote worker, and the company he works for said he doesn't have an assignment due for several days yet."

Ava exhaled deeply. "Dead ends, dead ends," she muttered, pacing the length of the room. "How to get around them; open them up." She continued to pace. She stopped and pointed at Ashton. "Ashton," she said.

He turned quickly. "Yes?"

"Run Silas Grey's financials. Find out where he spends most of his money. I need to find him. He's the only loose end we have from Ethan's case."

"Right now?"

"Yes, now."

Ava's phone rang. It was Chief Panko's number. "Hold up. The chief's calling me. Maybe…" She punched the button and put the phone to her ear. "Special Agent James speaking."

After several moments, she said, "We're on our way." She put the phone in her pocket. "We've got another one."

"What? Another death?" Metford asked.

"Another murder."

"Why are we getting the call? Doesn't Baltimore PD have a homicide department?" Santos asked.

"Victim is another CBP agent. James Lawson. Come on, we all know how this goes."

Metford caught up to her at the elevator, as did the others. "Where are we headed this time?"

"To 76 Charm City Crescent. A townhouse about twenty minutes from Patapsco Bay Terminal."

"Not so charming this morning," Santos said, stepping into the elevator.

"Three CBP agents in less than a week. That's ridiculous," Dane said. "Someone is targeting them."

"If not, this is the biggest coincidence I've ever seen," Santos said.

"I don't believe in coincidences," Ava said. "But who is targeting them, and why?"

***

The townhouse was on the end of a seven-unit, three-story building. The windows of Mr. Lawson's unit had been tinted, and they glinted bright shards of light back into Ava's eyes as she approached the crowded front of the unit in question. Officers had been stationed and a police line was being put up, but none of the neighbors were heeding the orders shouted by the cops, and they screamed indignantly when they were physically removed from the area.

"What is it with the citizens around here?" Santos asked, disgruntled. "They act like they're so interested after their neighbors get murdered. Why couldn't they be half that concerned and nosy before they were murdered, or at least while they're being attacked? Maybe if they had, a victim could be saved every now and then."

"Nobody wants to be accused of being nosy, or putting their nose in other people's business," Dane said. "In New York City, we always taught women to scream 'fire' instead of screaming for help if they were being attacked. The rape whistles were great for a while, but even the public's response to them flagged after a while. People will go out of their way to look the other way. In cities, it's always worse."

"Way worse," Metford said.

"I'm going in," Ava said. "The rest of you stay out here and help get this under control."

Ava made her way through the questioning, clamoring onlookers. No way all of them were simply neighbors.

She met with the lead detective.

"What do we have so far?"

"A bad day, just like most." He motioned for her to go down the short hall ahead of him. "Take a right at the end. He's in the living room."

Ava gloved up as she walked. The interior of the townhouse wasn't rich or luxurious, but it was way out of her budget. Out of budget for most regular working Joes.

"Looks like he was watching television," Detective Coffey said. "He was killed with a knife, just like the last two."

Ava entered and stood in front of James Lawson. The footrest of the recliner was up. One leg had flopped off the side and dangled. He was slumped to one side. The attacker had stabbed him in the heart, the side of the neck, and just below the right collarbone. There was a deep laceration wound on the outside edge of his right hand, and one on his right forearm. Blood had soaked his shirt, pants to his thighs, and had sprayed all the way to the fireplace three feet away. Ava thought that was probably from being stabbed in the neck. The deep cuts on his hand and forearm looked to be defensive wounds, and there were only two shallower ones.

"Doesn't seem like he put up much of a fight," Detective Coffey said.

"More than the other two. Look how deep these two defensive wounds are." She stood and looked over the scene, playing out scenarios in her mind. "Maybe he was dozing when the killer struck the first blow, but it didn't kill him. He reflexively swung his arm…" She looked at the scene a bit more and nodded. "The killer attacked from James' right side. Probably the first stab was the one below the collarbone, or possibly the side of his neck there. I think the one under the collarbone, though. He swung his arm reflexively at the killer who then cut his hand. James drew the hand back, tried to get up, the killer panicked and stabbed him in the neck. James grabbed the wound, fell back, and the killer struck again, only James tried to protect himself with his right arm again, and it was cut. As he recoiled, the killer landed the final and fatal blow to his heart."

"That's quite a story just from looking at this for three minutes. Almost played out like a movie," Coffey said through light laughter.

"You have a different scenario in mind?"

"No, not really. I just have questions."

"Like?"

"Like, how do you know the wound under the collarbone was inflicted before the one on his neck? How do you know the wound on his hand was inflicted before the one on his arm? How do you know the killer attacked from Mr. Lawson's right side at all? Maybe he stood in front of him."

"These are just the most likely scenarios, Detective Coffey. It's all based on logic." She pointed to the blood spatter on the white stones of the fireplace. "And observation. See the way the blood spray fans outward from that spot right there?"

"Yeah. We can agree that probably came from him being stabbed in the neck."

"The killer was standing there. Forensics can probably study this and tell us about how tall the killer was, too."

"Why do you say that?" Coffey turned his head and looked at the spatter. "It's just spatter."

"And there is a very clear edge to the spray. Something was blocking the blood when it sprayed from Lawson's neck, otherwise, the spatter would be present there." Ava pointed out the remarkably clean outline.

"I see that now. You're right. Not bad for a…" He cleared his throat and chuckled. "How about the order of the wounds? How do you determine that?"

"That's where logic comes in. Reflexes are strange things. When something hurts the neck, a human will almost always slap the palm of their hand over it. Before they even know what it was, they put pressure on it with the hand on that side, whereas, if something hurts their upper chest, say just under the collarbone on the right side, they take a swing at the offender, whatever it might be. In a split-second, he deduced that the chest wound nor the cut hand were deadly, and he would have tried to get up to defend himself better. He would've used both hands to press down on the arms of the recliner while pushing downward with his feet on the footrest. His neck was exposed, and the killer took the opportunity. Lawson was shocked, hurt, and probably knew that wound could be fatal. He grabbed it, causing his weight to shift and he fell back into the seat. While he was still gripping his throat, the killer lunged for the last blow, but as the knife descended, Lawson threw up that right elbow. His left hand was probably still clutching the armrest on that side. His legs were probably still tensed. The killer might have had to try twice for that kill shot, but he eventually got it, didn't he?"

"He did. Unfortunately, he did. What can we do to help further the investigation? You are pursuing this as a serial killer, right?"

"We don't know that it's the work of a serial killer, Detective, and I would highly suggest that you don't say that where it could get out to anyone unless and until there is sufficient evidence."

"Wouldn't want to panic the public, right? And God forbid we tell the workers at Patapsco Bay that they might be the next target, no doubt."

"Legally, we can't cause a panic like that either, but I think they are smart enough to know they should be more vigilant. Especially after Mr. Lawson's murder. If you want to help, do your job and make sure we have access to the information as soon as you get it. And if you could put a rush on the autopsy, that would be great."

"Dr. Blake will be here in a few minutes. If we find anything not in the reports already, I'll make sure you get it ASAP. I want the bastard found before he kills again."

"We do, too."

The rest of the team came in. Ava walked them through the scene and her scenarios. Ashton said she was right about the blood spatter and that the killer had attacked from Lawson's right side. He also agreed on the order of the attack she laid out.

"I would add one thing," he said, looking at the pattern of blood spray on the white bricks. "The killer likely wasn't over five-five, or at the most, five-seven, and he isn't very broad. Of course, it could be that he was standing sideways, but that's a longshot." Ashton made a stabbing gesture toward Lawson's neck, and one of the forensic team yelled, rushing toward him.

"Don't touch anything, dude. We haven't processed everything," the man barked, holding out his hands to block any attempt Ashton might make to touch Lawson's body.

"I am aware that you aren't finished. I wasn't going to touch anything. I'm playing out a theory."

"Could you do it somewhere else? You're making me nervous."

"Actually, I can't." Ignoring the man, Ashton made the lunging, stabbing gesture again. "Unless I'm excruciatingly wrong, the killer is of smaller stature. Not tall. Not broad. Very quick with the attack and the movements to execute it."

"Are you doing my job?" the forensic tech asked, squinting at Ashton.

"Kinda, but not really," Ashton said, sidestepping him and moving to the team. "A small attacker, just like I said with Emily's situation. Evidence is starting to show it might really be the same killer in all three murders."

"So, what, do we have a petite serial killer running around covered in blood, and nobody sees or hears anything?" Metford asked. "Because if the killer's body blocked the spatter, it had to hit him, right?"

"We don't know if he wore something to protect his clothing," Ashton said. "But yes, the blood hit him, and there would have been a lot more than there was with Emily. Lawson's artery was cut, and there was..." He turned to point at the bricks as he spoke. "One, two, three jets of arterial spray that hit the bricks there."

"So, you're saying the killer would have been covered, not just splattered?" Dane asked.

"Exactly. And since we think he leaned closer to deliver the killing wound, that means it's likely that at least one arm was covered as well."

"Thank you," Ava said, appreciative of Ashton's knowledge and instant insight. "You just narrowed down the suspect pool, and gave us a better idea of what kind of person we're looking for here. This isn't just your run-of-the-mill killer. If he killed all three of the victims, we're looking at revenge killings."

"Revenge for what?" Santos asked.

"That's what we need to find out. You know the routine, everybody. Let's get this thing rolling."

With that, the search of the property and the questioning began in full force. Chief Panko sent a couple of extra officers to help with the questioning, and it went quicker than before. Three hours later, Ava and Metford finished collecting evidence. The others were still questioning neighbors and taking notes when Ava and Metford left.

CHAPTER NINETEEN

"Can you please explain why we're going back there again? If we push our luck, he's going to file a harassment charge against us," Metford said sternly.

"He won't." Ava white-knuckled the steering wheel to keep her resolve from slipping.

"Last time you said he would let us have access to the files, too."

"I have a plan," she said.

"Care to let me in on it?"

"I have an idea about the killings. If it's revenge, it might be a jealous lover, girlfriend, boyfriend, something like that. But if it's not, there's something else that could cause someone to snap and kill people in this way. Methodical and brutal. We're not talking about a bullet to the brain; quick and clean. These are horribly painful deaths, and the killer doesn't mind getting up close and personal."

"None of the vics has a significant other. They've never been married, and don't have kids either."

"I don't think it's that sort of revenge." She paused for a moment while she was stopped at a four-way. "What if it has something to do with smuggling that's going on at Patapsco Bay Terminal?"

"What, like smuggling drugs? You think the vics were smugglers?" He scoffed.

"Think about it. If they were supposed to be helping somebody smuggle something, and then stopped. If they caught a smuggler and shut down the operation. I'm just spitballing here, but you get the idea, right?"

"You know, come to think about it, this is something drug dealers would do."

"Yeah, we've seen it before. All ports have trouble with smuggling. Either people are trying to get stuff into the States, or they're trying to get it out, and I'm sure Patapsco is no exception. I just need to get someone to admit it's a problem."

"Wouldn't it have been in the reports and files we got from Patapsco?"

"Maybe. Should have been, but who really knows? Never hurts to try another angle when the current one isn't working."

Metford thought about it for the rest of the ride.

As they walked toward the entrance of the CBP building, Metford said, "It's worth a shot. I just hope we get some sort of traction here. I'm tired of the same tired lines from this guy, and he's not the most pleasant person to be around. He's a nice jerk. I've been around too many of his kind all my life."

"Agreed. I prefer outright hostility to his specially patented brand of hostility wrapped up in fake niceties."

Deputy Commissioner Halloway made them wait an hour before he conceded to let them into his inner sanctum for a brief interview. His demeanor was annoyed but resigned to being civil at the least amount possible for it to still be considered civil. Without a word, and without getting up, he motioned for them to take a seat in front of his desk. He then folded his hands on the desk and pasted on a thin smile that said he was only humoring them because he had to.

"I'll start," Ava said after the man refused to even greet them.

"Very well."

"Another of your agents from Patapsco has been murdered. That's three in less than a week."

"So I've been informed."

"Don't you think that warrants allowing us access to the employee files now?"

"Absolutely not." He held out a hand, palm-up. "Unless you have the proper documentation this time."

Ava breathed in and straightened her shoulders.

He pulled back his hand, straightened his glasses, and pulled closer to the desk. "Do I need to define proper documentation to you, Special Agent James?"

"Do I need to define human decency to you, Deputy Commissioner?" Her anger flared, and she reined it back in. It wouldn't further the case to fly off the handle before the meeting had even properly begun.

"I'm afraid I'm going to have to ask you to leave. I don't have time for this. As you know, three of our Patapsco agents have lost their lives this past week, and I'm up to my eyeballs in paperwork and phone calls over it. I have people to answer to in this situation, and you are hindering my progress on all fronts."

"Oh, I apologize for hindering your work, Mr. Halloway. That's the last thing I intended to do. And those agents didn't lose their lives; their lives were brutally taken from them. I need to know why, and I have reason to think the answers might lie in the files you're guarding like a mad dog."

"Is there even one judge who agrees with you, or is this some kind of last-ditch effort to get me to hand over the files without proceeding with proper protocol? A kind of Hail Mary, if you will."

Ava bit her tongue for a second and sat back in her seat. She pulled her jacket and adjusted it, ran a hand down the sides as if making sure it was straight, and then she smiled at him.

"What is it, Agent?" Halloway looked from her to Metford expectantly. "I think the meeting is—"

"What kind of corruption is going on here?" she asked bluntly.

His mouth formed a little 'o,' then his lips pulled into a tight, thin line, and his brows took a dive toward his nose. "I'm not sure what you're getting at here, but I assure you that you do not want to be throwing around false accusations in a bid to get what you want. Now, if you would see yourselves out. I have work to do. Work that doesn't include tossing about inflammatory statements and trying to threaten people into doing what they should. Goodbye."

Metford nudged her elbow with one finger and cut his eyes toward the door. She shook her head once.

"Mr. Halloway, I know things that aren't strictly legal go on in ports all over the world. Sometimes, it just can't be helped. Other times?" She shrugged. "Other times, it gets...*overlooked*. Has there been something like that going on at Patapsco Bay Terminal recently?"

"That's enough of your nonsense. It's that kind of idiocrasy that ruins careers on both sides of this desk. Stop with your inane, juvenile attempts to threaten me and get out before I—"

"Before you what? Call my boss? The head of the Bureau? The President himself? Your phone's right there. Go ahead." She sat back and made herself comfortable again. "I have all day."

He pulled his phone close and eyed her closely. "What's your angle, Agent? Because I fail to see the benefit of possibly being brought up on charges and losing your career over this when all you have to do is get the warrants."

"I'll bring you a warrant if I don't get some answers. Today."

He let his hand fall away from the phone and looked at her suspiciously. "We're not still talking about the employee files, are we?" His tone and demeanor changed, slowly morphing into something less haughty, less superior, and more equal to her.

"If you don't tell me what corruption and smuggling has been going on in Patapsco Bay, I'll see to it that an investigation is opened against you for suspected corruption. You and all of the CBP."

"That would never be approved." His tone implied he didn't really believe his own words. The color slipped from his cheeks.

"Wouldn't it? I can weave a good story of how it all intertwines with the recent deaths, or how it might be linked to them. I can be pretty convincing when I need to be."

Metford cleared his throat. "She's not exaggerating."

Halloway interlocked his fingers again and stared at them hard for a few moments in silence. The muscles of his jaw worked as if he were repeatedly clamping his teeth together to keep from saying something he shouldn't.

"So help me, if you continue to block me and my investigation at every turn, I will open an investigation into you and everyone at Customs and Border Protection. That's a promise, Mr. Halloway. I'll make sure to turn everyone's lives here inside out, air out their deepest, darkest for the world to see; for the media to pick apart like a murder of starving crows. You'll be in the headlines, on every news station for months on end. Longer maybe. I'll dig up every piece of dirt on you all the way back to your college days. Is that what you want?"

Halloway inhaled sharply and motioned to Metford. "Leave us. I want to speak to her alone."

Metford started to protest, but Ava cut him off. "It's okay. Go. I'm fine." She never took her eyes off Halloway.

Metford stood looking from one to the other making it known that he was highly displeased and more than a little distrustful of Halloway's intentions. "I'll be right outside the door."

Halloway and Ava were locked on each other and didn't acknowledge Metford's words. He left and the door shut.

They sat there for several interminable seconds in silence before Ava said, "Well?"

Halloway shifted nervously in his seat. "I don't want to even speak to you about it. It's done. Forgotten. In the past. But if I don't tell you, I believe that you will rip it right back open and splash it all over the front pages with as much gusto as you can muster just to get back at me for doing my job." He sighed and wrung his hands as he swiveled the chair to the side. "You would be wreaking havoc in the lives of innocent people, but I don't think you would care, would you?"

"Not if it helped solve these three murders." That wasn't exactly the truth. It depended on who the innocents were, and just how innocent they really were in whatever scandal he was referencing. "Was it smuggling? Or corruption? Here in the offices, or at Patapsco Bay Terminal?"

He held up a hand to halt her rapid-fire questions. "There was an incident over a year ago that involved two CBP officers."

"At Patapsco?"

"Yes, at Patapsco Bay Terminal. It was over a year ago now, however, and it's been taken care of."

"How so?"

"All the employees involved have been fired. Charges were handed down by the local PD, and the two men, the main players, were put in jail for two years each. I'm surprised Chief Panko didn't tell you all this already. He was in office when it happened. He was there when the two men were arrested."

That shocked Ava. Why hadn't Panko mentioned it? Why had he not thought it might be relevant if it only happened a little over a year ago? "What were the charges for?" she asked, choosing not to play into the mention of Chief Panko.

He sighed and ran his hands over his face. "For facilitating the importation of drugs. In very small quantities. It's not like they were facilitating a dump truck load. It was small quantities."

"How long had they been doing that?"

"Three years. That we know about."

"You mean, that you found out about. How long had they worked there?"

"One was there for ten years; the other for almost fourteen."

"Why did they only get two years?"

He turned to face her again. "They were connected; they pulled strings. The wheels of the justice system got greased with money, and they got highly reduced sentences."

"When will they be up for parole; or will they?"

"Any time. It's not like I keep personal tabs on that sort of thing, but I know they could parole out sometime after the first twelve months."

"So they could actually be out right now? They could have gotten out this past week, in fact."

"It's possible." His head snapped up and his eyes were bright with understanding. "No. That's not possible. They weren't violent. They'd never do that. And why would they? Miss Harper, Mr. Holt, and Mr. Lawson had nothing to do with that situation."

"At least, not that you know of. I need all the information you have on these two men, and I need it now."

Halloway didn't do as he usually did when she requested anything. There was no dickering back and forth, no request for warrants or other documentation, and no hesitation. He worked at his computer's keyboard for a minute, and then the printer behind him whirred to life. He spun the chair, snatched the papers from the tray, and spun back to face Ava with the papers held out.

She took them. "Thank you, Mr. Halloway. I'll be in touch."

"I've no doubt," he said wearily.

She left and filled Metford in on the changed situation as they made their way back to the hotel.

In the room, she informed the rest of the team, who had finished at Lawson's place and returned as well. After everyone was up to speed, she checked the messages on her phone. It was almost three, and Dr. Blake had sent her the autopsy reports at eleven just as promised. She moved to a laptop and pulled them up. After scanning through them, she printed them.

"Ethan Holt and Emily Harper have similar superficial defensive wounds, stab wounds, and cuts. Dr. Blake is of the opinion that the same weapon made the wounds on both victims, and that both had been attacked while they were asleep."

"We were right, then," Santos said.

"Not to mention that both had the weird poker chips in their house," Ashton piped up. "We still don't know what that's about."

"Yeah, and he also found something else they had in common." Ava put the printed reports on the table and opened them to the photos. She pointed to the pictures. "See that?"

Dane squinted. "It looks like three dots in the shape of a triangle maybe. Freckles?"

"No. Tattoos," Ava said.

"That's a photo behind the ear," Metford said, touching behind his right ear absently.

"It is. It is behind the right ear on both of them. We need to find out what this tattoo means. Why do they have matching ones in an area where it won't be seen?"

"Maybe they were having an affair," Dane said. "And they got the matching ink to symbolize they belonged to each other. Like wedding rings, except without announcing it to the world."

"Why would they do that?" Metford asked. "At least, if you have a falling out, you can take off a ring."

"CBP agents aren't supposed to get romantically involved," Ashton supplied.

"And we haven't come across anything from their houses that would imply that they were involved romantically or otherwise," Santos said. "I don't think it has anything to do with a relationship. At least not that kind. It's something else, I believe."

"Like a secret club or something?" Metford asked.

"Don't know. Maybe. Give me a while to think on it, and I'll come up with some ideas."

"Let me know when you do," Ava said. "While you're all working on your assignments, Metford and I are going to be working the new angle. The two men who were arrested for facilitating smugglers at Patapsco."

"Or, the two who took the fall for it," Santos said, clicking her tongue and winking as she turned back to her computer.

"Or that, yeah." Ava motioned to Metford. "Pick one of the men and start digging. I'll take the other and do the same."

CHAPTER TWENTY

METFORD ROLLED HIS CHAIR TO AVA'S SIDE AND HELD OUT A PAPER. "Ethan Holt took over Derek Hayes' position after Hayes was arrested."

Ava took the paper and read the short article in the local section of the newspaper. It was a sidenote meant to keep the case alive in the minds of the residents of Baltimore, but not too much on their minds. She gave it back.

"More than I found on Ryan Brooks. I found one article about the snafu at Patapsco, another one announcing the sentencing phase of the trial, and that's about it other than the official arrest records and such."

"I say we go to Patapsco and ask them why they didn't mention this when we were there."

"I say that's a great idea. It's five-thirty; we're going to get the second shift crew and management."

He bobbed one shoulder as he slid into his jacket. "Might not be such a bad thing."

"Might not be a bad thing. Never hurts to get a fresh perspective on things."

Grinning, he raised his eyebrows and opened the door.

At Patapsco Bay Terminal, Alexandra Sutton, the assistant port director, met Ava and Metford.

"Please, come in and have a seat." Ms. Sutton's eyes stopped on Metford, and her smile broadened. She tucked a strand of hair behind her left ear and looked down, clearing her throat as he stepped into the small office. "What can I help you with today?" She sat at the desk.

"We need some information about Derek Hayes and Ryan Brooks," Ava said.

Alexandra's face fell and a worried expression settled there. "I'm... I'm sorry. I don't understand. They...uhm..." She exhaled deeply and looked uncomfortable. "They don't work here anymore. I'm sure that you know what happened, or you wouldn't be asking for information about them."

"We know," Metford said.

"Do you think they tie into the current deaths somehow?"

"We can't talk about an open investigation," Metford said in a smooth, low tone that Ava had rarely heard from him before.

"Oh. Okay. What do you want to know? I'll help with what I can." Alexandra shifted in her seat and her gaze flitted around the room and over its sparse furnishings.

"How did Mr. Hayes and Mr. Brooks get along with everyone here?" Ava asked.

"You mean, how did they get along with Ethan, Emily, and James, I assume?"

"How did they get along with them? Any differently than with the other workers?" Ava prodded.

"Wow. You do think they had something to do with..." Alexandra looked levelly at Ava. "Okay, this is my experience of working with Derek and Ryan. They were both outstanding employees. They were never late, followed protocols and procedures right down to the letter, and I don't remember them ever making any big mistakes with anything at work. They were meticulous and dedicated. They seemed like all-around nice guys, too. They treated coworkers and bosses with respect. They were courteous. I don't know what else to say that could convey how good these two men were."

"But?" Ava asked, knowing there was more. "I'm sure I hear an unspoken 'but' lingering at the end of that statement."

Alexandra nodded and looked down again. "There is. About a week before they were arrested and this place was turned upside down, Derek and Ryan started acting odd. As that week went on, it got worse."

"Odd how?"

"I don't know exactly how to explain it except that they seemed nervous and quieter than usual at first. By the end of the week, they were hardly speaking to anyone other than each other and they seemed almost paranoid, always looking over their shoulders. Once, I walked into their department and they were talking. They looked upset, like in a heated debate over something. They didn't see me at first, and I was just going to check that everything was all right. Derek looked up and saw me, and immediately, his expression changed. Ryan did the same, but they were sweating something. And Derek stopped paying as much attention to his personal appearance during that time, too."

"What did you think was going on with them?"

"I didn't know what to think because they had always been so different from the way they were acting." She tucked the strand of hair again. "Honestly, I worried that maybe they were on something."

"What do you mean, 'on something'?" Metford asked.

"You know. Drugs or something."

"Their demeanors changed that drastically?" he asked.

She nodded. "And it was quick. Like I said, about a week before the arrests. Their supervisors might have more insight than I do. They worked more closely with them."

"Who were the supervisors?" Ava asked.

"Aaron Gallagher and Tamish Hawke. They've both been here for twenty years, and the last seven have been in their current supervisory positions."

"Where can we find them?"

"I could call them in here right now, if you want to speak with them. They never leave before six in the evening."

"Why so late?"

"It's just the shift they work while we're swamped with work from now until winter."

"We'll talk to them now." Ava glanced at Metford to make sure he didn't disagree, but his eyes were locked on Alexandra. He looked like a lovestruck teenager, and she wanted to kick him to snap him out of it. Instead, she cleared her throat.

Metford looked at her, and she gave him a 'straighten up and stop mooning over the woman' expression. Deigning to look confused, he sat a little straighter and scoffed under his breath.

Alexandra called Aaron and Tamish over the walkie and then replaced it on the charging base. "They're on their way. Shouldn't take more than a couple of minutes."

"Had anything happened here before the Derek and Ryan incident? I mean, any smuggling or other illegal activities going on?"

"There are always people, low-level dock workers and such, who try. Most of them are caught before anything happens. We're good at our jobs, and we know where to look for things like that. We don't want any of the drugs and guns hitting our streets. It's our home. Our families live here. Kids live here."

"What about human trafficking? Any of that ever happen in the past?"

"Not during my time here."

There was a knock at the door and then two men entered. Ava's first thought was that the men looked much younger than she expected. They looked to be in their mid-to-late forties.

"Aaron, Tamish," Alexandra said. "This is Special Agents James and Metford." She motioned to Ava and then Metford. "They'd like to ask you some questions about Derek Hayes and Ryan Brooks."

Tamish was average height and build with hair as red as Metford's. Aaron was over six feet with salt-and-pepper hair and looked like he worked out regularly. They all shook hands and then Tamish sat on the extra chair and Aaron propped on the edge of the table behind Alexandra.

"That business has been over for more than a year," Aaron said. "Looks like FBI would have access to all the files on the matter."

"We thought it would save some time if we could just talk to people who knew them and experienced first-hand what happened," Ava said.

"Why are you even looking into it again?" Tamish asked. "It was closed. They went to jail."

"We just want to know what kind of people they were. How were they as workers? Who did they chum around with? Where did they hang out? Things like that."

"What's that got to do with anything?" Tamish asked through a light chuckle.

"We can't go into that right now," Metford said.

"Wait, does this have something to do with the murders this last week? Do you think Derek and Ryan had something to do with them?" He laughed. "No way. You're barking up the wrong tree there. They might have gotten into some trouble, but they wouldn't hurt anybody."

"Not those two," Aaron said. "Does this have something to do with the recent murders? Do we need to warn our employees that they might have a target on their backs?"

Ava and Metford exchanged a look, and Metford gave a small nod.

"I wouldn't do anything to panic the workers, but they would be wise to keep their heads on swivels, yeah," Ava said bluntly. "Three of your workers have been murdered in less than a week, and we still don't know why. Now, back to the matter at hand." She looked at each man in turn with an expectant expression.

Tamish and Aaron made brief eye contact and then Tamish spoke. "I worked very close to Derek Hayes. He was a supervisor's dream employee. He never complained. At least, not to me. He was always on time, and the man never called out a single day that I remember. He wasn't the most outgoing guy, but he was nice to everyone, and he was always respectful. Even when things didn't go his way, or he was having a trash-fire-in-a-dumpster day, he was always respectful. I don't know who he hung around with outside of work, but…" He glanced back to Aaron, who gave the minutest bob of his shoulders as he flipped two fingers forward in a 'go ahead' gesture.

"But what, Mr. Hawke?" Ava asked.

"When they worked the same days, Derek and Ethan and James took lunch together."

"How often did that happen?"

"It wasn't like I kept tabs on them. I just happened to see them leaving the area together at lunchtime."

"Once? Twice? Often? Rarely?" Ava urged.

Flustered, Tamish said, "More than rarely but less than often. I don't know. I saw it enough that it stuck." He tapped his temple with two fingers.

"But it's safe to assume they were all on friendly terms."

"I suppose. You'd have to be on friendly terms to do that, right?"

Ava nodded. "What about Ryan?"

"He was the same kind of employee as Derek was," Aaron said. "No complaints from me at all. I wished I had a whole department like him." He chuffed and shook his head. "Boy, I'm glad that didn't happen now."

"We all are," Tamish said.

"He was pretty outgoing; always making people smile or laugh. He just had such a gusto for life. Sometimes, it was intimidating."

"How so?"

"The man never seemed to have a bad day, and looking back, that's just not right. Everybody has bad days. Everybody gets grumpy, or down every now and then. God knows, I do. Even then, it struck me as odd, but he had passed all his drug tests and his psych eval, so it was intimidating to work with someone who enjoyed life so much every single day."

"Sounds like someone we'd all like to have more of in our lives."

"Except that he was facilitating smuggling and caused everybody here a lot of damn trouble that should have never happened."

"There's always a catch, right?" Metford said.

"That's one we could have all done without."

"Who were his friends here?" Metford asked.

"Don't know that they were all friends, but I saw him hanging around with Emily a few times. Lunch, breaks, tagging along behind her when shift was over. Things like that, but she never seemed to reciprocate whatever he was trying for with her. She was never interested in relationships at work that I could see. And he sometimes went to Ethan Holt's department and helped out, but I don't know that they were friends either."

"Where did they go after work?" Ava asked.

"Home, I suppose," Aaron said. "Some of us go to a bar down the road after work and then go home, but I don't know how often they went there. I didn't see them more than a dozen times. You, Tamish?"

"Nah. But I do know that they started hitting the casino a few months before the arrests."

"Porter Casino and Hotel?" Ava asked, suddenly more interested.

"Yeah."

"Did you go there? Is that how you knew they started going?"

"No. My wife would kill me if I took up gambling. She lights me up just for going to the bar a couple of times a week. Derek talked about it. To everyone who would listen, I think."

Aaron smiled. "He's not kidding. She would."

Metford grinned. "Well, if anything ever happens to you, we know where to start with the questioning."

"Thanks," Tamish said good-naturedly.

"Who else went with them?"

"Oh, he never said. I assumed it was just him and Ryan because they did just about everything together. Thick as thieves, as the old saying goes."

"What about Mr. Brooks, Mr. Gallagher? Did he ever mention going to the casino to you?"

"Yeah. Why? Is it important?"

"Just for clarity," Ava assured him.

"Why do I get the feeling that something else is going on and that we should be worried?"

"I don't know. Why would you be worried? Do you suspect something is happening here again?"

He laughed dryly and tossed up his hands. "Wouldn't you? If three of your employees and coworkers were brutally murdered in their own houses while they're sleeping, wouldn't you suspect that *something* was going on *somewhere*, or is it just me being paranoid?"

"Aaron," Alexandra said in a warning tone.

"How can you not know why they were killed? You're the FBI. I thought solving cases quickly was what you did." Aaron was on a roll. He was upset, and it was justified.

"James Lawson worked right there with Ryan Brooks but I never saw them together otherwise," Tamish said. "Isn't that right, Aaron? They worked side by side."

Aaron's face paled. "And James still had that job until he was killed."

"And Ethan took over Derek's job after he was arrested," Alexandra said.

"Why didn't you tell us this earlier?" Ava asked. "You should have led with that."

"Sorry, I honestly just didn't think about it. Your employees have designated work areas and job titles, and I hate to say it, but you can get snowblind to it until something or someone draws your attention to it."

"Like getting desensitized to violence and death like Finnigan said," Metford said.

"Who's Finnigan? We don't have a Finnigan here," Alexandra said.

"No, it's someone else," Ava said. "Is there something special about what all these employees were working on? Something that sets that department apart from the others?"

Alexandra considered it a moment, and shook her head. "Nothing I can think of. We all do pretty much the same job. We inspect. We run the X-ray machine. We check paperwork. We investigate when something is wrong, or when there is reason to suspect something is amiss. And we fill out a ton of reports for everything we do. There's follow-ups, further investigation when necessary, and release of goods if the shipment is cleared. Just the regular work."

"They didn't have a dog in their department," Aaron said. "None of us over here have a dog. Yet."

"Dog?" Ava asked. "What does a dog have to do with anything?"

"They're specially trained to sniff out contraband. We're getting two beagles per shift in our departments later this year. The other departments have German Shepherds and Labs."

Ava got as much information as she could about the policies and procedures at Patapsco Bay Terminal, and then she thanked them and left.

In the car, she handed Metford the stack of papers.

"They have as many rules and regs and policies as we do," he said.

"You'd think. What do you think about all this?"

"I'm still processing it all, but my gut tells me there's something going on in that department that is less than legit."

"I think there is, too. And I believe that if they'd had those dogs sooner, Ryan and Derek wouldn't have gotten away with the smuggling."

"It's strange that no one told us about James and Ethan before now, too."

"Yeah, Alexandra sure knows how to bury a lede."

CHAPTER TWENTY-ONE

AFTER GOING THROUGH ALL THE WORK HISTORIES OF ALL THE departmental employees at Patapsco Bay Terminal, Ava was ready for a break. Dead ends were one of the most frustrating parts of her job, and frustration led to tunnel vision, which inevitably sent her running in a circle instead of a straight line in the investigation.

Ashton was still scrubbing every venue online to pick up digital trails on the three victims, and he was now trying to tie their online presences to Derek Hayes and Ryan Brooks in any way possible. Had they been in contact for any reason since the men went to jail?

Ava and Metford had gone to the jail and interviewed both men, who implicated no other person in their actions. All they were interested in was proclaiming their innocence. If they were so innocent, though, there would have been no need to grease the wheels of the justice system with money or to pull strings for lighter sentences, which they both vehemently denied.

It was one of those out-in-the-open secrets. Everybody knew what had happened but nobody admitted it. The judge had since retired, conveniently removing himself from the picture. The defense lawyers had stopped practicing in Baltimore, again, conveniently removing themselves from the scene. The police officers, guards, and everyone else who had taken a cut of the money to give the two men an easier time and a lesser sentence had moved on to somewhere far away.

"It's a shame we can't go after all of them, too," Dane said, looking over all the names on Metford's list. "You know all these dirtbags moved on because they didn't want to get caught."

"How much money was spilled to give those two the lightest sentence possible?" Santos asked in amazement at the long list of names.

"More than we'll ever see," Ashton said.

"And I owe you, Ash," Metford said. "I would never have been able to find all these people without your help."

Ashton looked uncomfortable and mumbled, "Yep." He turned back to his computer without further input.

Metford mouthed, "What's up with him?" to Ava.

She shrugged. She had no idea. Ashton was never over-friendly, and always seemed more comfortable with his electronics than with people. The most social interaction the man had was when they solved a case, he'd join them at the bar for beer and burgers to celebrate. He seemed mostly normal during those times, but she had long believed it was a charade. The mask Ashton put on for the sake of camaraderie among the team members. She suspected he was always glad when the celebration was over.

"How do you know these are the people who took bribes?" Santos asked.

"We don't know for sure," Metford said, taking back the list. "It just seems fishy that they all decided to stop working in Baltimore right after the sentence was handed down. Within six months, they were all gone from the city. Some of them kept their professions, a couple retired, and a few found new lines of work altogether. What sucks is that it's mostly useless information. Does nothing for our current investigations."

Ava's phone rang. Her heart sank when she saw Chief Panko's number. She answered as she walked away from the team. A few moments later, she put the phone in her pocket and kept looking out the window at the scene on the street. "Guys, we got another one. Another two, I should say."

In unison, the team exclaimed, and all their voices clamored to be heard.

"I know. I know. This is ridiculous, but it's true. And, yes, it's two more Patapsco Bay workers. Christopher Wells and Vanessa Morales, 1720 Crabapple Court, apartment 9A."

They left as a group, questions flying in every direction as they got into the elevator. Ava didn't have any answers for them, and it was maddening. What was she missing? What vital thing was she not seeing that could have stopped the madness before the two newest victims became victims?

She beat herself up all the way to Crabapple Court. If the scenes at the other murders had been bad, the new one was horrible. There were more people, less cops outside, and even news cameras and reporters. Traffic was clogged, horns blared, people shouted, and only a few were paying attention to the police tape.

"Crowd control, everybody," Ava said when they got out of their cars.

The collective groan was one she felt to her bones.

More cops showed up with barricades, which they set up quickly. The new crews unloaded from the cars and helped get the crowd moved back and under control after twenty minutes of hell.

Ava and the team made their way to the elevator only to find that the cops had to cut off access to it so they could clear the hallway on nine.

"It'll be working by the time you leave," the guard said. "They had to do something to be able to keep them out up there. Damn people went crazy when they found out about the murders."

Ava and the others took the stairs. On their way up, they passed a small group of people on a landing. Ava flashed her badge and told them to move on. Most didn't put up any argument, but one younger woman tried to stand her ground.

"I live here, you can't make me leave. We're not up there. We're out of the way and we can't see or hear anything."

"I can, and I am. If you don't leave, I'll have you arrested for obstruction."

"You can't do that. I know my rights." She jutted out her chin and crossed her arms defiantly.

"And I know mine." Ava turned to Santos. "Special Agent Santos, would you please arrest this young woman and put her in the vehicle?"

Santos immediately moved around the others and toward the woman.

"Hey, no, you can't do that," she blurted in a panic. "I'll go. Jeez." She went all the way down the stairs grumbling about how inept the cops were and how the FBI was only bullies.

Detective Coffey stood in the hallway with his arms crossed, deep in thought.

"Detective," Ava said.

"Ah, good. I'm glad you guys are here. This is..." He sighed and tossed up his hands. "I don't even know. This is a freaking mess. That's what it is."

"What have you got so far?"

"Well, not much. I'm just now getting all these tenants out of the way so we can work. Forensics is still in there. I went in but had to come back out here to help. There are even reporters with all kinds of cameras. They're talking about a serial killer who's targeting Patapsco Bay workers."

"Christopher Wells and Vanessa Morales," Ava said. "What do you know so far?"

"He's younger than the others. He's in his bedroom. On the bed. She's in the bathroom. Looks like she was attacked when she got out of the shower. Looks like a damn slaughterhouse in that bathroom."

"And they both worked at Patapsco?"

"As far as I know."

"This is a much less affluent neighborhood than the others were," Santos said.

"Like I said, he's pretty young. Probably hasn't been at the job very long. According to his driver's license, he's only just turned twenty-seven a few days ago."

"His license wasn't taken?" Ava asked.

"No."

"All the others were taken. All forms of ID had been taken, as a matter of fact."

"Not his. All his personal and work stuff was there. Least it looked that way to me."

"What about hers?" Dane asked.

"Yep. Her purse was sitting right there. Nothing was missing that I could tell, but then again, women's purses are mysterious things to us men. Am I right?" he asked Metford.

"The great abyss of secrets," Metford agreed.

Ava walked into the apartment. It wasn't nearly as large as the homes of the other murdered agents. The paint was stained in places, nail holes decorated the wall behind the flatscreen, and the furniture had a well-loved look to it.

"Wow, he didn't spend much on living accommodations or décor," Santos said.

"If he's young and hasn't been at the job long, he's just starting to make enough money to think about those things," Ashton said.

"Good point," Metford said.

In the bedroom, Ava studied the scene. Christopher lay on the bed in a position that made it seem as if maybe he had passed out. With all the beer and liquor bottles sitting around, she didn't doubt that he had.

"Are there any defensive wounds on his arms?" she asked a forensic team member.

"Not that we found. Looks like he was stabbed in the heart and the side of the neck and didn't put up any fight. Poor bastard just laid there and bled out from the looks of it."

The blood had soaked the thick comforter underneath Christopher. Spatter had hit the bedside lamp, floor, wall, and had speckled Christopher's arm and one side of his face.

Moving to the bathroom doorway, Ava stopped. Coffey had not been exaggerating when he said it looked like a slaughterhouse. The floor and walls were white tiles. The blood stood out starkly against all that white and under the bright fluorescent ring light in the center of the ceiling. The dark splotches of blood that had hit the light ring cast odd shadows on the room.

The shower curtain lay crumpled behind the very pretty woman on the floor. Her arms were covered in defensive wounds as were her hands. She had been stabbed randomly all over, her face and neck had slash marks. She had fought hard for her life.

The forensic unit tiptoed, moving carefully over and around the wide streaks and smears and puddles and spatters.

"We're going to be a while yet," the woman said. "Don't come in. There's not room for any more."

"Not coming in, thanks," Ava said, backing up a step.

The others moved toward the door, and each had the same expression of disgust once they saw the room. It wasn't a look of disgust at the blood and gore, Ava knew. They were disgusted that the victim had been so brutalized, had fought so hard to live, and yet one maniac with a knife had still won the battle. How could bad come out on top so many times?

"Who is she to him?" Ava asked Coffey.

"Girlfriend, I suppose."

"She has a light circle around her ring finger like there was a ring there."

"Divorcee, maybe. I told you I don't know much yet. She looks older than him, though."

"She does. I see his work ID and other items, how did you know she worked at Patapsco?"

"The ID and all her pertinent work badges are in her purse."

"But no wedding ring?"

"Not that I saw."

"Did you look in the zipper pockets in the purse and on the wallet?"

"I opened them, yeah. Hey, it's over there in the big brown bag. Knock yourself out."

Ava went to the bag and carefully removed items from the purse. The inventory listed nothing, so she filled it out as she went. She put the cellphone in a separate plastic bag. When she opened the wallet, she unzipped the change compartment and ran her finger through the coins. A slim gold band glinted behind the pennies, and she took it out.

"Found a woman's wedding band in the change compartment," she said, holding it up for Coffey to see.

"Well, this probably just got more convoluted and difficult to deal with than it already was."

"Probably. Unless she was divorced and just saving the ring for sentimental reasons. Maybe Christopher was a rebound boyfriend, or a very close friend."

From the bathroom, the female tech answered. "Used condom in the trash. I'd say close friends."

"If it's an affair, the husband has to be located and someone has to tell him the bad news," Coffey said.

"What? That his wife was having an affair, or that she was stabbed to death while having that affair?" Santos asked, her lip curling in distaste. "People never cease to amaze me." She made her way to the collected evidence.

"Her attack doesn't fit with the pattern so far," Dane announced from the bathroom doorway.

"It's almost like she surprised the attacker," Ashton said. "This looks more frenzied and uncertain."

"The killer has been leaving the scenes without being noticed," Metford said. "Maybe he's cleaning up before he leaves. Maybe he was going to the bathroom, where there's a mirror and bright light, to clean up before leaving, and she was in there."

"And the killer was taken by surprise," Ava said.

"She might have even attacked him when he walked into the bathroom," Santos said. "They surprised each other. Vanessa might have been expecting it to be Christopher when the door opened, and the killer expected an empty room."

"Possible. At this point, though, almost anything is possible," Ava said. "Ashton, as soon as the electronics are logged, take them. Santos, go with him and start looking into whether Ms. Morales was married, single, divorced. If she was married, find an address. We have to inform her husband before someone splashes her picture on the internet or the news."

"Ava," Metford said from the bedroom. "Does he look familiar to you?"

Ava moved so that she could get a clear look at Christopher's face. "Maybe. I don't know, but he does. Where from, though?"

They waited for forensics to be finished, and Dr. Blake to start loading the body for removal.

"Wait," Ava said, drawing a scowl from Dr. Blake.

"I've waited about all I'm inclined to wait. I need to get the bodies back to the office."

Ava stepped close to the gurney and looked at the man's face. "I recognize him from somewhere."

"The CBP building," Metford said over her shoulder. "He was there when we went to talk with the deputy commissioner about Ethan."

"Where? He's too young to work there, I think. They were all much older than him."

"No, he was there talking to a man in one of the outer offices. It looked like they were discussing something really important and really private because they stopped talking and looked guilty when we went by the room they were in. I'm sure that was him."

"I remember seeing the two men because I thought they looked guilty, too, but I didn't think anything of it because that's not why we were there."

"Can I take the body now?"

"Yes," Ava said curtly, stepping back and returning Dr. Blake's scowl.

"Thanks," Metford said to him.

"Mm." That one sound and the slight lift of one graying eyebrow were the only sign of acknowledgement.

"How can you be sure that's the same man from the CBP headquarters?"

"He had a scar on his temple."

"Okay, so he was at CBP headquarters, and now he's dead."

"Along with his girlfriend, who was collateral damage, in my opinion."

"That's how it seems. Let's do a final sweep after everybody's gone. I want to make sure we didn't miss something important. I feel like whatever the link is, it's right in front of me and I'm just not seeing it."

CHAPTER TWENTY-TWO

Ava put her phone to her ear as she unlocked the car and got in. "James," she said, already knowing it was Santos on the other end.

"Yeah, Santos, boss. Vanessa Morales is, or was, very much married. To Javier Morales, who works for the mayor. Sending her address to you now. It's the same as on her driver's license."

"Great, thanks."

Metford got in, and Ava put the phone in the console tray and buckled her seatbelt.

"That seems like it was a bad phone call. Who was it?"

"Santos. Our Ms. Morales was a Mrs. Morales."

"Well, Mr. Morales isn't going to have a very good day, is he?" Metford huffed out a sigh and buckled up.

"Nope. Not at all. And we're the lucky ducks who get to tell him about his late wife."

THE FORGOTTEN GIRLS

The house at 9143 Blue Heron Drive had a meticulously manicured lawn, paved drive, and a large, ornate birdbath surrounded by flowers and mulch as the centerpiece. It added a pop of color to the otherwise monotone palette of the white brick, white vinyl siding, white mailbox, and super-white window frames that looked relatively new.

"Nice place," Metford noted aloud.

"Kind of place that probably has a nice payment to go with it. Husband works in the mayor's office. Combined incomes probably made that payment easier."

"I doubt he'll be thinking much about the next mortgage payment, just to be honest."

Ava got out. He was right.

"Says a lot about your priorities, you know?"

She stopped walking. "What do you mean? What about *my* priorities?"

"That you thought first about how the man was going to make the mortgage payment instead of that his life was about to be turned upside down and ripped apart so badly that he might not even care about the house."

Stunned, Ava had no response. "What are you now, Dr. Bran's replacement?" She walked ahead toward the door. She neither waited for, wanted, nor expected a response from him.

Ava rang the doorbell and then knocked. Metford stepped up beside her and straightened his jacket idly. His expression was professionally unreadable, which was a little out of character for him. She had half-expected at least a wry smile, or a glint in his eyes because he had ruffled her, but there was nothing. Did that mean he hadn't been aiming to merely ruffle her feathers? Had he said that to make her think about her priorities? And if so, was he right to do it?

If her priorities were screwed up, it was for a good reason. The ordeal with Jason Ellis would have been enough to screw up anyone's priorities. At least, for a while.

After all the months that had passed, maybe she should start to force things back into their rightful places.

Like my priorities, she thought darkly, not wanting to analyze that part of herself yet. Being screwed up was easier than making a change.

She knocked again, louder.

Metford bounded off the porch to the garage. He looked through the windows on the rolling doors. "Not here. At least, there are no cars here."

Ava looked at her watch and exhaled a long breath. The road was empty and still in both directions. Near the end of the block, a few kids were in a yard laughing as they tossed a ball over the head of a smaller kid who would try to jump for it, fall, and laugh with them.

She turned back and rang the doorbell again in frustration before heading toward the car. Metford ambled down the drive to the passenger door and got in slowly, irritating Ava even more. She said nothing, just let it go. She didn't want to open her mouth while she was upset and cause another useless argument that she wasn't even sure she would be in the right about.

"We can send somebody back later," Metford suggested.

Ava nodded and started the engine. Just as she put the car in reverse, a large black Tahoe turned into the drive and stopped behind them.

"That him?" Ava asked, looking in the rearview.

"Beats me." He got out.

Ava stepped out, too, but was more cautious as she approached the vehicle. Federal workers had been murdered left and right, and she couldn't be sure the person in the Tahoe wasn't the killer. Maybe it was an overabundance of caution on her part, and she was okay with that.

Metford on the other hand, flipped out his ID and held it up as he smiled and motioned the car to pull forward. His hand never went close to his gun, and his steps never faltered.

"FBI," he called. "Mr. Morales?"

The man in the driver seat squinted at the badge with a dubious expression. He turned and shot Ava a suspicious look as she moved into view with a much more dour expression. His hands gripped the wheel, and a look of anger settled on his face.

"Mr. Morales?" Ava said, holding out her ID as well. "FBI, Mr. Morales. It's about your wife," she said loudly, hoping he could hear her with the windows rolled up and likely with the AC running. She mouthed, 'Your wife' for emphasis.

His hands loosened on the wheel and he looked back to Metford, who motioned for him to pull forward. The man nodded and gestured that he would pull into the garage.

Dressed in a suit and tie, carrying a briefcase, Mr. Morales stood outside the Tahoe and waited for the agents to approach him.

"You're FBI."

"Yes, sir," Ava said, showing her badge again.

"Why are you here about my wife? That is what you were saying back there, isn't it?"

Ava cleared her throat and put away her badge. "Yes, sir. Could we maybe go inside and talk?" She tilted her head toward the house.

THE FORGOTTEN GIRLS

"Why can't you just tell me what she's done right here? How did she get mixed up with something so bad that you're here?"

Ava and Metford shared a look.

"Mr. Morales, could we please speak inside?" Metford asked. "I think it would be better if we did this in private."

"Oh, God," Mr. Morales said, turning toward the house. He opened the door and left it as he stepped inside.

Ava and Metford didn't prompt the man to offer entrance. He was getting ready to have a bad enough day without the added small irritations of being overly polite.

"This is bad, bad, isn't it?" Mr. Morales asked, dropping his briefcase, keys, and jacket on an armchair in the living room.

Metford indicated Ava should break the news.

"Mr. Morales, how is your marriage?" Ava started off. She motioned for him to sit on the sofa across the room.

Mr. Morales sat and shook his head. "I don't know. How is any marriage after twelve years? Going as expected? Good? We're still married, anyway. What's going on? What does it have to do with how my marriage is going?"

"I have some bad news, Mr. Morales." Ava glanced at Metford. He conveniently didn't make eye contact. "Your wife, Vanessa Morales, was having an affair, it seems."

Mr. Morales gave her a doubtful look and shook his head. "No. She was having a fling, not an affair. There's a big difference. In case you didn't notice, she is seven years my junior, and my job keeps me away from home. A lot."

Metford did make eye contact then, and his expression was one of disbelief.

"I'm sorry," Ava said, trying to understand the situation. "You knew about the affair?"

"Fling. I know about the fling, yes. Some young guy at her work." He shifted uneasily. "Don't judge me. Vanessa has always been more… *active* than me. She needs these little flings every now and then. I know you probably think that's stupid, but we do what we can to make things work and to keep each other happy. I knew what I was getting into when we married."

Ava nodded, opening and closing her hands once. "No judgment here, Mr. Morales. None at all. Thank you for being open and honest about the situation."

"Why would the FBI be here about a fling my wife is having. It's still that Chris Wells at her work, isn't it? He seemed harmless enough the one time we met. I can't imagine he is into something that would draw the attention of the FBI."

Ava cleared her throat and shook her head. "No. The aff—fling isn't the only reason we're here today. It's your wife, Mr. Morales. She's gone, sir. She's…she's dead. I'm sorry, but she was murdered at Mr. Wells's apartment."

Ava wanted to be anywhere but with Mr. Morales at that moment. She watched as his body language and his expression changed. His emotions were winding up for the mother of all emotional storms, and Ava would have to sit through the worst of it.

After he calmed enough to talk again, Ava gave him the few details she could.

"Did they get into an argument? Kill each other? Vanessa is confrontational, and I can see an argument going sideways with a young, hot-headed guy."

"Was Mr. Wells hot-headed?" Metford asked.

"Aren't all young guys?" Mr. Morales said, looking at Metford as if he should know.

"Fair enough," Ava said. "You said you knew about the fling, and that you had met Mr. Wells?"

"Yes. We, Vanessa and I, always agreed that she could have these flings as long as I met the man at least once. For her safety, you see."

"And how long had this been going on between Mrs. Morales and Mr. Wells?"

"A little longer than her usual. Maybe five months, maybe six."

"And you were okay with it. Really?" Ava asked, unable to hide the astonishment.

"I thought you said you weren't judging me for this."

"I'm not. I genuinely want to know. Were you really okay with your wife going out and sleeping with younger men?"

"No, okay. No. I was never really okay with it, but it's something I had to do to keep her happy. How would it look if I was going through a divorce and all this shit came out in court? The public would know about it before I got home that evening. It would be humiliating, and it would make my job unbearable. I'm a public figure, you do realize?"

"So, it wasn't something you agreed to just to make her happy. It was something you did to save face." Ava stood and laid her card on his coffee table.

"That's not what I said. I did agree to it because it kept her happy." His tone became argumentative, defensive.

"I'm sorry for your loss, Mr. Morales. I've left my card and the number for a grief counselor; in case you need it. We'll see ourselves out."

"I love my wife," he said, not following them to the door.

Ava stepped outside. Metford followed quickly.

"Shut the door," she said.

"I did. I wasn't raised in a barn. I have manners. Do you?"

"Not now, Metford. Not the time or the place."

They got into the car.

"We should have stayed a few more minutes, shouldn't we?" Metford asked. "I mean, he was messed up, and we just left him there. Didn't even offer to call a family member or friend for him."

"I left him the card for the counselor. I don't think he would have let us call anyone for him."

"Wait a minute." Metford opened the door and headed stubbornly back into the house.

Ten minutes later, he returned and got back into the car. "There. I feel better now."

"What the hell?"

"I called his cousin. He said he'd be here in about twenty minutes. That's the only family he has in Maryland." Metford scowled. "Why are you looking at me like that? I couldn't leave him that way. My conscience would have eaten me alive tonight. I have enough trouble trying to sleep without adding to it."

"Okay, so I was wrong not to offer, but I think maybe Mr. Morales should be investigated in the deaths of Mrs. Morales and Christopher Wells. Sorry, I was thinking maybe all his emotions in there weren't genuine. That it was an act. Didn't you hear how defensive he got?"

"I'd get defensive, too. You were pretty hard on him in there. Anybody would have seen where your mind was going with the questions. He just wanted you to know he didn't have anything to do with it. I'm not judging him or his wife for the lifestyle choices they made."

"You heard the anger in his voice when he finally admitted that he didn't like it. He only agreed to let her have affairs—"

"Flings."

"—flings, whatever, so he wouldn't have to go through a very embarrassing public divorce that could have impacted his profession."

"Well, how is it any better now that she was found dead at her lover's apartment? The details will get out no matter what."

"But this way, he was wronged. He's a victim of circumstance. In public, he can say that he had no idea she was having the affair, and now she's dead. The love of his life who he worked so hard to keep happy for the last twelve years. Don't you see the pity angle he'll be working? If they had divorced, there would have been no angle to work. I think I have to investigate him for possible involvement."

Metford chuckled dryly. "I'm sorry, but did we meet the same Javier Morales? I mean, you met him, talked to him, saw how he acted, right? If that man was capable of murder…" He exhaled sharply and tossed up his hands. "I don't know. I know people sometimes do things in fits of anger they later regret, and even are capable of murder under certain circumstances when they otherwise seem like a humble, gentle person, but him? I think if he had committed these murders, he would have been riddled with guilt. At the very least, he would have been super nervous when he saw us."

"And you think he wasn't?"

"I think he was shocked and wondering why the hell two FBI agents were at his house, but not guilty. I'd call it cautious, instead."

Ava backed out of the drive. "Call it what you like, but I'm putting him on my list."

Metford looked out the passenger window. "Of course, you are."

"What's that supposed to mean?"

"Nothing. Just that I knew you would. When you make up your mind about something or someone, nothing changes it. Not that it's a bad thing; just sorta your trademark move, as I've learned."

It was getting harder to let things go and not argue her point, but Ava did just that. Dr. Bran had given her a few guidelines to help with thinking before acting or speaking. Ava had argued adamantly that her job, her career, her chosen path in life dictated that she be able to make snap decisions without a ton of thinking involved. People's lives depended on it; not least of all, her own.

After several sessions, Ava understood that Dr. Bran only wanted her to implement the guidelines in her personal life, in her personal relationships, but somehow, those guidances had bled over into all facets of her life, leaving her unsure if she should react, or just let it go in certain situations.

She and Metford didn't have a personal relationship. She and the team were coworkers with professional ties to each other. But hadn't they all, at one time, or several, acted in ways that meant they thought of each other as more than friends? Hadn't they all, at some point, said out loud that they thought of the team as 'family'?

She gripped the wheel and bit her tongue. As she parked in the hotel parking lot, she could no longer keep her thoughts quiet on the subject of Javier. "If Vanessa was sleeping with Christopher, who's to say she wasn't messing around with the others who were killed?" She put the car in park and switched off the engine.

Metford looked like she had kicked him. "What?"

"Well? What if she was? She and Javier were down with that kind of thing. Maybe she was racking up the body count at work, and Javier finally had all he could take and snapped."

"Now you're saying you think he killed all the other agents, too? Not just a killer, but a serial killer?"

"All the deaths have one thing in common."

"Yeah, they were all killed with a knife."

"Besides that." She unbuckled her seatbelt.

"They were all Patapsco Bay Terminal employees."

She huffed. "Besides that, Metford. Besides the obvious. They were all coworkers of Vanessa Morales, which meant they all had her in common."

"Some of them didn't even work in the same departments. How can you say they all had her in common? There's no evidence of any of them sleeping with her."

"There might be. We didn't look for any evidence of that because we didn't know to. Not until now."

He shook his head. "I don't think this is a good route to take. You're reaching here. You're not following the evidence."

"What evidence?!" she shouted, fed up with the frustration of the dead ends in the case.

"The evidence that suggests some of the Patapsco workers were possibly into something less than legal with those home-printed poker chips and money, remember?"

After several minutes of useless back-and-forth with him, Ava snatched the key from the ignition and got out.

"I'm going to update Sal and then I'm going to check on those warrants. If they're not in my hand by this evening, I'm going to look into Javier and see what he's been up to lately. Like over the last two weeks. I can't let it go. You're right. I just can't. When you're team lead, you can make these decisions, but until then, I'm lead, and I say he needs to be looked at."

"I'm not trying to tell you how to do your job, and I don't want to be team lead. I don't even know where that came from, but it's unjustified. That was a low-blow, Ava."

She turned to him in shock. "That's how it feels every time you undermine me, too. Like I've been sucker-punched in the gut." She grabbed the door and flung it wide to walk through alone.

As she turned the slight corner to the bank of elevators, she glanced over her shoulder to the entrance. Metford had taken off his jacket and was walking down the sidewalk to the left. There was a coffee and pastry shop that way. Maybe a little diner, too, she couldn't really remember.

She got in the elevator and hit the button to go up. Metford would be upset for a while, but he would walk it off, or go to a diner and have a burger, after which he'd most assuredly feel better and return. She decided to deal with him then. For now, it was okay that he went the other way and left her alone. Probably more than okay. It was the first time since they'd arrived in Baltimore that he had done something to avoid more friction and conflict between them.

CHAPTER TWENTY-THREE

Sal wasn't happy about the warrants, or the fact that Ava suggested there was corruption at CBP.

"I know Deputy Commissioner Jasper Halloway is hiding something he was involved in, or maybe still is involved in. Who knows, maybe it's something to do with all these CBP agents getting murdered in their homes," Ava argued, fighting to hold a civil tone.

Maybe it had not been a good idea to call Sal right after getting upset with Metford and holding that in. The frustration built in Ava's chest until she felt that screaming would be the only way to release it, but she still tamped it down, put it back in its box, and tried to lock the lid. She recalled the advice her grandmother always gave about honey and vinegar and flies or the lack of. Though she couldn't quite summon the honey, she could at least avoid the vinegar part.

"No, Ava. Stand down on this. Especially right now. It's not a request. You can't go off on this while you're investigating the brutal murders of five federal customs agents. Do you really think the whole of CBP is involved?"

"Okay. Maybe that is a little over-the-top, but can we at least agree that all the murders are related somehow?"

After a brief silence, Sal agreed. "The murders might be related. They seem to be, but you can't always assume the worst of everybody just because they act strange, or guilty, or however."

"I get that. I do."

"Good," Sal said. "Now, these five murders are connected. Do what you do best, and get in there and figure out what that connection is. Logically. Follow the facts, and nothing else."

"Yes, ma'am," Ava said, still choked up with the need to argue about how right she was and how wrong Sal was on this one.

"Update me when you get something new."

"Will do. Thank you." Ava hung up and put away her phone. She picked up her laptop and moved to the end of the long table away from everyone else and with her back to the large window overlooking the busy street.

"You okay?" Metford asked.

"Fine," Ava said without looking at him.

"Call with Sal didn't go as planned, I take it."

"Your instincts are impeccable, as usual."

"What about—"

Ava shut her laptop. "What about you, Santos, take Dane and go question people at the mayor's office about Javier. Character statements, alibis, anything about him and his whereabouts last night. Got it?" Her tone snapped with tension and irritation.

Santos stood abruptly. "Right now?"

"Yeah, right now. Ashton, where are you with the electronics?"

Ashton spread his hands to indicate the exorbitant number of electronics meticulously placed on the table he worked at alone. "Not far. There are tablets, phones, computers, smart watches, you name it, I have it here in spades."

"What's taking so long? Usually, you're finished with your work before I get to ask about it."

"My lab is back in Fairhaven, and I am working with a limited number of portable tools."

"Right. Sorry." Ava opened her computer again. "How long do you think it's going to take to get through all of that?"

"If you mean all the electronics here…days, most likely."

"That's your only assignment until you're finished with them." She started searching records for Javier Morales and noticed Metford staring at her from his seat midway down the table. "You can help me. Find anything you can about Javier Morales. I'm going through police records for him back until he was eighteen. You choose any other path and start looking."

Metford didn't say anything, and just went to work at his laptop.

Two hours later, Ava stood and stretched. "You find anything useful?" she asked Metford.

"Not much. He's popular. All his social media posts seem to have a political angle. The guy seems clean. People like him, and from what I've read online, he's a big activist for animal rights, the environment, underprivileged people, and after-school community programs for kids from age twelve to eighteen."

"I'm not painting any halos on his picture just yet," Ava said.

"Did you find something?"

"Yeah, a speeding ticket dated for 2017."

Metford laughed. "So, we're done right? I mean, I feel like we just investigated Ghandi and Mother Teresa. Javier is just a grieving widower." He stood and closed the laptop.

"Oh, no. Nothing of the sort." Ava walked to the printer and picked up the papers she had printed out. Shuffling through them one at a time, she read snippets of information aloud. "Bailey's Burlesque Bar, Sovereign Sudz for Studz, The Fuzzy Hole, The Fox's Ear. That's just a few of the strip bars he likes to frequent. There are scores of other bars, sports bars, dives, all kinds of them, and they all have shady reputations from what I saw online. He also likes to stay at cheap motels a few nights a month. Again, real shady, out-of-the-way places. So, I'd say he likes the ladies a lot. Ladies, alcohol, and cheap motels."

"He and his wife had an agreement about that sort of thing, though. It doesn't prove anything. Maybe he was having an affair, or maybe he was just looking. Guys do that without having affairs sometimes."

"Right." She turned and grabbed her jacket from the back of her chair. "Not in my experience. And the agreement he told us about went only one way—in favor of Vanessa's desires, not his."

"Where are you going?"

"To visit The Fuzzy Hole. It seems to be his favorite place. Drops a lot of money there every week. Especially over the last month. Somebody there must know him."

"I'm right behind you." Metford tipped his chair in his haste to grab his own jacket.

Ava stepped out of the room. "If you're going just for the peepshow, don't bother. I don't have time to wipe the drool and snap you back to the questioning."

"I wipe my own drool, thank you." He pushed the button for the elevator and grinned like a schoolboy.

Ava barely contained her eyeroll of exasperation. "Do guys ever grow up?"

They stepped into the elevator.

"Not if we can help it."

∽

The flashing neon lights and blasting techno beats inside The Fuzzy Hole were enough to set off epileptic seizures. Ava groaned as the smell of alcohol and stale cigarette smoke blasted her just inside the front doors. She gasped and coughed lightly, trying to acclimate. The stench of body odor, dozens of different, loud perfumes and colognes, and something that smelled faintly like deep-fried food hung thickly in the air like a cloud of toxic smog.

"I thought there was a no smoking law in all public places," Metford said, fanning the air as they walked past a man in jeans and cowboy boots, smoking a fat cigar.

"Look around, Metford," Ava practically yelled over her shoulder to be heard. "Honestly, smoking is the least of their worries in here."

He laughed, and the sound was lost in the wild, industrial hammering of the music.

It was amazing that every facet and station of normal, everyday people seemed to be represented in the crowd. The people had segregated into cliques the same as they had in high school, but they were there, under the same roof, sharing the same tight space. The motorcycle club wannabes in one section, the truckers in another, office boys occupied yet another space, college guys and girls in another, thugs, barflies, and the awkward men looking to pick them up all seemed to find space at the long bar. All the groups that would normally clash with each other out on the street had come together mostly peacefully, and for the common goal of seeing bare tits. Ava didn't know whether it was sad, scary, or just ironic.

The bartender slapped a folded white towel over his shoulder, expertly leaving the embroidered logo in view.

"What can I get for you two cops?" He grinned and winked.

Ava scoffed. "Nothing to drink. Just some information." She pulled out her phone to show a picture of Javier.

"Drinks are expensive, but information is even more so."

"Just need to know if you know this man." She turned her phone to face him.

"Never seen him before." The bartender turned to another customer.

"Hey!" Ava yelled, stepping between two barstools and holding out the picture to the bartender again. "You barely even looked—"

The man snapped his head back toward her. "I told you I don't know him. Never seen him before. I've got a job to do here."

Metford put a hand on her shoulder, and she stepped back. The man and woman she had stepped between craned to look at the picture as she did so.

"Hey, I know him. That's Javvy," the skinny woman in the too-short, form-fitting, hot pink dress said, putting her finger in the center of the phone screen.

"You know him?" Ava asked, pulling the phone roughly from under the pinning finger. God only knew where it had been before it was on her screen.

"Yeah, I told you, that's Javvy," the woman leaned closer so she didn't have to yell.

Hot, sour breath enveloped Ava's face, and she jerked her head to the side, disgusted to the point of gagging.

Miss Hot Pink turned to Metford and ran her hand down his forearm. "Hiya, Sexy. God, I love a man with muscle," she slurred.

"Hey, don't touch," Ava ordered. "Can we talk to you about...*Javvy*? Somewhere we don't have to scream, please."

"Sure, honey. You two just follow Auntie Candy to the back and we'll have a chat about him. I hope he's not in any trouble or nothing."

Ava followed at a distance as Candy opened a door and went down a dim, narrow hallway with dirty tile floors and grimy tan walls. A woman used an ancient landline a few feet down the hall, and there was no room to get around her without brushing against her. Ava turned her back to the woman and gritted her teeth as her clothes brushed the filthy wall.

The woman smiled as Metford turned sideways to get past her. Just as he was almost clear of her, she stepped backward, pressing herself into him.

To Ava's surprise, his hands shot up into the air, and he stepped away fast enough that the woman lost balance and stumbled backward into the opposite wall.

"Asshole," she blurted at him as she got the stiletto heels under her again and regained her balance.

Candy pulled back a multi-colored, fringed satin curtain at the end of the hallway, revealing a cramped dressing room full of mirrors with bright lights, makeup on the vanities and on the floor and smeared on the whitewashed cinderblock walls, and a crush of women in varying stages of drunkenness. Laughter, conversations, and cursing mingled into a droning cacophony of background noise. Candy led them through the room and toward a dented metal door with a push bar.

"This is about as quiet as it gets, unless you think we should step into the alley back here. I don't recommend that, not with you two being cops and all." She chuckled. Red lipstick had tinted her front top teeth.

"FBI, actually," Ava said.

Candy stopped laughing and pulled a smashed pack of Marlboros from her sequined clutch. She lit up. Ava and Metford took a step back. There was no ventilation and nowhere to get away from the slowly drifting cloud.

"What the hell? FBI? Javvy's alright, isn't he?"

"How well do you know him?"

She shrugged, the bones at the tops of her shoulders standing out starkly in the sickly light of the single yellowing bulb over the door. "Well enough, I guess. I mean, it's not like we were besties or anything, but he's a regular." She looked shocked and held out her hands toward Ava. "One of the *good* regulars," she said.

Ava recoiled, bumping Metford's arm, to avoid the contact.

"What does that mean?" Metford asked when Ava's brain ground to a momentary halt in her bid to not be groped by the woman.

"It means he was a real gentleman," Candy said, looking as if it was a given.

Ava scoffed and looked toward the women clamoring in the dressing room. "I suspect the standards of gentlemanly behavior are pretty low in a place like this."

Metford elbowed her lightly and looked shocked.

Candy pulled back against the wall, crossed her arms, and dragged from the cigarette. "You think we're too stupid to know how a gentleman acts? That it?"

"I'm sorry," Ava said, immediately regretting her words. She spent a third of her time helping women just like Candy, not insulting them. "I didn't mean it like that."

Candy glared at her, immediately distrustful and resentful. "Whatever, sister. Who knows, with one tiny little difference in your life, or even in your parents' lives before you were a twinkle in your daddy's eye, and this could have been your life."

Chagrined, Ava nodded. "I'm sorry. Like I said, I didn't—"

"Don't matter. I have nothing more to tell you about Javvy. You obviously think I'm too dumb to have any useful information anyway." She plowed between them and threw the cigarette on the tiles at their feet. "Thanks for wasting my time."

"Candy, I'm sorry," Ava said. "Come back and tell us about Javvy."

Candy stopped.

Metford gave Ava a concerned look as he crushed the cigarette underfoot.

"Did Javvy ever talk to you about his marriage, his job, anything personal?" Ava continued.

Candy returned to them. "Sometimes. Is he okay?"

"He's okay, Candy," Metford said. "We just need to know what kind of person he is when he's around the girls here. He ever cause any trouble, maybe get rough with one of them, or anything like that?"

Candy looked shocked. "No, never. I told you..." She sneered at Ava. "Never mind." She made eye contact with Metford and held it. "Javvy is a nice man. Real respectable, and I know how that sounds, but he is. He never got tossed out, and nobody ever got manhandled or groped by him."

"Did he ever..." Ava glanced down the hall and lowered her voice. "He ever sleep with any of the women here?"

"No. We don't do that here. It's not legal, you know."

"Did he ever get a private dance from anyone?" Metford asked.

"He requested them from me sometimes." She looked down at her glittering clutch. "And before you ask, no, we never slept together. Truth be told, he never even got the private dances. Not what he wanted."

"What did he want?" Ava urged.

"Someone to listen to him, mostly. He talks about everything under the sun. He's super smart, witty, too. Likes a good laugh. Hard to find a man who's good and has a sense of humor. Weren't never any talk about anything that should make a difference to you guys, though. Just his wife, her boyfriends, his job, her job, the mayor and what a shit he is to work with sometimes, all the penny dreadfuls he volunteers for, and that he would love to just leave everything behind one day and become a beach bum in Jamaica." She laughed. "He dreams like a teenage girl. That's what I told him last time he was here."

"Penny dreadfuls?" Ava asked.

"Yeah, that's what he calls all those programs, or whatever you call them, where he volunteers. He just does that so he doesn't have to sit at home and think about where his wife is."

"Is that what he told you?"

"More or less. It's more like the feeling I got from him. Sorta sad and lonely, I think."

"He ever say anything about having affairs himself?"

"No. I offered to be his…you know, but he didn't want that. Said it would ruin him if it ever got out. I asked how it would look if it got out about his wife, and he didn't like that. Told me to never say anything about that to anyone but him." She scoffed and chucked a thumb over her shoulder toward the dressing area. "Like I would. If I did, it's not like anyone here would even remember it an hour later."

"Did you ever tell anyone?" Ava asked.

"No. Of course not."

"You have feelings for him?" Metford asked.

"'Course I do. He's a…friend, sorta."

"He ever suggest that the two of you would go away together?"

She blew a raspberry. "In my wettest dream, yeah, but not in real life. I'm not stupid. I know someone like him would never be with anyone like me. I'm just glad I can call him friend for now. If it threatened to tarnish his shining armor in public, though, he'd turn on me in a split-second. I ain't living in a fantasy world."

After a few more minutes, Ava and Metford thanked Candy and left.

They made a few more stops, and it seemed they were met with the same kind of responses about Javier Morales. He was a respectable guy who was lonely and worried about his public image.

"How can he be worried about his public image if he's out in places like this all the time?" Ava asked as they drove back to the hotel.

"He's really lonely. Maybe he thinks as long as he keeps a low profile out here on the seedier side of Baltimore, no one will really recognize him. And honestly, in one of these places, if someone does recognize him, I don't think they'd run and tell the mayor and the news outlets, do you?"

"Probably not. You think if he got really worried about his wife's affairs affecting his image he would do something to her?"

"Anything is possible," Metford said.

"I'm surprised you even went as far as to say that much."

"Why? I'm not saying it's impossible that he killed his wife, but it is very improbable. Did you check his finances to see where he was last night, the night before, or the night before that?"

Ava sighed and readjusted her grip on the wheel. "Yeah."

"Well, where was he?"

"We just left there. Sudz for Studz. While you were supposed to be questioning people, I went and got a quick look at the outside security camera footage. He didn't leave until two in the morning, and that was by cab. That was last night. I have to check with Silver Taxi to find out where he was dropped."

"How about I call them and find out right now?" He reached for her phone lying in the console tray.

"Might want to wipe that down before you stick it to your ear. Candy fingered it at the bar, remember?"

He laughed. "Is that why you didn't put it back in your pocket?" He swiped through cab company listings.

"Yes, it is."

He punched a button and moved the phone toward his ear. "Jasmine might have put her tongue on this ear when she was telling me about Javier, so it's fine."

"Toss the phone out the window when you're done," Ava said.

Metford hung up three minutes later. "Silver Taxi dropped Javier Morales off at home at five minutes before three this morning. It's possible that's why he looked and acted a little off when we were at his house. Obviously, he hadn't slept if he worked today."

"Did he work, though? Do we know that?"

"God, you're not going to give this up until you're forced to, are you?"

"Nope. That's the final dangling loose end with him, and if he was at work, we can close the book on him."

"Thankfully. Santos and Dane will know if he worked. They've had time to find out what drink he had with his lunch, and what color socks he wore, too."

"He didn't have lunch."

"How do you know that?"

"He was bombed at two this morning. Do you eat lunch with a hangover?"

"I do. How else are you supposed to get over one?"

Ava hadn't had a hangover since college, it seemed. It felt like the only time she loosened up even a little bit was at the end of a successful case, and even then, she didn't always stay as long as the others at the bar.

She had become accustomed to sticking around long enough to drink a beer and eat a little food, and then she bowed out.

CHAPTER TWENTY-FOUR

The next morning, Ashton was already at the table with the electronics. Three large coffee cups and empty sugar packets littered a portion of the tabletop.

"You're at it early this morning," Ava said as she entered.

He turned toward her with dark circles under his eyes and messy hair. That's when she realized he was wearing the same clothes he had worn the day before.

"Wells and Morales," he said, his eyes flitting back to the computer screen. He picked up printouts, pressed a napkin on the top page to remove coffee drips, and handed them to her.

"What about them, Ashton?" She took the pages.

"I don't think they were serious about each other. I read so many messages." He paused, rubbed his eyes, and shook his head. "So many messages that were not meant to be read by anyone but them."

Ava glanced over the printouts and spotted a few rather lascivious messages between the two. She snickered. "Oh, you got to read some romance. No wonder you look disheveled this morning."

"Haven't been to bed. I spent the entire night foraging through the wasteland of dirty minds in search of something useful."

"And did you find it?"

He looked blank for a second. "Find what? Was I looking for something in particular? No one told me, if I was."

"No. Did you find something useful?"

"Oh," he said with relief. "No. At least, I don't think so. And definitely not in that hot mess." He pointed to the printouts in Ava's hand before turning back to the electronics. He picked up a laptop and motioned for Ava to move closer. "This is Wells' personal laptop. I found these messages that just seem off. They don't make much sense, and they're going out to recipients that are never named. Just the usernames are ever used."

Bigdaddy, Theanthol, Sealwasonjm, Chellswisr, Leprayerhim, Snatchamber, and Notaletuxs were the very unusual recipient names. They were all tied to darkmail dot com accounts. Ava had never heard of the domain.

"What's darkmail?"

"Oh, that's a site that charges extortionists' rates and hosts disposable email accounts. Every thirty days, they delete all the accounts and any mail in them." He turned back to his tools and coffee.

"That sounds like a lot of trouble and anxiety. Who would want to make a new email account every thirty days? And who would want their account wiped like that?" She stopped short on the last word. "People who don't want to be traced."

"Bingo," Ashton said. "But I've been working around in the guts of his computer for a while, and I dug out two similar messages to the same recipients dated two months ago. It's almost the same message with only a few words changed. There's a code here, I'm sure of it. I just need time to unravel it."

"Can you trace the usernames to any IP or physical address?"

"No. They seem to be unique to these messages. I wouldn't even have the messages if Wells hadn't saved them in a separate folder. His password was ridiculous to break, so, I assume he was at least tech savvy." He glanced at her.

"I know. I should take classes. Catch up on the tech stuff."

He nodded. "All of you should."

"One day, I will."

"I'll hold you to that."

"Okay, work your magic, Ash. See if you can figure out who these letter salads belong to. I'll keep this and keep them in mind, too."

He chuckled dryly and bobbed his head in the semblance of a nod.

"And don't forget to get some sleep while we're out today. Couple of hours anyway."

He gave her a thumbs up and then kept working.

She wanted to ask if he heard the clacking of the keys in his sleep. Or, in his nightmares, perhaps. Instead, she mused the question for a full minute before the others joined her at the table for the morning updates and assignments.

She made a copy of the usernames for everybody. "While you're scanning through files and records online, keep these handy. If one of the usernames pops up, get it to Ashton ASAP."

Metford joined her after Dane and Santos left.

"Ash, which username was Christopher Wells using? Any of these?"

"Yes. He used c-h-e-l-l-s-w-i-s-r."

Metford leaned over and read the name. "See-hells-wis-er," he said, sounding it out.

"I read it as Chell's wiser, actually."

Ashton turned to them. "And in my head, I hear Shell Swisher."

Ava groaned and got up. "And that makes my head hurt. I'm going to make an educated guess here and say that I think at least some of the names belong to the murdered agents."

"Well, Shell Swisher belongs to one for sure. Chris Wells."

"Why do you think these names belong to the murder victims?" Metford asked.

Metford reached for Ava's paper and she pushed his hand away. "Get yours. It's right there." She pointed to the table.

He turned from hers to his like a puppy going from a carrot to a piece of steak.

"Because I still say they were into something illegal," Ava said.

"It tracks," Ashton said. "People don't usually end up as murder victims if they're not."

Metford snickered sarcastically.

"Don't be facetious. It doesn't suit you," Ava said.

"I'm not being."

"What's facetious?" Metford asked, looking up from his paper.

"Silly or foolish for the sake of," Ava said.

"Just say that instead." He turned his attention to the paper again.

"Anyway," Ava said. She paused long enough to make sure there were going to be no further interruptions. "I think they were all into something illegal because they were targeted by someone, and it looks to be the same person killing them, so, it must be something they were all doing to piss off that one person. Make sense?"

"All but Vanessa Morales," Ashton said, turning back to his work. "I'm not sure that she fits with the others. Her murder was all kinds of messy and chaotic. The male victims were stronger and larger than her, yet hers was the one that looked like it took the most effort."

"Like she surprised the killer," Metford said.

"Exactly," Ashton said. "Like she surprised him."

"So, maybe she isn't going to be connected to the usernames, but I'm willing to bet the others will. Christopher Wells' name is tied to one of them, so…"

"So, it's something I'll definitely look into," Ashton said.

"Thank you. Take a nap, would you? You look awful."

"Knows how to stroke an ego, don't she?" Metford asked, giving a quick cockeyed grin before putting the paper back in his face.

"Let's just go. The ME's office is expecting us to pick up that report."

"Why didn't you just have them send it over the computer?" Ashton asked.

"Because if I have to be cooped up in this room one minute longer than absolutely necessary, I'm going to blow a fuse."

She went to the door and opened it. Standing there for ten seconds staring at Metford. He didn't notice. Not that she truly expected him to.

"Earth to Metford?" she said.

"Yeah?" He looked at her and a shocked expression crossed his face. "Oh, yeah. Coming."

All the way to the car, he had the paper in his face, mouthing letters and words. It was amusing.

"You know if Ash is having trouble deciphering this stuff, we stand no chance at all."

"Speak for yourself. It's right here. I just have to look at it long enough, and it'll come clear."

"Knock yourself out."

They got in and buckled up.

"Where are we going again?" Metford asked, eyes on the paper.

"Medical examiner's office. The reports for Ethan Holt are back."

"Oh," he said, keeping his eyes on the scramble of letters.

"You let me know if you figure out something there. And lower the paper; you've got it right in my line of vision. Don't want to pull out in front of somebody because you're playing Sherlock Holmes over there."

"Who says I'm playing?" He chuckled. "You have a pencil in here anywhere? One with an eraser." He flipped open the glove box and shuffled everything around.

"I seriously doubt you'll find a pencil, but there might be a spare notepad in there with a pen, if that helps."

"Got it. Thanks." He flipped it open and started writing furiously.

On the way to the ME's office, she glanced at Metford's work a few times. He had written usernames and crossed out the letters one at a time. Below the crossed-out letters, he had made another letter salad using all the letters.

"Are you seriously scrambling the scramble there?"

"Don't judge. I'm telling you, something is staring us right in the face here. I just can't figure out what it is."

She pulled into the parking garage and shut off the engine. "Can I see it for a minute?"

"You want to play Sherlock, too?" He handed her the notebook. "Don't mess them up, please."

She flipped the page deliberately making sure he saw that she was nowhere near his dubious work.

"What are you doing? I thought that was a spare notepad?" He leaned to look at the paper.

"It is." She wrote the name Christopher Wells and underlined it. Below the line, she wrote CHELLSWISR and then tipped it so Metford could see. "That's the one we know for sure was linked to one of the victims." A few lines down, she wrote the name Ethan Holt and underlined it. Moving to another line, she wrote Emily Harper and finally James Lawson. She handed the notepad and pen back to Metford.

He read over it and at the bottom, he wrote Vanessa Morales and underlined it. "She deserves a place on the list until we figure out what's going on and if one of the usernames belonged to her."

"Deserves a place on there? With possible criminals?"

He nodded. "Why not? She was killed just like the rest of them. Why wouldn't we consider it?"

Ava thought about it. "You're right." It was as good as admitting she was wrong, wasn't it? It was as close as she was getting to saying it out loud anyway.

He closed the notebook and unbuckled the seatbelt, letting it zing and clank into the holder above his shoulder. "I am."

"Don't get too cocky. The day is young; plenty of time to make a fool of yourself before bedtime."

He got out and laughed as he closed the door.

CHAPTER TWENTY-FIVE

"Do you know what an anthology is?" Metford asked as they walked toward the door.

"Yeah, why?"

"I think one of those usernames is referencing that."

"How so?" Ava stepped through the front door.

"The Anthol," he said, and then spelled out the name. "It's just short a few letters at the end."

"I don't know. Why not just put all the letters if that's the word you're going for?"

"Maybe that username was already taken. You know how that goes."

"But you can usually just add numbers at the end and still use it. There wouldn't be much use in making hard-to-remember usernames for a throwaway email account that's just going to be wiped out within thirty days."

THE FORGOTTEN GIRLS

Dr. Blake was his usual sunny self as he delivered the full printed reports for Ethan Holt and Emily Harper. "Tox was clean. Got the prelim on Lawson, too. Want it?"

"I'd very much appreciate it, yes," Ava said, barely even bothering to be annoyed at the man as she flipped through the reports and handed them to Metford.

Blake walked off, or maybe penguin waddled was a better description. Ava shook the comparison away and pinched the bridge of her nose.

"Don't let Mr. Goodtimes get to you. It's just his personality," Metford said. "He spends all day with dead bodies. I'm guessing he doesn't have much time to hone those social skills."

"And it shows. Why didn't he just bring Lawson's report with him? What's taking him so long?"

"He just left the room," Metford said. "Patience is a virtue."

She shot him a scowl.

"Or, so I'm told. Maybe not."

"Not one of mine," she said and walked to the door. She pulled it open and stepped through.

"Where are you going?"

"I want to see if Lawson had that same tattoo behind his left ear." She walked down the hallway with long strides and entered the autopsy suite without knocking.

"Hell-o," Blake said grumpily, turning from the desk to her. "Ever heard of knocking?"

"Did Lawson have the tattoo?" She looked around at several bodies under sheets. "Which one?"

"Depends on what you want to see," Blake said. He pointed to the bodies as he spoke. "Heart attack, self-inflicted gunshot to the forehead, drowning, undetermined, last stages of decomp, another heart attack."

"Lawson," Ava said.

Blake pointed to a cooler door. "Number seven. And yes, he had the same tattoo." He had made his way to her side and flicked the papers in front of her hand as she reached for the cooler's handle. "Hands off."

Ava hesitated for a moment as they locked eyes. Part of her wanted to open the cooler anyway. Probably only because she had been stopped mid-action; or possibly only because she had been told 'no.' That last thought stopped her, and she took the papers as she stepped back one stride.

Blake opened the door and pulled out the table. "Still testing DNA. He died like the others. Stabbed and sliced, only he had some deep defensive wounds to go with it." He pulled back the sheet and rolled the corpse's head to the side and folded the ear forward. "Same tattoo. Same place."

"Do you have any clue what the tattoos represent?" Ava asked, studying the marks closely.

Blake let go of the ear. "A triangle, best I can figure."

"I know that. I mean what else it signifies. I mean, is it like a military tattoo, or gang tattoo?"

He flipped the sheet back over Lawson's face. "How the hell should I know?"

"What about his tox screen? It come back clean?"

He shut the cooler door. "Why do I bother with the reports if I'm just going to have to stand here and tell you every detail in them?" He ripped off his gloves and dropped them in a trashcan as he went back toward the door.

"Right. Because God forbid you take a minute of your precious time to give insight that might be helpful in solving five murders."

"And God forbid you actually get your head out of there for five minutes and look around this room," he said, his voice growing louder. "There are only seven bodies in here right now because that's all the tables I have in this room. There are twenty-six coolers, and not one of them is empty. Go through that door and into the next room, and you'll find seventeen more bodies that I have yet to even look at. And that's just the past week. More bodies come in every day, and every day, we work on them, clean them, and write up reports that entitled agents like you don't even bother reading." He slammed one big hand against the swinging door and held it against the outer hall wall. "Now, if you don't mind, I need to get back to work. Yours isn't the only case here."

Metford stood just outside the open door with wide eyes.

Ava walked past Blake and Metford without a word and stormed to the car outside. Metford followed, trying to hail her, but she got in and slammed the door. The report fluttered against the windshield as she flung it in anger. She jammed the key into the ignition and turned it just as Metford got in.

"What was that all about? Are you okay?"

"I'm fine. He's fine. We're all fine," she snipped.

Metford got Lawson's report from the dashboard and added to the other two as Ava headed for the road. "There's really nothing new in the Holt or Harper reports." He flipped open Lawson's. "Anything unexpected in Lawson's?"

"I didn't have time to read it. I was too busy being chewed up by Blake because I asked a question."

"I caught part of it. What did you ask that set him off?"

She didn't want to get into it. Mostly because Blake had been right, but also because she hadn't been able to say anything back to the man about his rant. She always had a rebuttal; she had always been right before. Except with this case.

And with Jason, she thought miserably.

"I asked him something that he said was in the report. He said I should just read the report. I snapped at him, and he told me to get my head out of my…"

Metford's eyes widened. "He said that to you?"

"Not explicitly, but yeah. He told me to get my head out of there and look around. Then he said I should stop acting entitled and do my job."

"And you let him live?" he asked with a tone of awe. "Unbelievable. Why didn't you light him up like you do everybody else who ever talked to you like that?"

"Shut up, Metford."

"Right. I'll just read over the reports."

Back at the hotel, Ashton looked like he had just woken up. Santos was there working on files and a laptop. Dane was absent.

"Where's Dane?"

"Grabbing coffee," Santos said, tilting her head toward Ashton. "What's up?"

"Got the prelim report from the ME on Lawson," Ava said.

Metford held up the papers. "Nothing unexpected, but he had that same tat behind his left ear."

"Did you ever find anything out about that?" Ava asked Santos.

"That's actually what I'm working on right now. I stopped at a few of the tattoo parlors yesterday, but they didn't know. All of them said their people had not done the work in their shops."

"How many more shops are there to check out in town?" Ava asked.

"Way too many for us to go to all of them. Some are reputable. Others? Fly-by-nighters. Here for a few weeks and gone without warning or a trace."

"Just about anyone can order a tattoo gun and all the supplies online nowadays," Ashton said. He yawned and then apologized for it as it spread through the group one at a time like a nasty, aggressive virus.

Dane came in with the coffee. "Want me to get more for you guys?" she asked Ava and Metford.

"No," Ava said.

"I'll put on a pot of the hotel stuff just in case. What's new with the case?"

"Got the prelim on Lawson," Ava said.

"And I think I'm onto something with those usernames," Metford said.

Santos held out a hand. "Can I see the Lawson report?"

Ava gave it to her. "Nothing we didn't already suspect."

"He had the tattoo," Metford said.

"Three for three. What about Wells and Morales? Did you find out if they had the ink, too?" Santos asked, handing back the report.

Ava cleared her throat. "No."

Metford chuckled. "It'll be in Dr. Blake's report. Right, Ava?"

"I'm sure it will."

"I still say that if they all have the same ink, they were into something illegal together."

"Maybe we should go back to Patapsco and find out who else has the tattoo," Dane suggested.

"That would take a month of Sundays," Santos said. "Too many employees there at once. It would just be chaos and mayhem. Then you'd have the ones who are on vacation, leaves, or just called out the day we show up."

"I planned on hitting up all the tattoo parlors in Baltimore to check on it. Guess I'll kick that up to the top of my list." She nodded to Ava. "If that's okay."

"They didn't get that ink in a parlor," Santos said. "You're wasting your time."

"Why do you say that?" Dane asked.

"Because when you're in a secret group, it kinda defeats the first tenet of being secret. It would eventually get out if all the members were showing up one at a time in some shop to get the tattoo."

Dane gave Ava a questioning look.

"Go ahead and ask around. Santos, give her the list of places you've already checked with. Dane, don't try to visit all the brick-and-mortar shops; call as many as you can, or you'll be at this forever."

"Got it." Dane waited around until Santos gave her the list, and then she left.

"I say we do a search online and see if any of the victims, or any other Patapsco workers, have recently ordered a tattoo kit online."

"How many places sell them?" Ava asked.

"All the online marketplaces," Ashton said. "The biggest would be Amazon."

Ava smiled. "Santos, you have your assignment for the day."

"What? No. I don't want to sit here all day tied to a computer screen. I'll go nuts. Ashton can do it. He's way better at that stuff than I am."

"He's got all the work he can handle right now. Start with the victims. Run them and let me know what you dig up."

Crestfallen, Santos turned to her computer. "They could have used the tat to gain entry into places regular Joes can't access. Like the backrooms in bars where shady crap happens."

Ava stopped and thought about it for a minute. "I didn't think about that, but you're right."

"Sometimes tats like that—small, inconspicuous, innocent-looking—are done when someone passes a street gang initiation. Prostitutes get them like a brand. Shows which pimp they belong to, but those are usually on top of the hand between the thumb and index finger. Guess how many of those are done in parlors?" She spun her chair to face Ava.

"None, right?"

Santos grinned. "None. A high-ranked gang member does it, and the pimp, or the pimp's trusted buddy who is also in on the prostitution ring and has a lot to lose. Have to be able to trust everybody involved. Same thing applies to high society gangs or groups. There was a group of rich people who hunted humans as a pastime. The members of that elite, very rich, influential, and powerful group all had a tattoo of crosshairs on their right ankle. Right on the bone."

"You know a lot about this sort of thing," Metford said.

"I do. I'm well-versed in high-society gang initiations and markings, if I do say so myself. I worked the gang task force for years before landing here with you."

"Put that knowledge to good use and get to work, then," Ava said. "We need to cover as many angles as possible as quickly as possible with this case. It's getting out of hand, and I don't want any more murders, if we can help it. Let's find out who's killing these federal agents. Come on, everybody. Let's light a fire here and get this case solved."

CHAPTER TWENTY-SIX

"I can't believe we're going to a car lot called Vic's Used Vehicles because three of our vics bought their last cars there," Metford said.

"It's strange, but that's where they got them," Ava said. "And who knows if there's some connection? I feel like this case is stalling out right under our feet. If I have to look at one more financial report today, I think I'll scream."

"I don't know how Ashton does it all the time. It takes a special type of person to do that job, and I'm not the right type."

"Me neither. I have enough paperwork to look at every day as it is." Ava steered to the turn lane and maneuvered the SUV into the car lot.

"Polished, shiny troubles sitting around to tempt passersby into throwing their hard-earned cash away," Metford said.

"Kind of like some of the women at the strip bars, huh?"

Metford laughed and then sobered straight away. "The women at least dance and entertain people, too. They earn the cash thrown their way."

"I'm sure some of these cars end up dancing all the way to the nearest garage within the first month of being bought."

"But that's not entertainment. That's trouble that nobody needs."

Ava cut her eyes at him with a one-sided smirk.

"Don't say it."

It was her turn to laugh. She pulled up in front of a flat, ugly building that looked like it had been built around 1965. The sun glinted off the windows that wrapped around three sides of the structure.

"Building is as spotless and shiny as the cars," she noted with amusement.

"It's like the road grime doesn't touch the place."

They got out and started for the front door. A portly man in a cheap suit rushed out with a big, bright smile and a face full of completely unwarranted glee. He stuck out his hand.

"Hiya, folks. My name's Bernie. I'm Vic's son, but I never had the heart to change the name of the place. What can I do you for today?" He looked around Metford to the SUV. "Looking to trade that beauty in on something a little more efficient on the gas and easier on the environment?"

"No, we're FBI, Bernie," Ava said, showing her badge.

The overly-cheerful expression fell flat and all the twinkle left Bernie's eyes. "FBI, eh? What can I do for you?"

"Well, three people who bought vehicles here over the last eight months are dead," Ava said.

Bernie blanched and backed up a couple of steps. "Now hold on a minute. These cars are sold 'as is.' We have a mechanic who checks that all the cars are up to par, safe, and comply with all the required road safety laws in Maryland and in Baltimore."

"Let's have a chat inside, shall we?" Metford said, motioning to the door.

"Sure. Yeah, come on in." Bernie turned to the door and walked with a noticeably less enthusiastic gait.

Much later, Ava and Metford left.

"I'm pretty sure Bernie was thrilled that we were leaving," Metford said.

"I think you're absolutely right, but not as glad as I am."

"At least all his paperwork was in order and easy to get to. We didn't have to wait hours or days to get a look at it. I thought Bernie and the car lot were going to be shady. It was a nice surprise."

"I guess so, but it just makes me feel like we hit yet another brick wall."

"Did you really believe we'd find something here that would help the case?"

"Of course. I was hoping anyway."

Her phone rang before she got out of the lot. She spoke shortly with Dr. Blake and hung up. "That was the ME."

"And?"

"He's finished with all the autopsies of our vics."

"Three days to finish Wells and Morales?"

"At least it wasn't longer. Considering the sheer volume of work he has in there every day, I'm just glad he made ours a priority."

"Did he have a choice?"

"Yes. A man like Dr. Blake always has a choice."

"What about the tox screens and DNA tests?"

"I don't know. He didn't say."

Metford chuckled low and tried to stifle it, but not very hard. "It'll be in the reports, right?"

She smirked at him and turned right, pulling into the flow of traffic. At the next light, she turned right again. She turned on her signal at the next light as she waited in line.

"Are we going to the ME's office?"

"We are."

"You're just going by there to get under his skin, aren't you?"

"Absolutely not. I'm going because if he thinks he intimidated me, he'll be sure to try talking to me like that again, and men like him only make a point with me once."

"Was it a valid point?"

"It was. That's why it'll only happen once. Further outbursts would only be a show of authority on his part, and I won't let that happen. He's put me in my place and opened my eyes a little, but he didn't intimidate me."

Metford gave her a quizzical look.

"Women have to address situations like this differently than men do. Or, differently than most men. Even though there are a lot of women in positions of authority now, it's still largely a man's world, and women have to figure out how to navigate through it without being run over and without becoming a tyrant themselves if they want to be successful."

"Wow. Good thing I'm not a woman, then."

"Not to be mean, but you don't have the balls to be a woman, Metford."

The trip to Blake's office went off without a hitch. He was respectful even if short with his words and curt with his tone. Those things were just part of his personality, and Ava suspected even his genetic makeup.

She left with the reports. Blake had even reprinted the partials she had picked up before so that each file was complete.

"Let's take this back and share with the team. It's time to go over all our evidence and timeline again," Ava said.

"Maybe now we can get some forward movement on this thing."

"It's been three days with nothing so, I hope so."

In the makeshift headquarters, Ava went over all the autopsy reports until the whole team showed up. When everyone was present, she stood with her back to the whiteboard and laid the reports on the table in front of her.

"I got the autopsy reports back for all our vics. Ethan Holt, Emily Harper, James Lawson, and Christopher Wells had the same tattoo in the same place." She placed pictures of the tattoos under the victims' pictures on the caseboard.

"Wait, what about Vanessa Morales?" Santos asked.

"She did not have the tattoo," Ava replied, still placing pictures on the board.

"But she was the most brutal of all the murders," Dane said. "I was considering the possibility that she was the target and that it was a crime of passion like a jealous lover." Dane pulled a notepad from her portfolio and flipped it open.

"What's that?" Santos asked, leaning for a better view.

"It's the list of men who might have killed her. I was working through a 'what if' scenario. What if she had slept with all the victims, and one of her past lovers didn't like it. That type of thing."

"But Emily Harper wouldn't fit," Ashton said.

"Maybe. Maybe not. We don't know that Vanessa only slept with men."

"That's good thinking," Santos said, looking impressed. "If she's onto something, that puts the gang thing right out the window."

"It would," Ava agreed. "Ashton, have you found anything on the electronics yet?"

"I have. I'm still working, too. Mr. Wells' laptop is synced with his phone. If the laptop is sleeping or powered down, the phone can be utilized as if it's a standalone tool. Once you power up the laptop, however, they immediately sync. The calendar apps are always synced, so it doesn't matter which calendar you enter an event or reminder into, it lands on both. Mr. Wells' calendar has a reminder set for one day each week. It's a different day each time, and I compared those days to the ones in Ethan's planner. They're always different."

"So, what does that mean?" Metford asked.

"I'm not sure. There are no explanations, no labels of any kind. Just the time notation with a reminder set to go off an hour before."

"His reminder was set to go off at five in the morning on those days?" Ava asked.

"Yes. And that's not all I found. I compared Mr. Wells' planner with Ethan's planner. Never do any of the days from either one overlap. If Ethan's planner had 6:00 a.m. written on Monday, that same week in Mr. Wells' calendar has 6:00 a.m. written on Wednesday. Every time."

"Okay, they are both taking care of something. One thing between the two of them," Santos said. "Something that has to be done on Monday and Wednesday. At six in the morning. I don't get it."

"Me neither," Metford said. "We don't know what that one thing is, and we definitely don't know if they were taking care of it together. What was it, a puppy? Watering a garden? Washing a car? Maybe they took turns cleaning something at work."

"Maybe. I just think if there's a connection, it's worth looking into."

"Can you print out those calendars for me, Ashton?" Ava asked.

"Yes. How far back and how many months per page?"

"One month per page, and go back to when the first unlabeled times start popping up. Namely, the six in the morning ones."

"I'll have it to you in five minutes." He went to his table and started working.

"Are we still working the gang angle?" Santos asked.

"Yes, we are," Ava said. "I can't help but think there's something to those tattoos. We might find that it's nothing, but I doubt it. We need to find out what group they were part of." She picked up the poker chip and turned it over and over in her hand. "Any luck finding more of these?"

"No, but I'm still looking," Santos said. "There are a lot of places around here that take chips and tokens, but none like that."

"Maybe it's unique to the group the victims were in," Ava said, thinking aloud.

"Like the tattoos," Dane said.

"Like that," Ava agreed.

"What would they use them for?" Santos asked. "They have the tats to gain access to something that regular people can't, or aren't, allowed to access."

"I don't know. Maybe they used them to buy something the group has."

"Like what?" Metford asked.

Ava put the chip down again. "I don't know. It's just a thought right now."

Ashton gave her the printed calendars. "Two copies of each one."

"Thank you. Metford, come with me."

"Where are we going?"

"Back to Patapsco Bay."

"Why?" He followed her out the door.

"I'm going to see if these dates and times mean anything to the port director or any of the supervisors."

CHAPTER TWENTY-SEVEN

Patapsco Bay Terminal bustled with activity, and the noise level was much louder than on the previous visits. As Ava and Metford walked toward Nathaniel Chambers' building, they looked toward the massive shipping containers stacked in rows closer to the water. People yelled instructions, engines droned and revved, and every now and then, the sound of horns and buzzers could be heard in the mix. Bobtailed big rigs trundled from their lot toward the seemingly endless rows of containers on their way to deliver goods to one of the hundreds of thousands of businesses all eagerly waiting for their shipment to arrive.

"I wonder how many shipping containers are over there?" Metford asked.

"Thousands, I would guess," Ava said. "This is like a look behind the curtains. A side of the business that everyday consumers don't normally get to see. It's loud and nasty and nerve-wracking, but all they see is that new item when it arrives safe and sound in their mailbox or dropped on their front porch."

"And how many people handle it before it reaches its destination?"

Ava blew air and widened her eyes. "Jeez. I don't even want to think about that."

They made their way inside the building. Ava showed her badge and told the man they needed to speak with Nathaniel Chambers.

"He's not in his office right now."

"Okay, where is he?"

"He had to go to the yard about an hour ago."

"Where in the yard? Did he say?"

The man shook his head.

"Will he be back soon?"

"Depends on your definition of soon. He could be back any minute, or it might be hours from now. Want me to give him a message?"

Ava considered it. She didn't want to be sitting around at Patapsco any more than she wanted to be sitting around back at the hotel. "No. We'll wait a while. See if he shows up. Can we wait in his office?"

A few minutes later, she and Metford followed the man down various hallways until they came to the port director's office. The man showed them in.

"Have to admit this office is better than the others we've seen here," Ava said.

"At least there's elbow room in this one, but I still wouldn't give a dime for that view."

Ava looked out the window. The view was a slash of sky, the side of the neighboring building, and a corner of a distant parking lot. If she put her face close to the glass, she could just see the huge brick buildings looming at the city's edge.

"Nope. Me neither," she said, sitting again.

They talked about the case. Finally, that conversation turned into one revolving around Ashton's lack of sleep. Somehow that chat ended with them sharing stories about their time in college.

Metford looked at his watch. "Not that you're not good company, but it's been almost an hour. How much longer are you going to give this guy?"

"It's been forty-five minutes. I'll give him another fifteen. If he's not here, we'll come back later."

"And call ahead first, right?"

"I didn't want to give him time to prepare for the visit. I like to see people's candid reactions to things when I talk to them."

Seven minutes later, the door swung open and Nathaniel Chambers walked in. He gave a small smile and brief nod as he closed the door behind himself and then went to his desk. Sitting across from them, he exhaled heavily and plunked down his hardhat. "Sorry, Agents. It's been a busy day. How can I help you?" He looked at his watch. "I don't have much time, but I'll do what I can."

"Thank you," Ava said. She pushed the papers toward him. "These are pages from the planners of Ethan Holt and Christopher Wells. Do the highlighted dates and times mean anything to you?"

Chambers pulled the pages closer, picked them up, and seemed to look over them closely. His brow furrowed a couple of times, and it seemed that he was only looking closely at the pages in an effort to construct some response. Ava had been reading people her whole life, and with the exception of Jason Ellis, no one had ever been able to dupe her completely. Her gut said Chambers was flustered by the pages, but her brain had to throw doubt in the mix. That had been happening ever since the Jason Ellis situation. Thankfully, the doubt lessened each time she proved it wrong.

The port director made a show of pulling pages out and looking at them again. At last, he put them all back in a stack and slid them across the desk to Ava. "I'm sorry, but no. They mean nothing to me. I don't know why you'd think they would, though, to be honest. Why would pages out of an employee's personal planner mean anything to me? I'm just their boss; not their brother or best friend."

"The dates and times aren't something they were doing for their work here?" Ava asked. "Like a duty that needed doing maybe before a shift started, or after one ended? A special task they had been assigned? Anything?"

"No. Nothing that I know of." He laced his fingers on the desktop. Sweat had beaded across his top lip and at his temples. It glistened in the slant of sunlight from the window.

Seeing that he was starting to sweat bullets, Ava kept going. She picked up a page from Ethan's planner. "This one is from three months ago. Ethan was doing something at six in the morning on these days. You say it was nothing for work."

"Not that I know of, no." Using his thumb, Chambers brushed the budding sweat from his temple and toward his hairline.

"Did you ever assign either man a special shift in the last three months?"

"No, I didn't."

Ava nodded. "Did their direct supervisors ever ask employees to come in early and perform some task on certain days of the week? Like maybe Mondays and Wednesdays?"

"Okay, listen, I don't know anything about those dates and times. What I do know is that I have a port to run, and I need to get back to work, if you don't mind. Those mean nothing to me, just so we're clear." He stood and opened the door. "Now, if you'll excuse me, I need to make a call before my meeting."

"Of course, Mr. Chambers," Ava said, standing. "Thank you for your time and cooperation." She held out her card. He grudgingly took it. "If you happen to suddenly recall something about those days." She tapped the card with one finger. "Give me a ring, would you?"

"Yes. Thanks. You can find your way out, right?" He pointed down the hall and forced a slight smile before shutting the door.

"I think you rattled him," Metford said.

"I didn't rattle him. The calendars did." She looked at the last page Chambers had stared at. "He recognized those dates and times. I'd bet money on it."

As they stepped out of the building and turned toward the parking area, Ava stopped. "I don't want to leave just yet. I want to see where he goes. Over here." She motioned for Metford to follow her between two short buildings. They made their way to the other end of the long building they had just exited and went left toward the smaller metal building in front of the hill to the parking lot.

"Where are we going?"

"Taking the scenic route," Ava said. "They come out this end to smoke, remember?"

"What are we going to do, turn him in if he comes out and lights up? He might not even come out. He might already be two miles in the other direction."

"That's why we're going up the hill. So we can see if he goes out the other end of the building. I want to see where he goes. I don't think he had a meeting to get to. I think he just wanted rid of us."

They moved to stand at the back of the smaller building, giving them a decent view between the long buildings below and the paved area at the opposite end.

"If he comes out either end of the building, we'll see him from here," Ava said.

They didn't have to wait long for someone to exit through the closest door.

"That's not Chambers," Metford said.

"No, it's Cody Stillwell."

Stillwell had a cellphone plastered to his ear, and he seemed to be arguing with someone on the other end of the line. Two minutes later, the door opened again and Chambers stepped out.

"There he is," Ava said.

The two men were agitated as they spoke.

"Looks like Chambers is telling him something he doesn't like," Metford said. "Wish we could hear them."

There was animated pointing and head shaking and what looked to be yelling from both parties. Ava shielded her eyes from the sun and squinted. If she were only closer, she could perhaps read Chambers' lips as he was facing her.

"Stay still," she told Metford. "Chambers is facing us and any movement will catch his eye."

"Excuse me, what are you doing here?" a male voice she didn't recognize boomed, startling her.

Ava spun at the unexpected voice. "FBI," she said.

"You can't be here," the man said.

"Yes, we can," Ava said, turning back to the two men. They were gone. There was no sign of them. She turned to the man. "We were just leaving." She pointed to the parking lot up the hill.

"You should stay on the pavement." He pointed to the paved roadway leading up the hill.

"Yeah, thanks." She moved in that direction.

Metford followed. When they were far enough away, she stopped and scanned the buildings and property below one more time for signs of Stillwell and Chambers. There was no sign.

"Did you see where they went?" she asked.

"No, I turned around, too, when that guy spoke. They probably saw the movement and went back inside."

"And now at least Chambers will suspect that we were watching him."

"It looked like he was explaining something to Stillwell. The way he moved his hands looked like he was talking about the papers you showed him. Of course, that's just a guess, but it seems suspicious to me."

"Yeah, to me, too."

They made their way to the car and left.

CHAPTER TWENTY-EIGHT

Later that day, the warrants came through for the collection of employee records pertaining to the victims. Ava took Metford with her to get the physical files.

"The deputy commissioner is not going to be happy to see us," Metford said. "Correction: he is not going to be happy to see *you*."

"He'll be even less happy when he sees the warrants. I gave him chances to comply without these, but he refused." She handed the warrants to Metford as they got in the car.

The Customs and Border Protection building was at least quieter and much cleaner than Patapsco Bay Terminal, though the levels of stress exhibited by the employees at both places seemed to be similarly high.

Ava and Metford had mused that most of the workers at Patapsco had seemed highly stressed because of the constant high level of noise and the uncertainty of their daily jobs as far as never knowing what they might encounter on a daily basis. After entering the CBP building, and really watching the people there, she changed her mind.

"Guess it doesn't matter how nice your work environment is; a stressful job is a stressful job," she mused.

They asked to see the commissioner, and as usual, he was away and wasn't expected back that day. It seemed convenient that every time they visited, he was gone and wouldn't be back in time to speak with them.

"That's shocking," Ava said to the man. She tapped the warrants into her palm. "The deputy commissioner, then."

"And your names?" He put a phone to his ear.

"FBI Special Agents James and Metford," she said.

The man stepped away from them and spoke low into the phone for a few seconds. He hung up and joined them again. "He said he would be ready for you in ten minutes. I can escort you—"

"We know where his office is." Ava motioned to Metford to follow her as she headed in the direction of Halloway's office.

"Wait. He's not ready for you yet. He said to give him ten minutes." The man scurried to catch up with them.

Ava held up the warrants. "He'll be ready when we get there. We're calling the shots today." She turned and continued walking, leaving the flustered man standing in the wide corridor.

"He looks like he's about to have a seizure back there," Metford said.

"He'll be fine. Probably already calling Halloway to tell him we're coming up now."

"Maybe he's in an important meeting."

"Ten minutes gives him time to destroy or remove things from those files. I don't intend to let that happen."

She opened the door and held the warrants out in front of her when a man rushed in her direction. "FBI." She held up her badge in the other hand. "Deputy Commissioner Jasper Halloway? Where is he?"

A woman with wide eyes pointed toward Halloway's inner office.

Ava and Metford went to the door. Ava opened it without knocking. Halloway was on the other side of the room at a filing cabinet. He slammed it shut and spun to face them.

"Deputy Commissioner Jasper Halloway, we have warrants for those employee files." She extended the hand with the warrants. "Where are they? In that filing cabinet?" She went over to it and yanked open the drawer he had been in. After only seconds, she pulled out a bottle of whiskey and a plastic tumbler. A tiny amount of amber liquid remained in the plastic cup. She held them up. "Really? On the job?" She set the bottle and cup on top of the cabinet and went back to flipping through folders.

THE FORGOTTEN GIRLS

"The files you're looking for aren't in there."

"Then where are they? You'll find that the warrants are for the complete employee records for each of the five victims."

"I'll have to call someone to get them. They're in digital format as well." He pointed to the computer on his desk. "The file manager can bring the physical copies from the file room downstairs."

"Call him, then." Ava motioned to the phone on his desk. "Be sure he gets all the records."

"Do the digital files match the physical files?" Metford asked.

"Yes, they're the same information."

Halloway was sweating as he made the call. While it was warm in the office, it was not uncomfortably so. Ava moved to the side of the desk. Sweat glistened on Halloway's bald head. The overheads reflected pinpoints of bright light in each little bead of perspiration.

An image of Ethan's tattoo popped into her head, and she wondered if Halloway might have the same one, too. She had not thought about it while talking to Chambers, but when the thought came to her about Halloway, she had to see for herself.

She moved so that she was partially behind him. As he spoke briefly to the file clerk, she leaned, trying to get a clear view behind his ear.

Metford gave her a questioning look, and she pointed to Halloway and then her own ear. Metford nodded understanding.

Halloway hung up the phone and turned to eye Ava suspiciously. "He said it would take a few minutes, but he'll bring them up right away. Would you like to sit?" He smiled tightly at Ava and pointed to the empty seat in front of his desk.

She looked at the chair and shook her head. "No, but thank you for offering. I'm more comfortable standing, actually."

Metford took the planner printouts from a folder and drew Halloway's attention to them. "Mr. Halloway, would you mind having a look at these and tell me what you think?" He left the papers purposefully almost out of the man's reach.

Halloway gave him a pursed look of irritation and then partially stood and stretched his arm to grab them. Snatching them unceremoniously, he sat heavily and snapped them as he adjusted his glasses.

Taking the opportunity to step one stride closer, Ava leaned toward Halloway's ear. She was unsurprised to see the three dots in the shape of a triangle behind his ear. She stood and nodded to Metford. She moved to the front of the desk.

Halloway scoffed at the printouts and tossed them to the desk. "What even is this?"

"It's pages from a couple of different planners," Metford said.

"Not my planners," Halloway snapped.

"No, not yours, you are absolutely right. Do the dates and times mean anything to you?"

Halloway's gaze slid to the pages again. The color steadily drained from his cheeks leaving only two high red spots on his cheeks. He shrugged one shoulder and tilted his head as he pulled the glasses from his face. "No. Why would I have any idea what something written in the planners of others meant?" He ran a hand over his sweaty head and replaced the glasses.

"I was just asking if the days or times or both meant anything—"

"I have a secretary who keeps up with my appointments; maybe the owners of these planners should do the same."

"What do you mean?" Metford retrieved the papers and put them back into the file.

It wasn't lost on Ava that Halloway had left them just beyond Metford's comfortable reach. Turnabout is fair play sometimes, but she suspected it was a power play.

"Someone obviously doesn't know how planners work. The times are there, but there are no labels to indicate the appointment, or even the type of appointment."

The file clerk knocked at the door and asked where to put the cart with the files.

"I requested them, didn't I?" Halloway asked. "Common sense would dictate that the files need to be placed in here. With me." He motioned hotly with one hand for the clerk to bring the cart to the desk.

The clerk lowered his gaze, and Ava imagined that he bit his tongue hard to keep from snapping back at his boss. He rolled the large two-shelf utility cart into the room, turned on his heel, and left with barely a glance at any of them. He looked to be in his early-to-mid-twenties.

"That generation is going to be the downfall of the whole civilization, I tell you," Halloway grumbled. Color seeped back into his face, but the sweating continued. "Now, could you take what you need and go? I need to get back to work. Thanks to having so many of that generation starting out here, I have to keep a tight lead on everyone. I don't want the whole CBP crumbling on my watch."

"You have a lot of young blood working here, don't you?" Metford asked, moving to the cart and boxes of neatly labeled boxes.

Halloway scoffed. "That wouldn't be a bad thing normally, but these kids?" He shook his head and palmed sweat again. "Most of them couldn't find their asses with both hands, a map, and a full-time guide."

Metford chuckled as he opened the first box.

"Mr. Halloway?" Ava asked, taking a seat in front of him.

"Yes, Agent?" He huffed and glanced at his watch. "Do you need help getting the files to your vehicle? I don't think that's our problem."

"No, we don't need help with that. I was just wondering about that tattoo you have."

He blanched again and moved his hands to his lap. "Tattoo?" He held out his arms and turned them over as if unable to find a tattoo.

"Behind your ear. Just there." Ava touched her own head to show where she meant. "Pretty hidden spot for ink, isn't it?"

His hand moved upward and his fingers ducked behind his ear. "Ah, that old thing? I hadn't thought of it in...well, probably twenty years at least."

"Where did you get it?"

"College."

"Did you get any other tattoos in college?"

"No."

"Why not? That's usually the age group that ends up with the most tattoos."

"You don't put bumper stickers on a Rolls Royce, do you?"

"Makes sense," Metford said, replacing the lid and moving to the next box.

"Why did you get that one, then?"

"It was for a fraternity that I was in back then. Fraternities always have something you have to do to be a member. With some, it was a secret handshake, with others it was a humiliation ritual, another had a special ring that all the members wore so they could recognize each other, and mine just happened to want all the members to get this silly tattoo. At the time, I had hair. We all did, and the thing was hidden. At twenty, you don't think much about how your body and genetics might betray you as you age." He grinned wryly.

"No, most young people never give it a thought," Ava said. "What was the name of the frat?"

His finger caressed behind his ear once more and his gaze shifted out the window. "Delta Aeternum."

"That's a cool name. I've never heard of it before. Which college did you attend? Something out in California, I bet," she said with a slight smile that she hoped came off as admiration.

"No. I went to the esteemed Wharton Hills right in the heart of New England. I've only ever been to California once, found it completely disagreeable, and I've never returned. I understand you might think it's a much better place to be, it's always sunny, warm, Hollywood is there with all its celebrities, and all the good TV shows are set there, but you're young. The fascination with The Sunshine State proves it."

"I've been to California, Mr. Halloway. More times than you could imagine. It has its disagreeable components. With that I can totally agree." She stood once Metford had checked the last box. "Thank you for your cooperation, Mr. Halloway."

"Don't thank me. I didn't have a choice, did I?"

Metford pushed the cart through the doorway. Ava glanced back at Halloway and smiled. "No, you didn't." She stepped out and closed the door.

"I'm shocked that he talked to you about that tattoo," Metford said.

"Like the man said, he didn't have much choice. After he knew I'd seen it, I'm sure he knew why I had even looked for it. He gave me a good story about it, but I wonder how much of it is even close to true?"

"Guess we'll find out."

"Right now, we're going to Javier's house to recover all of Vanessa's electronics that we might have missed."

CHAPTER TWENTY-NINE

Javier Morales opened the door for Ava and Metford. He showed them to the living room.

Ava gave him the warrant for the electronics and any planners, notebooks, journals, and ledgers, and explained that they needed all of them. Even the home computer and jointly used calendars in the house.

"My wife was a good woman. I know you think otherwise because of her lifestyle, but she was good. She prided herself in her work and in her life."

"Mr. Morales, I'm sorry, but we need those items. Any that haven't already been collected."

"What do you think you're going to find in them? I don't understand. She was having a fling, sure, but that was it. People do that all the time. What is there to find?"

"That's why we need them; to find out if there was more."

Fifteen minutes later, he returned with a box containing Vanessa's electronics, planners, notebooks, and calendars. "This is everything. All the devices, thumb drives, charging cords, and cases. Everything I could find, anyway. The paper stuff is under the electronics."

"What about the home computer?" Metford asked, eyeing the contents of the box as he took it.

"She barely ever used it. She used that laptop and her work laptop mostly."

"We need the computer, Mr. Morales," Ava said.

Angrily, he left the room again and returned moments later carrying an HP tower. Its power cord dragged behind on the floor. "Anything else? Would you like her clothes, perhaps her makeup, or a list of her favorite meals? I have all that, too, and you're welcome to it." His lower lip quivered. "I don't know what I'm going to do with all of it anyway." He backed up to the sofa and sat fighting tears.

"I'm very sorry, Mr. Morales," Ava said. She motioned for Metford to take the box to the car. "Thank you for your cooperation. We'll show ourselves out and leave you alone."

"Is that supposed to be funny?"

"No, sir. We'll leave you to your day."

"My day of planning my wife's funeral. When will her body be released?"

"That's a matter for the ME. Do you have the number?"

"I can find it. Will I get any of her devices back, or do they belong to the FBI now?"

"We'll return what we can as soon as we're finished with this investigation. Again, I'm sorry." Remembering what Metford had done for the man before, she paused with the door open. "Mr. Morales, would you like me to call someone for you? A relative, or a friend?"

"No. I'd very much appreciate being left alone now. You've done quite enough."

She slipped out the door and closed it quietly.

In the car, she let out a pent-up breath. "Before you ask, he didn't want me to call anyone for him. He just wanted me to leave. Seems to be in the air the past few days."

"It's a symptom of our jobs."

That it was. And she honestly didn't mind it too much most of the time.

Back at the hotel, Ashton took possession of the electronics after they were logged. Ava took the non-electronics to the table and spread them out. She took the other planners in the evidence and laid them out as well.

"Going to compare all of them?" Metford asked.

"I am. If any of her calendars match up with any of theirs, maybe we can figure out what Holt and Wells were up to."

Metford stepped up to help her go through comparisons carefully. Everything written in Vanessa's calendars checked out as being legit appointments. Myriad phone calls later, Ava hung up the phone and put her hands on her hips.

"Well, that's it. Nothing lines up across the three planners. Vanessa was going to the doctor regularly to have her diabetes monitored. She went to yoga three times a week, paid for a membership at an all-women's gym on the other side of the city where she also went three times a week, and she even spent time volunteering as an advocate for domestic abuse victims every other Saturday and at the soup kitchen in the middle of the city one Sunday a month. And not once does she have any appointment marked for six in the morning. Ever."

"That's good news, though, right?" Metford asked as he straightened all the planners and notebooks back into their proper boxes. "It means she was innocent. It means that she was at the wrong place at the wrong time. It means that she likely surprised the killer at Wells' apartment just like we thought."

"And it does nothing to further the investigation. Does nothing to get us closer to who the killer is. Or killers."

"But it does further the investigation. This is one path we can drop. Now, we can focus on another path. Process of elimination."

"And which path do you suggest we focus on next? The poker chip, Silas Grey's fingerprints all over Ethan's place, the casino, the tattoo that, like all the other paths, have led us nowhere so far?"

Metford was silent for a moment and then snapped his fingers. "The tattoo. That's it. Halloway had it. He said he got it in college when he joined Delta Eternity, or whatever it was."

"Delta Aeternum," Ava said dully. "So, he got the mark and joined the group over two decades ago. If that was even the truth. Probably wasn't. It felt like a cover story to me. He fumbled over his words. Did you see the way his eyes kept darting to the side when he was telling me that story?"

She wanted to throw her hands up and toss in the towel. No matter how much she felt like doing that, she knew she would never be able to walk away from it.

"Wharton Hills," Metford said. "That's the college he went to. That part's easy enough to check out." He pulled up Wharton Hills College on the computer within seconds. "Here it is. Wharton Hills College. Stillwater, Connecticut."

"That much was real," she said.

"Want me to pull up the student records from when Halloway might have been there?"

"No, we're going to work on one of the other leads. Divide and conquer. That's the only way I see to get through this any faster."

Ava pulled out her phone and called Santos. She assigned Santos and Dane the task of finding out about Delta Aeternum at the college.

"To be clear, you just want us to research from here; in Baltimore, right?" Santos asked.

"Yes, unless you fancy driving for about six hours to get to Wharton Hills," Ava said.

"I'm good right here."

"Check records for all of our victims' names. I want to know if any of them attended Wharton Hills. Find out all you can about Delta Aeternum and what it requires for membership now and in the past."

"Namely, find out if they ink their members."

"Yes. If it's a tiered membership, find out about all tiers. Also, see which of our victims might have been members of the fraternity, what tier they were initiated to, and any other information you can dig up."

"Where'd you come up with this college and frat house name?"

"Jasper Halloway, of all people. He has the tattoo. When we served the warrants earlier, I saw it, and he gave me a story about the college and Delta Aeternum membership."

"That's a shock."

"And might be a pack of lies. That's why I need you two to find out."

"We're on it. I'll update you as soon as we know anything."

"What about the tattoo shops? Dane have any luck with that?"

"No."

"Okay, thanks. Get back to me as soon as you have something about Jasper Halloway and Delta Aeternum."

They ended the call, and Ava stared at the caseboard.

"What's up?" Metford asked.

"I don't know. It's like something is trying to come together, but I'm still not seeing it fully. Like a blurry picture trying to come into focus."

"Which lead are we checking next?" Metford stood and looked at the caseboard, too.

"The tattoo didn't come from any of the major tattoo parlors in the city, so, I think Santos might have been right about that. They didn't get it from a parlor. Halloway's story about Delta Aeternum giving him the tattoo is being checked out. I say we locate Silas Grey, and we don't stop until we find him this time. No more running back and forth with that lead. We keep at it until we find him, get him in for questioning, and find out what he was looking for at Ethan's house." She tapped the poker chip. "Might have been this. It was hidden."

"Could have been cash or drugs, too. Maybe he found whatever he was looking for and took it."

Ava shot him a look.

"Or, it could have been the poker chip, but I don't know why anyone would go to all that trouble for only one chip." He shrugged.

"We still don't know what the chips were being used for. Emily Harper was printing them at home. The 3-D printer was hidden. This chip was hidden. What were the chips being used for? To gain access to something illegal? To purchase illicit items? It couldn't have been anything legal and legit, or no one would have gone to such trouble to hide them."

"You're right. I just don't know that Silas Grey had anything to do with the poker chip. Maybe he's the one doing the killing. Or, maybe he knows who is doing it. Or, he's part of the group killing these people. It might be more than one person."

"That's doubtful," Ashton said. "Reading the crime scenes and the blood spatter suggests a small person. One small person. Unless there are multiple people of similar height, weight, and general strength all working together to perpetrate the murders. It's more likely it's just one person. Teams and multiples are more likely to get caught, be noticed, or turn on one another when things heat up from law enforcement."

Metford took the sheet with Silas Grey's information off the board and went to the printer. He lifted the lid and placed the paper facedown. "Two copies?"

"Thank you," Ava said.

She went to Ashton's table. "Getting anywhere on any of this?"

"I finally got into the locations on Wells' phone." He worked at the computer keyboard for a minute and a map came into view with red pins on it. "These red dots are where the phone pinged over the last month. There are more for previous months, but I decided to do focus sessions for each month so I could really dive in and see where he was going."

"Did you try to line any of the times and dates up with his planner?"

"I did." He worked at the keyboard again, and many of the red pins disappeared, narrowing the field of Wells' movements significantly.

CHAPTER THIRTY

"Where is that?" Ava pointed to the tight grouping of red pins.

"That is an abandoned Victorian on Ashburn Street. Almost everything on that street is abandoned now."

"Why would Wells be going to an abandoned house there?"

"I don't know, but he was going there often." He handed her a printout of Wells' planner. "I've marked the times and days that he went there over the last month. You can see that it fits with the marked days in his planner. Sometimes, he went early in the morning, and other times, he went in the evenings. But when he was going to Ethan's house, it never aligns with marked days in the planner."

"Visits to Ethan were not planned events. They were spontaneous, maybe. But the abandoned property…that was planned every time." She looked back and forth between the planner and the pins. Hovering over the pins with the mouse brought up the location, date, and time of the visit.

"Looks that way. I'm working now to get into the location of Ethan's phones," Ashton said.

"What's so important on Ashburn Street?" Ava leaned close and zoomed in on the satellite image of the rundown Victorian. She moved the view along the street. Other buildings had decayed, their windows broken or boarded over, none of the residences looked inhabited, and all the exteriors were weathered and covered with graffiti.

"It's not somewhere most decent people would want to go so often," Ashton said.

"No. The whole street looks like a haven for illicit activities of all kinds. Do a property search and see if anyone owns that Victorian. Run the locations from all the victims' phones and see if any of them were visiting that house."

"You got it."

"Metford, change of plans," she said, putting the abandoned house address into her phone's GPS. "Well, not a complete change. More like a sidestep while we're heading over to Silas Grey's place."

Metford held up a finger and darted back to the room.

"What are you—"

"Be right back." He opened the door and rushed inside.

Ava turned toward the elevators and waited. A few seconds later, Metford returned holding up the poker chip in its evidence bag.

"Maybe whatever is going on there has something to do with the chips. I thought we should bring it along just in case." He put it in his pocket.

"Ashton is checking the other vics' phone locations. If they were all going to that house, something was definitely going on."

She pressed the button, and the doors slid shut. "We will go by Grey's workplace first."

"The sign shop over on East Fisher?"

"That's it."

"Didn't they say they hadn't heard from him in a while?"

"Not surprisingly, they hadn't heard from him since the day of Ethan's murder," she said.

"Does he fit with Ashton's description of the killer's size?"

Ava shook her head. "Not unless he's changed since that picture of him was taken."

"The one we have was taken in 2020. He could look a lot different now. Don't we have a recent ID photo, driver's license, anything more up to date?"

"Ashton couldn't find one. And, if he couldn't find one…"

"Yeah, it probably doesn't exist. At least not online."

Breckinridge Signs was a small shop crammed between an Italian bistro and a medical office. On the same street, there was a florist, a dry cleaner, two ice cream shops, an expensive coffee shop, and a women's clothing boutique. Traffic was nonstop. The sidewalks were busy with foot traffic that came in waves like the tide ebbing and flowing. The smells from all the different businesses mingled with that of car exhaust making the air feel heavy in Ava's lungs.

Metford stopped under the dark green awning over the door to Breckinridge Signs. "This is a good location for a business. Plenty of exposure here."

Ava glanced around again and then walked inside.

They left only a few minutes later with Silas Grey's employee records, and no information at all on his whereabouts. No one had seen him since the day of Ethan's murder. Phone calls and text messages had gone unanswered. The owner, Grey's boss, was worried that Grey might have been injured and was in the hospital or incarcerated.

"Bosses don't typically get so worried about their employees that they call the local hospitals to check if they're there, do they?" Metford asked.

"Not in my experience. Not unless they're friends."

"Maybe they are," Metford suggested.

"Do you think he really doesn't know where Grey is?"

Metford shrugged. "I say we call the hospitals and have somebody check that he's not in jail, too. It's worth a shot."

Ava grinned. "Pull up a list of all the hospitals on my phone. You can use your phone to call them while we drive." She took out her phone and handed it to him, then set the GPS while Metford pulled up the local hospitals on her phone. The traffic was heavy and slow as they made their way toward Ashburn Street. The navigation said they should make their destination in thirty-seven minutes, but with the state of the traffic, Ava thought it would take closer to an hour.

Twenty minutes into the drive, Metford hung up with the last hospital. "He's not in the hospital. Not in Baltimore anyway."

Ava's phone rang. Metford looked at the screen. "It's Santos."

He answered and put the phone on speaker.

"Dane and I did some digging about Wharton Hills College and Delta Aeternum. We actually scored a video call with one of the officials there. Turns out that frat never existed at Wharton Hills. Also, none of the frat houses there require anyone to get a tattoo to join up. They said that would be stupid. College is transitory, to quote the man. You attend, go into debt, get your degree, and graduate. And nobody wanted a permanent mark for some college fraternity to deal with when they were eighty."

"He has a point, but we had to check out the story. Was that all you found out?"

"We found out that three of our vics attended Wharton Hills, too. Ethan Holt, Emily Harper, and James Lawson. All at different times and for different lengths of time. Emily is the only one who stayed until graduation. Holt made it to the end of freshman year. Lawson left six weeks into his junior year."

"Do you know why they left?"

"No. Grades were good, attendance was satisfactory, and they were active in a few sports."

"Since the tattoo didn't come from a fraternity, you and Dane go back to Patapsco and ask around about it. See if anyone is willing to talk to you about it. Maybe they know why some of their coworkers have a hidden tattoo. Maybe some of them even have the same one. Somebody knows something."

"On it."

CHAPTER THIRTY-ONE

Dane pulled into the parking area at Patapsco and shut off the engine. "I guess, here goes nothing." She opened her door and got out.

Santos got out and stretched. "I hate to say it, but I like this better than being in the city, and I dang sure like it better than being in the 'office.'"

"I like the city part better. It smells bad out here."

Santos inhaled deeply and smiled. "Nah. Although, all that exhaust in the city stinks. And the rotten undertone you smell in certain areas where there are a lot of homeless and drug users. It's like everything good about the city gets underlined with that stench."

"I agree. It's just bad enough to not let you forget there's a lot of bad in cities. There's a lot of good things, but the bad is always there."

They walked toward the offices.

"Where do you want to start this questioning, and do you want to split up or stay together?"

"I vote that we stay together. It's safer that way."

They went inside and asked to see the port director.

"Mr. Chambers is in his office," the man told them. He let his boss know where he was going, and then he led Dane and Santos to Chambers' office.

"That felt like a two-mile trek through a rat maze," Santos said as the man left them. "How do they all stand working in here? I never understood the appeal of office work anywhere."

"It's definitely not for everyone." Dane knocked on the door and waited for a reply before she opened the door and they went inside.

"Mr. Chambers," Dane said by way of greeting.

"Ah, I was expecting the other two; they've been here so often." He stood and extended his hand. "What can I do for you ladies today?"

"Agents," Santos said with the tiniest smile.

"Sorry. Agents. What can I do for you agents today?"

"We need to speak to your employees," Dane said. "We wanted to give you a heads-up that we might be here for a while, walking around to different areas and speaking with people."

He looked confused. "Okay, but which employees do you need to speak with? I could just call them here for you and save you all that walking."

"All of them," Santos said. "Or, as close to all of them as possible in one day."

Chambers' eyes widened. "All of them? Are you serious?"

"Yes, sir," Dane said. "Is there a problem?"

"No, no. Would you like an escort? Someone to show you around?"

"Not necessary. We've been here before," Santos said.

"Thanks anyway," Dane said.

"You have to wear a hardhat in certain areas. Please do so. There are safety guidelines on signage at each department."

"We will," Santos said. "Safety first, right?"

Chambers narrowed his eyes and nodded once. "Right. Absolutely."

Dane paused at the door. "You don't happen to have a tattoo, do you?"

Chambers' grin crawled up one side of his face making him look like a rogue from the cover of one of the old romance novels her aunt used to read.

"Why, Agent, I believe that's a question best answered after work hours. Say, at the Wharfman's Pub. Around seven."

"I wasn't asking for personal reasons," Dane said flatly.

His self-satisfied grin remained in place. "That's disappointing. No, I don't have any tattoos."

"Thank you," Dane said, opening the door.

In the hallway, she huffed and shook her head. "Can you believe that guy? What a sleaze."

"He'll be at Wharfman's Pub at seven, if you want to tell him what a sleaze he is," Santos teased.

"That's not funny."

"Was to me."

They started in the office building, asking employees if they knew anything about the tattoo, if they knew anyone who had it, and asking to see behind their ears just to make sure they didn't have it.

Throughout the offices, things went smoothly, though it was obvious that many of the office workers were not in their offices, or even in the buildings. When Dane questioned anyone, they always answered that the missing workers were either off work that day, in a meeting, or possibly in the yard. No one had a direct answer ever.

"Let's move to the inspection departments," Santos said. "That's more like what all our victims were doing; not office work."

"Yeah, we've wasted enough time here."

They went to the inspection area in a huge warehouse close to the administration offices. The areas were separated by containers and long, waist-high silver tables. Goods of all kinds were on display as workers went through them to ensure they complied with current trade laws. Most of the workers didn't even pay attention when Dane and Santos entered. They just kept working diligently.

"Let's start there," Santos said. "We'll work our way through the place."

"We'll be here all day. Did you see the size of the place?"

"Yeah, I did. And I see how many busy worker bees are in here, too. Soonest begun…"

"Soonest done, yeah, I know."

They approached the first inspection area. There were twenty-eight workers in that area, and it looked to be one of the smallest areas.

Dane and Santos split up and started on opposite sides. They met in the middle and headed for the next area, repeating the process.

"Anyone refuse to show you behind their ears?" Santos asked. Quickly, she added, "God, I never thought I'd be saying that in this line of work."

Dane chuckled. "Honestly, I've had to ask worse. Everyone was compliant. I did have a couple of them laugh and tell me they felt like they were kids again and their mom was checking to make sure they washed behind their ears."

"Everybody I asked complied, too. But I feel like this is taking forever."

"We're going to have to group them," Dane said. "Realistically, we'll never get through them all if we don't."

Implementing the new questioning technique, Dane and Santos paid extra close attention to body language within each group. If anyone was hiding information, or a tattoo, they were undetectable.

Outside, in the first large, open inspection area, a dozen men worked. They moved in and out of shipping containers. Dane looked around as they walked. "I'm not seeing security cameras that could pick up what's going on inside those containers. I only see two high up on the roof of the warehouse behind us, as a matter of fact."

Santos laughed. "Yeah, because the employees are the security, Dane."

"We stick together, and we don't enter the containers."

"Seriously? You that worried? It's not like they're going to do anything to us right here in the open in broad daylight."

"And how many kidnap victims or murder victims had that very same thought running through their heads only minutes before their lives changed forever?"

Santos cleared her throat. She hadn't thought of it like that. "Yeah. Okay. We'll stick together, then." Grinning, she nudged Dane as they drew close to the first man and container. She whispered, "Don't worry, I won't let the bad man get you."

"I'm starting to understand why you and Metford don't work together alone in the field."

"Nah, that's because we argue. Gasoline and fire, us two."

The man stood straight and looked at Dane and Santos. He held an electronic device that was a little larger than a tablet. He didn't smile, but he did look behind the women as if expecting someone else to approach with them.

Dane and Santos showed their badges and introduced themselves. The man gripped the electronic device as if his life depended on it. His gaze flitted from Dane to Santos several times, and he never smiled.

"I don't know anything about any of that," he said. "I have a lot of work to do." He turned away from them.

"Mr. Jenkins," Dane called out.

The man kept walking but turned so he was walking backward. "Gotta get back to work. I told you I don't know anything about any of that."

Dane and Santos exchanged a look and then followed him around the side of the container.

"Mr. Jenkins, do you know anyone who has the tattoo?" Dane asked. "Maybe you've seen it on a coworker, or a friend here at work?"

He stopped walking and turned to face them. They were between two large containers and there was no one else there. Not for several yards in any direction.

The man dropped the hand holding the electronic device to his side. It hung there limply as he glared at them. His other hand went to his ear and one finger slipped behind it as he spoke. "I told you, I don't know anything about a tattoo." The hand dropped to his side.

"Get a little itch there, did you?" Santos asked. "Right behind your ear."

Jenkins' jaw muscles bulged as he clamped his teeth together. His gaze darted to his right, toward the warehouse, and then to his left, toward the endless rows of stacked shipping containers and the parking area beyond.

"Don't do it," Dane said.

Santos moved ahead of Dane. "Let me see behind your ear, Mr. Jenkins."

In an instant, Jenkins whipped the electronic device at Dane and bolted to his left.

"Dammit!" Santos yelled as she rocketed forward.

Dane was behind Santos until they exited the narrow space, and then she moved alongside. Jenkins was fast. He pulled away from them quickly and darted between rows of containers.

Dane motioned that she was going around the outside of the container area. Santos nodded and pushed her muscles harder and ran faster. Jenkins kept moving in the direction of the distant parking lot, he was just set on taking a zig-zagging path to get there.

Barely keeping him in sight, Santos feared he would slip past them. He shot from the last row of containers and slammed into a forklift. The impact was hard enough to bounce him backward into a container before he hit the ground. He scrambled to get off the ground. The man on the lift jumped down and moved toward him, yelling and panicked. Jenkins grabbed him by the shirt and yanked him to the ground as he struggled to get on his feet. He glanced down the row at Santos before turning to run again.

Santos was only a yard behind Jenkins when Dane ran from behind a parked lift and lunged for him. She stretched her arms out and grabbed at his ankle as she hit the pavement. Jenkins stumbled, cursed, and shunted to the right, screaming in pain, but he kept trying to get away. Santos caught up to him. She threw herself at his back, tackling him.

They hit half on the pavement and half on the mushy ground past it. The air whoofed out of him, and he rolled. Santos clung to him, snaking her arm around his throat as they rolled. He pinned her under his back and strained to break her hold, but she held tighter. He threw an elbow into her side several times. Each time, she clamped her teeth and grunted but never let up her grip.

Jenkins coughed and gasped for air. Santos didn't know how much longer she could hold him, but she hoped it would be long enough for him to wear out. She couldn't run another step if her life depended on it. Jenkins moved his legs enough for her to get hers out from under him. She wrapped them over his thighs. If she lost her grip around his neck, she still had him.

"Stop," Dane said as her shadow fell over Santos and Jenkins.

Santos heard the distinct metallic click of the gun. Jenkins went still and raised his hands. He still coughed and gasped even after Santos let him go.

Getting to her feet, Santos got her cuffs, put one knee in Jenkins' low back, and cuffed him. She stood and fist bumped Dane. "Good job," she said with a smile.

"You okay?" Dane asked.

"Yeah. Think I might need to notch up my exercise routine a bit, though." She rubbed her thighs as they walked.

At the car, Santos pulled Jenkins' ear down. "Why am I not surprised?"

Dane peeked over Santos' shoulder. "Would you look at that? No wonder he jackrabbited. Let's get Mr. Jenkins here to the station for questioning."

"I'm all for that."

CHAPTER THIRTY-TWO

"This is it," Ava said, pulling the car slowly toward the curb on the opposite side of the street.

Ashburn Street was a desolate place. Both sides of the street were lined with crumbling homes sitting in overgrown lots that used to be yards where people had barbecues, played with their kids, and dogs frolicked. In the distance, a five-story apartment building had partially crumbled. Caution tape flapped like ribbon around the pile of rubble near it. A skinny man holding a liquor bottle stumbled past the tape and into the hole in the wall. The darkness inside swallowed him.

Windows had been boarded over or shattered in every visible structure. The Victorian had only one boarded window on the third floor, and despite age and obvious neglect, it looked sturdy. The graffiti splashed over the exterior walls had long ago faded. In a few more years, it would be unreadable. Given the nature of most of the drawings and phrases, that would be a good thing.

A sedan sat near the house and in front of a building that had, at one time, been a two-car garage. The building had collapsed, and moss had grown over it in a thick blanket. The car had no glass, the wheels had been thrown in the yard, and the inside of the vehicle had been burned out.

Metford leaned forward and eyed the big house. "That's a lot of rooms to hide in. And if the exterior is any indication of what's inside, there might not be much left to check out."

"The house looks solid enough. We have to go inside and see what was bringing Wells out here. Look at this place. What would be here that's so important he would come on a regular basis?"

"I can think of nothing. It's obvious that nobody lives here anymore. Or, they don't own these houses anymore." He pointed up the road to the apartment building where the skinny old man had wandered back outside and there were two other men with him.

"Maybe this is a drug drop house."

"If it was, wouldn't there be some kind of security detail? They usually have people protecting places where large amounts of dope or money are being dropped off."

Ava craned to see the houses that would offer a good view of the Victorian. There were only three. The ones on either side of it, and the one where she had parked across the road. "I don't see anyone. All the windows that offer a decent enough view for security are boarded over solid."

Metford opened his door and got out. He ducked his head back in. "Unless the security team is inside the Victorian."

Ava got out and scanned the neighborhood. Metford was right. There might be someone, or multiple people, in the house. With guns.

"Only one way to find that out," she said, heading across the empty street.

Ivy had worked its way up one side of the house in thick, leafy ropes. Tendrils shot off from the wall, sending ivy runners into the gutters along the front. From there, the greenery had snaked its way through what was left of the intricate, ornate trim and down the porch columns.

Ava took the lead once they were at the porch steps. She drew her gun and moved cautiously up the four steps to the porch. The boards were weak and gave under her slight weight. She motioned to Metford so he would be careful. The last thing she wanted was to be fishing him out from under the porch if he fell through.

Ava called out at the door, announcing herself as FBI.

Metford gave her a wry look and shook his head.

She knocked and called out again.

"Are you serious?" Metford asked. He stepped forward and grabbed the doorknob. It rattled but didn't fully turn.

"Yeah, I kinda was," Ava said. "We don't know that someone doesn't live here. We're assuming that."

"There was no meter on the electric pole at the side of the house. I looked as we walked up."

She raised her hand to knock again, ignoring him. Before she could knock, his foot slammed into the door directly beside the knob. There was an audible pop followed by splintering wood and then the door flew inward.

"Metford, you can't—"

"I just did," he said, making a move toward the open doorway.

Ava grabbed his arm. "I'm taking lead." She couldn't trust his judgment after that stunt. What if someone did live there? They had just committed a crime: breaking and entering.

"You know, I remember not so long ago, you might have been okay with kicking in the door of an abandoned house that was also a suspected drug drop house."

"They call it growing, Metford. I've grown and progressed since then. And that's been quite a while back that I might not have worried too much about that."

"It's your ass in a sling if there are repercussions now, so that makes a big difference, I'm sure."

"I'm going to ignore that because I don't think you meant it as an insult." She crossed the threshold and paused, giving her eyes time to adjust to the dimness.

Dust motes danced in the shaft of light outside the first room on the right. She motioned for him to keep his eyes open as she stepped forward. Stopping at the doorway, she raised her gun and put her back to the wall. A whorl of dust and a puff of air exited the room as if in the wake of a runner. She turned, gun out, glanced around the room, and came back against the wall.

Metford gave her a questioning look.

She shook her head. Nothing. She looked again at a slower pace and saw the window had been left open about six inches. Air flowed through it and out the doorway. There was no door to blow shut, so it was free movement.

"Ventilation?" Metford whispered.

"Could be."

She moved to the end of the entrance hall and was met with a large, carpeted staircase. The carpet had rotted away years ago, and the boards underneath looked sketchy. She tested the first riser with her foot. She gave Metford the thumbs-up and stepped up on it with both feet. It held. She turned to look over the railing as light moved in the room across the way. She stepped onto the next riser and felt something offer resistance under her foot. She looked down to see what it was, and she was roughly jerked backward into Metford's chest. He wrapped his arm around her and spun to the side just as a long PVC pipe slammed downward from over top of the staircase. In the lower end of the pipe, someone had placed a long boning knife. It would have hit her in the lower throat.

She turned to Metford, her heart in her throat and her eyes wide.

He took a step back. "Are you all right?"

She nodded, unable to speak.

"That thing nearly killed you."

She looked back at it and nodded again, swallowing hard to clear the lump in her throat. "You saved my life. I wasn't even looking up." She touched her finger to the tip of the thin blade. Blood beaded on her fingertip.

Metford stepped in front of her. "Probably a booby trap set by some homeless person to protect his turf. I'm taking lead." He headed up the stairs, gun at the ready.

"No. I'll take lead. I'm fine."

"Another second there and you wouldn't have been fine. I got this."

"What if there are more booby traps?" she said louder.

"That's why I'm taking lead. You're the brains; can't afford to lose you." He continued upward with his head on a swivel.

They made the first landing and checked the first rooms. Finding nothing of importance, they went back to the hallway, moving as silently as the old house would allow. Working their way to the last room on the third floor, Ava stepped into a closet, shone her light around, and stepped back out.

"Clear."

Metford holstered his gun and exhaled deeply. "This is a big house. Two families could live here and not see each other but twice a week."

"That's a bit of an exaggeration, don't you think?"

"Have you seen my apartment? It would fit in the entrance hall of this place."

She chuckled. "Okay, Mr. Dramatic. Let's go check the rest of the first floor and see if the place has a basement."

"I think they were called root cellars back in the day, weren't they?"

She groaned and headed out. "I'm more interested in the bedframes in the rooms on the second floor."

"Yeah, something happened here. Might not have been recent, but I don't think handcuffs attached to headboards was normal at any time, was it?"

"Neither was rope that looks long enough only to tie someone's feet to the footboard. Did you notice that all the questionable frames were made of metal?"

"I did. Two of them were bolted to the floor, too."

As she approached the pipe and knife at the bottom of the stairs, a little stab of adrenaline hit her in the chest. They stepped into the entrance hall again, taking a moment to listen for movement.

"Thank you," she said.

"Huh?" Metford looked confused again. "Me? For what?"

"For saving my life. Thank you." Her gaze drifted to the knife.

"Yep. Glad I was there," he said, turning toward the kitchen. "If there's a basement, it would probably be this way."

Ava followed, not liking the idea of it, but knowing he wouldn't allow her in front of him without an argument that they didn't have time for.

Ava's phone rang, and she stopped to answer it. Metford stopped, too.

"Who is it?" he asked.

"Dane."

CHAPTER THIRTY-THREE

"Dane, what's up? Find something out?" Ava motioned to Metford to move into the kitchen. She stayed a few paces behind.

"We were at Patapsco forever, questioning employees. Everybody was cooperative, and nobody seemed to be hiding anything. Then we went outside to the first inspection area for the shipping containers; the smaller ones."

"And you found something?" Ava stopped just inside the kitchen. Nothing remarkable. Just an old kitchen full of outdated equipment and bad wallpaper that hung in strips from the walls.

"We found someone," she said. "Carl Jenkins. He didn't want to talk to us, and when we pressed him on it, he walked away from us. Of course, we followed, and after questioning him about the tattoo, he launched an iPad at me and bolted."

"Are you okay? Did you catch him?"

"Yes, I'm fine, and we caught him. We brought him down to the local police station to question him. He's cooling his heels in the interview room right now."

"And you think he knows something about the tattoo?"

"Yes, because he has it, too. Right behind his ear. He wouldn't speak at all on the way down here. He's not spoken a word since Santos cuffed him."

"All right. We'll head that way. We're on Ashburn Street checking out an abandoned house that Wells was visiting before he was killed."

"Anything there?"

"Couple of metal bedframes bolted to the floor. One has handcuffs attached to it; the other has nylon rope attached to the footboard."

"Suspicious—hold on a second."

"We clear here?" Ava asked Metford.

He scanned around the room again and nodded. "Looks like. This place is definitely abandoned and there's nobody here. Not even much sign that anybody's been here in the last decade."

"But Wells was definitely here very recently."

"I know, but he didn't leave any evidence." He motioned to indicate the whole house. "We've been through every room."

"Okay. Let's go. Dane and Santos have a man in custody down at the local PD. We should go question him. He's got the tattoo."

Dane came back on the line, and Ava halted in the hallway and put the call on speaker.

"Local cop just told me that we all need to go to the marina beside Porter Casino. It's Fair Weather Marina, and it's on the side of the casino that's farthest from Patapsco."

Ava and Metford headed for the front door. "What's going on at the marina?" From the sound of the noise on Dane's end of the line, she was headed out of the station and to her car, as well.

"The cop said Nathaniel Chambers and Cody Stillwell were caught after stealing a boat. They were trying to dump one of the short cargo containers like we saw at Patapsco. Coast Guard caught them and kept the container from sinking. Ava, it had three women in it. The Coast Guard is bringing the whole thing back to the marina now, and PD is already there."

"We're on our way." Ava hung up.

"What the hell?" Metford said as they sprinted out of the house, through the yard, and across the street to their car.

"Port director and supervisor were smuggling women. Bastards," she said, jumping into the driver seat.

"Cody Stillwell was Ethan Holt's direct supervisor," Metford said.

"Yes, he was. And I'm willing to bet that they all knew and facilitated the smuggling of women, and God knows what else."

Metford was silent for a portion of the ride to the marina. Five minutes before they reached their destination, he broke his silence. "Do you think the house wasn't a drug drop but a human drop instead?"

"My stomach just turned. I hope not, but it would explain the bedframes and accessories."

They arrived at Fair Weather Marina and inspected the cargo container along with Dane, Santos, and Ashton.

"How long had they been in this thing?" Ava asked the Coast Guard officer.

"One of the women, the only one who was lucid and coherent, said they were put in there after being grabbed in Morocco. She didn't even know for sure where they were when we opened the container."

"Did someone die in there?" a local police officer asked, putting his face in the bend of his elbow.

"No," Ava said. "That's what it smells like when you're stuck in a ventless container with a bucket for a toilet for the better part of a month."

The forensic duo stepped out dressed in respirators and Hazmat suits.

The lead held up a paper bag. "Hypos. I'm sure we'll find drugs in them. They still had half a bottle of water left. There was evidence of crackers, but not much else for sustenance."

The other agent held out a plastic bag. "I found part of a beef broth container. Someone ate part of the cardboard it's made from."

Ava wanted to turn away from the horrors but wouldn't allow herself that luxury. Those three women, and countless others, had not been able to turn away from the horrors in the container. She stared at it with her insides twisting like barbed wire around a pole. The feeling was hot, sharp, and sick.

"There were three of those little fluffy dog beds you can buy at PetSmart and Walmart in there, too. Looks like those were the only soft things in there."

Ava walked over to the local police detective and the officers with him. "You have anyone checking the containers at the yard?"

"We sent five units over, but we don't have any more to send. There are other homicides, drug cases, and two separate escapees that are active right now at this very moment."

"I'll get a team to Patapsco as soon as possible." She walked off with her phone in her hand.

"Metford, let's go back to the station. Ashton, get back to the electronics. Dane, you and Santos go to the hospital and be there when any of the women are able to talk. Take their statements; find out all you can about this." Ava flung her hand toward the deplorable container. She was sickened and angry by the thought of what those women, and probably many more, had suffered in containers like that one.

She dialed Sal's number and let her know the situation.

"I'll see how many I can send right now," Sal said. "I take it your team are all engaged in a different aspect of the case?"

"They are." Ava told her what everyone on the team was doing, thanked her for sending agents to Patapsco to help search the containers, and hung up. Starting the car, she looked at Metford. They didn't have to speak. Each knew what was running through the other's head just by their expression.

At the police station, Ava stopped at Panko's office.

"I need you to send a unit over to Ashburn Street," she said as she entered the room.

"If I have one to send."

"We're all short-handed given the turn of events, but I need someone to go over there and give an abandoned house a complete walk-through. My partner and I were called away before we could find a basement, and before we completed the walk-through. It's just the ground floor that we didn't finish. All your men would have to do is go room to room on that floor and check for a basement."

"And you couldn't stop by there on your way back here?" Panko's tone of irritation rubbed Ava the wrong way.

"On our way? It's not on our way. It would have been a half-hour *out* of our way, and we have three men here that we need to question. Getting information from them quickly might save lives."

"Those three women are safe now. They're in the county hospital."

"And there might be more women in danger at Patapsco. There might be women still trapped in shipping containers. That's how these bastards work: a few women in this container, a few in that one, a couple with minors in them. The containers are all spread out through the shipping yard so that if one is discovered, they still stand a chance at their ring making money off the others that aren't found. And there could be women or drugs or any number of other illicit, possibly dangerous items at that house on Ashburn Street."

Panko's expression soured and his eyebrows drew down. "All right. Point made." He flapped a dismissive hand at her as he picked up the phone. "Damn city is gonna be the death of me," he grumbled to himself. He dialed a number and scowled at Ava, motioning for her to leave already as he clamped the phone between his shoulder and ear and drew a paper and pen toward himself.

Ava left and headed down the corridor. She quickened her pace as they neared the hallway that would lead them to the interview rooms, Metford keeping up.

The officers told her who was in which room.

"Who are we questioning first?" Metford asked.

"The port director. He's the highest-ranking person we have right now." She opened the file and skimmed over it, picking out the highlights of his arrest and then she gave the file to Metford while she watched Chambers through the two-way mirror.

Chambers sat with his hands cuffed and lying in his lap. He stared down at them with an expression of disinterest as if his situation wasn't dire. As if he didn't worry at all that he had been caught trying to kill three women just to get rid of evidence of his wrongdoing. As if drowning three women was just another Tuesday for him. Righteous anger began to build to a fever pitch in her chest. The tremor in her bones was uncomfortable and way too familiar.

As soon as Metford closed the file, she spun and stalked to the door of the interview room. She didn't knock, didn't announce her intent to enter; he didn't deserve the heads-up. Had those women gotten a heads-up that they were about to be dragged, drugged, and tossed into a metal box for more than two weeks?

For thirty minutes, Chambers said nothing. No matter the questions; no matter how detrimental to him the charges were, he remained apathetic and silent.

"You're not helping yourself, or anyone involved by remaining silent, Mr. Chambers," Ava said. "You and Stillwell were caught red-handed trying to murder three women. We know they were going to be trafficked, and we know you and Stillwater weren't the only ones involved. My bet is that Ethan Holt, James Lawson, and even Emily Harper were part of this ring. Were they? Were they your partners in this scheme, Mr. Chambers?"

A blank stare was her answer.

"And the tattoo? Was that part of the organization, too?"

He shifted his indifferent gaze to the wall and sighed as if bored with her.

"What about Vanessa Morales? Was someone trying to recruit her into this thing? She didn't have the tattoo." When he remained unmoved, Ava and Metford left without further questions.

"He didn't even try to lawyer up," Metford said.

"He's not said a word since he was detained, according to all law enforcement. Maybe he thinks the silent route will help him in the long run somehow."

Looking through the two-way at Stillwater, he was a ball of nervous energy compared to Chambers. His leg bounced ceaselessly. He couldn't keep his hands still, and his eyes were in constant motion. Several times, he looked guiltily at the mirror.

"I think he's ashamed," Metford said. "Every time he looks at himself in the mirror, he looks away with disgust."

"No, that's not shame. He's looking over here because he knows someone is back here. He's scared. And that's good."

"He has a right to be scared. He's in more trouble than he'll ever be able to get out of."

"Yep. No plea deals are going to help him much."

They went into the room. Stillwater gave them a deer in the headlights look.

"I'll tell you what I know," he said. His chin and bottom lip quivered. "Everything, but you have to protect me. They will kill me, if they find out I said anything."

CHAPTER THIRTY-FOUR

Ava sat and gave Stillwater a level stare as she laced her fingers and put her hands on the closed casefile. "You were caught trying to drown three women. Why would you think you deserve protection from anyone?"

Stillwell's eyes flew wide and he leaned forward violently. "You can't do that. You can't not protect me. You have to protect me if I have information that will help you…" He glanced at Metford and then at the mirror and then at the red eye of the camera up in the corner of the room. He shook his head and sat back. The leg started bouncing, and he chewed on his thumbnail.

"Information that will help us with what, Mr. Stillwell? I think we have all the evidence we need to get you convicted of three counts of attempted murder." She turned to Metford. "That's at least life, right?"

"At the very least, on three counts." Metford nodded solemnly. "Without possibility of parole anytime in his lifetime."

"Yeah," she said reflectively. "So, Mr. Stillwell, why would we need anything more from you?"

He reluctantly stopped gnawing on his thumbnail and lowered his hands to his lap. "What did Chambers tell you?"

"Who says we've even talked to him yet?" Ava asked.

"Why else would I be sitting here for hours before you came in?" He chuckled. The sound was more air being forced through a straw than an actual laugh.

"Well, because of what you were caught doing. You're going to be sitting somewhere on someone else's schedule for the foreseeable future. And because of your involvement in the human trafficking ring, you will never be a free man again."

"You know about the Sea Wolves? I thought you said you hadn't talked to Chambers yet."

"No, I never said that. I asked what made you think we already had talked to him. There's a difference."

"What did he tell you? They'll kill him, too," Stillwell said loudly and obviously scared.

Ava and Metford shared a look, and Metford gave a slight nod.

Ava opened the file and tilted the papers so Stillwell was unable to see them. She flipped a couple of pages while she debated her tactic. If it backfired, it could be detrimental to the case. If it went smoothly, and Stillwell bought the idea that she already had some of the information, he would open up and give her what she needed as they progressed through the interview.

"It says here that you have a tattoo behind your ear, Mr. Stillwell."

"Yeah." He turned his head and folded down his ear, revealing the three dots in the shape of a triangle. "We all do. We had to get it to stay on the payroll."

"On the Sea Wolves' payroll," she said as if it weren't a question.

"Yeah. They branded us just like they did some of the women they kept."

"How many Sea Wolves are there at Patapsco Bay Terminal?"

"I don't know," he stuttered, shifting his gaze to his hands.

"That's not very helpful, Mr. Stillwell. What happened? Just minutes ago, you were swearing to tell us everything."

"You have to protect me from them if you want what I know."

She nudged Metford and tilted her head toward the door. They left together without another word.

"Where are you going? Why are you leaving? Hey, where are you going?" Stillwell sounded more frantic with each question.

Ava led Metford into the observation room. "Let him sweat it for a few minutes. He needs to think we know more than we do."

"Are we going to promise him protection for information?"

Ava scoffed. "Absolutely not. Those women weren't offered protection, were they?"

"What about the Sea Wolves?"

"He said they all had the tattoo. Ethan Holt, Emily Harper, James Lawson, Chris Wells, Nathaniel Chambers, Caleb Jenkins, Jasper Halloway, and Cody Stillwell. That's eight that we know about already, if we believe that all members have the tattoo. You know there have to be quite a few more for them to be able to pull this off. Halloway is proof that it goes beyond the scope of Patapsco Bay Terminal, too. There will be other officials involved."

"And probably law enforcement and Coast Guard," Metford said. "This could get messy."

"It already is."

Ava took time to inquire about the investigation happening at Patapsco Bay. Panko was stressed, and under stress, he was snippy. Most people were, Ava supposed.

"Inform your people to be on the lookout for anyone with a tattoo behind their ear."

"What the hell are they supposed to do, check containers for people, or go around and ask to look behind employees' ears?" he asked.

"They'll figure it out, I'm sure, Chief Panko. Also, let them know to be on the lookout for any evidence of a group called Sea Wolves. They don't have to ask about it. They don't have to launch a full investigation; just be on the lookout. It's information they need to have while they're there. The group is trafficking young women, and it might be part of a worldwide network of human traffickers and smugglers. That means they're dangerous."

"Sea Wolves and ear tattoos." He shook his head wearily and stood. "What the hell has happened to the world?"

Ava understood it was a rhetorical question. "Where are you going?"

He shot her a hard look. "Not that I answer to you, Special Agent, but I am going to the field to be with my officers and detectives. I will be more useful there than sitting here behind this desk."

Ava moved aside and followed him out of the office.

"Hey, Chief," she called after him as he walked away.

He turned and faced her but said nothing.

"If you find anything give me a call, would you?"

"When will your agents be here to help with this?"

"My boss was on it earlier. I'm sure they'll be here within a couple of hours at most."

"How many warm bodies?"

"Couldn't tell you. I'll know when they get here."

He nodded and headed toward the nearest exit.

Ava went back to the observation room and tapped the wall under the light switch. "Ready to go back in?" she asked Metford.

"Sure. He's really worked up in there. Leaving like that has him worried bad."

"Good. That was my intention."

They entered the room and sat across from Stillwell again.

"Where'd you go? Did you find someone to protect me?"

"No, we didn't. That's not why we left, Mr. Stillwell," Ava said.

Stillwell put his arms on the table and leaned over them. "They'll kill me in here before I have a chance to talk."

"You're in a police station. I don't really think you have to worry about an assassin getting in here."

"Yeah, we call that paranoia," Metford added.

"I can give you a real reason to be paranoid, though," Ava said. "See, I know that Sea Wolves is a worldwide network of smugglers and human traffickers. Your little clique at Patapsco Bay Terminal are like the Mickey Mouse Gang in comparison to the brutality of the bigger organization."

"What? Worldwide? I thought we were only a US group."

"No, Mr. Stillwell. You knew the organization stretched across the globe, surely."

He shook his head. "No. I didn't know, and neither did the others. If they'd known, they would have said something."

"Right. Anyway, I'm not offering you protection in exchange for information. What I will do, if you refuse to start talking, is lead you right outside, have a few news cameras recording, and release you. I'll pat you on the back and tell the world that we could never have figured out any of this without you. That you are solely responsible for giving us the names of all the Sea Wolves members in Baltimore, and a handful of foreign nationals involved with it." She leaned forward, close to Stillwell, who was still leaned over his arms on the table. "And I will turn around and leave you right there for whoever might want you. Does that sound like a good deal?"

He looked sick as he melted back in his seat. His hands fell limply into his lap, and his leg was still. "You can't do that. The police won't let you do that. I was caught trying to kill three women. No way will they allow you to let me go like that." A small smirk formed on his lips.

Ava took out her badge and tapped it with one finger. "They won't have much choice. We're FBI. FBI trumps local law enforcement." She hoped he was as misinformed as most citizens about what the FBI could and could not do.

He swallowed. His throat made a clicking sound. That was good.

"Now that you understand the situation a little better…" She questioned him with her expression. Did he understand the situation a little better? Did he understand that his ass belonged to the FBI?

He nodded, turning grayish around the edges.

"Now, we only have proof pertaining to the three women in the container. That's enough to put you away for a long time. Maybe not forever like I said before, but for long enough that you won't have much life left when you do get out. But we can tie you in with the murders of the other CBP agents, and that will definitely put you away forever."

"But I didn't have anything to do with that!" he yelled. "I never killed anybody! I was only working at Patapsco Bay Terminal. I worked inbound shipping, and nothing more."

"You worked inbound shipping?" Ava asked.

"Yes."

"Inbound shipments of goods and humans, right?"

"Yes," he answered through gritted teeth.

"Who helped you? Who helped you with the human cargo?"

"All I did was put *those* containers aside. I marked them for…" His head was lowered so that he looked to be navel-gazing. He rolled his eyes up to meet Ava's and held her gaze for a moment. "I marked them for Ethan, okay?"

"Okay." She made notes. "What did Ethan do with them?"

His head shot up. "I don't know. All I did was mark the containers for him. When he took them, they left my mind. I didn't think about them anymore after that. It's the only way I could keep doing it."

"In other words, you took the money and then forgot about the girls as if they never mattered at all. As if they were disposable like so many of the goods that come in through that port."

His eyes welled with tears. "That sounds—"

"Heartless, unconscionable, cruel beyond words, inexcusable, *inhuman*, right? Because that's only a few words to describe your actions."

"And I'm sure a jury will have more words to add to that," Metford said. "Along with the judge."

"And what about the parents of those girls?" Ava added, barely able to contain the anger boiling through her veins.

Stillwell's eyes widened. "Their parents?"

"Did you think they were orphans? Every woman is someone's daughter, sister, aunt, mother, grandmother. You didn't just affect these women, but everyone in each of their families who is missing them, loving them, fearing for their lives!" Ava was yelling. She sat back and took a breath and a moment to compose herself.

"I'm sorry," Stillwell said in a watery voice. "I'm sorry. I never thought about it like that."

"No, you wouldn't, would you? You were finally one of the cool kids on campus. One of the *in* crowd. You got your cool little secret tattoo, got to do God-knows-what and get away with it, you were part of a powerful group with a strong, intimidating presence and name: Sea Wolves. No, you wouldn't think about the wider impact of your actions." She clenched her hands into fists and put them in her lap to control the anger-induced trembling.

"You've got it all wrong. That's not it."

"I've got it all wrong. Then you should enlighten me. Why did you agree to join them? Why did you agree to take money and deliver women for the sole purpose of trafficking them for sex and worse?"

"Worse? I don't know anything about that."

"Right. I believe you. Who all was involved, and what else was inbound that you set aside for someone else to take away?"

"Nothing."

"I must say that the women are bad enough, but I don't believe they were all that was coming in through your inspection area. I just can't believe that."

"If there was anything else, it was going through another area, or while I wasn't there. I swear it."

"Jasper Halloway," Ava said.

Stillwell blanched. If he had been gray around the edges before, he was completely gray after that.

"How much higher does this go?"

Stillwell remained silent and looked at the tabletop, refusing to make eye contact with Ava or Metford.

After another five minutes of questions that produced no answers, Ava stood so suddenly that her chair flew back, the legs squealing against the tile floor. She jerked the door open and exited before she put hands on Stillwell. How much would it take to push her over the edge? To make her cross the line from law enforcement to breaking the law?

She didn't like to admit it even to herself, but she thought she was toeing that line when she left the room.

CHAPTER THIRTY-FIVE

Metford followed Ava down the hall to the corner. "Don't let this get to you on a personal level, Ava. Come on."

"How can I not? It is personal. It should be personal to everyone who loves a woman, who has a female family member or friend."

And it was more than that for her, too, but she didn't need to say that out loud.

"I understand that. I really do, but this is our job, and we're exposed to this kind of horror almost every day. It'll do some serious damage if you let every case get under your skin so deep. I just worry about you."

"I'm working on it, okay? I want to get hold of him…" She clenched her hands and didn't finish the thought. "Him, Chambers, Halloway, and Jenkins."

"But they're not the only ones involved. We need solid proof of their involvement before we do more. You know that. There has to be something concrete before we can go after Halloway or anyone else."

"I know, Metford," she said, biting back on her anger. He didn't deserve to endure the brunt of it. He had done nothing but try to talk her down. And that was for her own good.

Ava's phone rang, and she blew out a pent-up breath as she punched the button to answer.

"Special Agent James, it's Chief Panko. My officers at the house on Ashburn found something. You need to get over here right away."

Ava motioned for Metford to follow her, and she took off at a good clip down the long hallway with the phone on speaker. "What did they find?"

"A bunker under the house accessed through a hidden door in the back of the basement. There were more booby traps, and one of my guys is being hauled to the hospital in an ambulance right now."

"Was there anything in the bunker?"

"Evidence that somebody might have been kept there. Looks pretty recent, too."

"Secure the scene!" she yelled. "Don't let anyone in until we get there!"

Ava ran to the car and Metford was right beside her.

"I knew I should have gone on ahead and finished looking for that damn basement door," Metford said. "What if that someone was still in there while we were walking around the rest of the house?"

"Metford, you can't beat yourself up over it."

"Oh, right. Advice from the queen of beating herself up over everything. They probably had more women down there."

Ava turned on the lights and sirens and floored the gas. "Call forensics to meet us there. I want every centimeter of that place scoured for evidence. I want anything and everything they find."

Metford made the call. "Detective Coffey had already made the call. Forensics will be there before we get there."

"Fine by me."

They arrived at the house on Ashburn. The strobes painted the deserted neighborhood in staggered red and blue swathes, highlighting the deplorable state of neglect.

Detective Coffey met them outside and walked in with them. "We swept the place as well as we could for more traps, but I'm telling you, be careful what you touch, where you step, the place was like walking through a field of landmines. Ridiculous."

"How long has forensics been here?" Ava asked.

"About ten minutes, maybe a little less."

"How bad is your guy hurt?" Metford asked.

"Pretty bad, but he'll survive. Someone had rigged razor wire on a pulley system. When he kicked the lever, the wire dropped down and zipped around the pulley system. It cut the side of his face and took off the top of his ear. There's blood splattered everywhere. I'm just glad he reacted quick enough to turn his head and jerk away as far as he did. If not, it might have sliced his throat."

Ava went down the narrow, rickety steps into the basement. Cobwebs lay like blankets on every shelf and hung like party streamers from the ceiling in every direction save one. The one that led to the spot where the hidden door had been uncovered.

Two cops stood outside that opening. Bright light emanated from beyond the threshold. As she moved closer, Ava saw that there was yet another long corridor. Could it be called a hallway if it was merely carved into the dirt? She paused at the entrance. The support beams didn't look as if they were the sturdiest system. Taking a breath, she bucked up her courage and entered the path.

The dirt floor, walls, and ceiling seemed to absorb sound. Everything sounded muffled, as if she had a skiff of cotton in her ears.

"Can you imagine how dark it would be down here without the work lights?" Metford asked from behind her.

"I don't see any electricity down here."

The chill was evident, and there was no escaping it. It was all around, hugging her body, chilling her through.

The room wasn't large, and the ceiling was lower than the ceiling in the hallway. It was claustrophobic, and she could only imagine that in total darkness, it would be maddening. Someone alone in the hidden room, in the dark, with the door closed, would be in complete sensory deprivation.

A bright shaft of light shot through the wall into the hall. Ava looked at it, confused for a moment. She moved to the hole and bent down. The hole looked to be maybe a little more than a foot across. Someone moved and blocked the light from inside again. Ava stood and moved to the entrance of the room. Two people in forensic suits worked, gathering things, and pulling prints off every solid surface.

There was a metal folding chair in the far corner being slowly devoured by rust, a five-gallon bucket with a piece of rough wood covering its top, and a filthy mattress that had three filthier blankets piled in the middle of it. The putrid odor of human waste drifted out the open doorway and Ava's lungs locked for an instant. As she turned and put a hand over her mouth and nose, she heard Metford have the same reaction.

After a few seconds, she turned back to the team inside. "Have you run the prints yet?"

"Not yet. None have been clear enough until now," a red-haired woman said, holding up a full print she had pulled from the back of the chair. She used the portable print scanner and stood staring down at the screen. "Got a positive hit," the woman said. She walked to Ava and showed her the results.

"Chloe Williams," Ava read aloud. "Seventeen, missing from San Diego over a year ago. Send that to me." Ava's heart sank. "She was taken when she was only sixteen," she said, feeling nauseated. "Prints came from being picked up for shoplifting shortly before that." She turned to the woman again. "Was she held here that long? Was she stuck in this pit for a year?"

"I can't say for sure. Maybe some of the evidence will give us a better timeline, but what I can tell you is that she was here recently. Maybe until only a couple of weeks ago, give or take."

"What's this hole in the wall?" Ava asked.

"It looks like someone dug their way out. With their hands."

"If she could get through that, she's small." Ava thought about Ashton's profile of the killer based on the blood spatter.

"Well, she's probably malnourished, and no telling what she was enduring from her captors, so yeah, she is small."

"And you can't tell what happened to her? Do you think she's dead, alive, what?"

The woman sighed and turned away. "I'm a forensic technician expert, not a psychic."

"Metford, what if she's our killer?"

"What? A teenage girl who's been held captive for over a year and she's small enough to fit through that hole? I seriously doubt it."

Ava was already having Chloe Williams' prints run against all the prints found at the other crime scenes. "Let's go. If her prints were left at any of the murders, we'll know in a few minutes."

"If she did escape, what about all these booby traps? How would she have avoided all of them?"

"Depends on how many times she was walked in and out of here." Ava used her flashlight and studied the dirt path. "See how a path has been worn? Notice how that path veers to skirt around each place a trap was found? That's how she knew. God, she had been through here with her captors often enough that she memorized the exact path. Probably counted the steps so she would know how to get through in the dark."

"If she did all that, which would be a remarkable feat for an abducted, abused teenager, why wouldn't she just go to the cops? That would be the logical thing to do. Run to the nearest police station, hospital, church, or house with lights on."

Ava shook her head. "These men did unthinkable things to her and kept her in deplorable conditions possibly for more than a year. She probably had a psychological break. It would be inevitable. Nobody could withstand such treatment and not have a break. The fantasy of revenge is probably what got her through the torture, and once she was free, she could only enact that fantasy. There was no other option. Not in her mind, at least. These men facilitated her abduction and her incarceration. She wanted to make them pay."

Ava and Metford went up the stairs and into the kitchen. Panko and Coffey stood propped against a counter at the window.

"The forensic crew upstairs said there's evidence that someone was being trafficked out in a couple of the rooms," Coffey said.

Ava knew which rooms before she saw them, and she was sure Metford already knew, too.

She pointed to the nylon rope around the foot rail of the bed in the first room. "Be sure you test that for any trace of evidence."

"Already planned on it," the man said.

"And the rails."

"I got this. I have a teenage daughter at home. Trust me, I'm going to go through the paces on everything here and the rest of the house, too."

"Thank you," Ava said.

"Let's go back to the station and question Jenkins," Ava said to Metford.

"There's nothing more we can do here until something more is found."

"We could stand around and wait to hear about every scrap of evidence, but that would be wasting time," she said as they tromped down the stairs.

She took enough time to speak to Coffey and Panko before leaving the scene.

A mile from the station, Ava's phone rang.

Metford answered and put it on speaker. "Ashton, you're on speaker. Ava's driving. Go ahead."

"The lab got the prints back from the Wells and Morales crime scene. That print you sent out—the one for Chloe Williams—it was a match for a single print found on the wall tile of the bathroom at Wells' apartment."

"Chloe Williams was in the bathroom where Vanessa Morales was murdered," Ava said, sparing a glance toward Metford.

"Yes, that's what was found. It was a full print, too. Not just a partial. Middle finger, right hand."

"All right. Thanks, Ashton."

"Yep." He disconnected before Ava could tell him that they were headed back to the station.

"Not much for saying goodbye, is he?" Metford said.

"Guess not. That's okay. At least he's not awkward to get off the phone with."

"Are we going to put out a BOLO or APB on Chloe Williams?"

"They've already been issued. I heard Panko giving the order back at the house. It won't do much good unless she's ready to be caught. If one of our suspects happens to be her next target, she'll figure out soon enough that they've been locked up. If there are others she's looking for, that's our best bet to find her."

"What, wait for her to go after her next victim?"

"Exactly."

"How are we going to figure out who to watch? We don't even know who she might be looking for next, or how many were involved."

"I know. I know." The feeling of treading water and waiting for something to happen was beyond irritating, but she didn't know what to do other than go back to the station. At least there, she could try to wrest some information from one of the suspects.

"I was wrong about the girl. It looks like you were right about that, too."

Ava nodded. "I've worked on a lot of these cases. I've seen what the brutality does to some of them. Adding the isolation and darkness and you've got the perfect recipe for a mental snap."

"She couldn't be very big. I mean, she must be tiny to have fit through that hole. How the heck is she killing these people with such ferocity? How are they not just tossing her around like a ragdoll?"

"Because she attacks while they're asleep. She's got a single mission: kill the people who did this to her. She's not enjoying the hunt or playing with them beforehand like some killers do to get their kicks. She just wants them dead, and she takes the simplest route to achieve that goal."

"She must be pretty smart, too. Especially for a girl so young. She's not leaving evidence everywhere, and so far, there have been no reports of seeing a young girl covered in blood walking around after these murders."

"That's probably from all the time she had to think about how to do it. She's been missing for sixteen months."

"To think that she will be locked up for the rest of her life for the murders… It seems unfair."

The girl had to be found. She had to be stopped. No matter what, she couldn't be allowed to kill and walk free. It was obvious that her mind had been damaged by the horrors she had endured, and it was nothing she asked for, nothing she did wrong that put her in that situation. The outcome, however, was still the same. She needed professional help, and even with it, there was no guarantee she could ever recover her mental well-being.

CHAPTER THIRTY-SIX

Jenkins was almost as dedicated to being silent and stoic as Chambers had been. Almost.

"Mr. Jenkins, you might as well give us what you can. We have a couple of your friends here, too, you know," Ava said. "Just because you don't talk to us doesn't mean they won't."

He flashed a grin at her and shook his head.

"You don't believe me? That's fine. I bet you think your friends got rid of the evidence, don't you?"

He looked at her with his eyebrows wrinkling toward the bridge of his nose.

"They tried," Metford said. "I mean, you gotta give them an A for effort, right?"

"Yeah. They tried, all right. Didn't quite succeed, though. Coast Guard caught them moments before the container started to sink."

Jenkins' expression turned to shock. He recovered quickly. "I don't know what you're talking about."

"Sure, you do," Ava said. She tapped behind her ear. "It has a little something to do with that funky tattoo behind your ear. Remember getting that?"

"No, I was twenty-one and drunk. Woke up with it."

"And that's why you ran from my agents when they asked you about it back at Patapsco?"

He clammed up and looked toward the wall, just the way Chambers had earlier.

"Who else is involved with the trafficking ring you're in?"

Color rose to his cheeks, but he remained silent.

"Those three women survived, you know," Ava continued. "They'll identify every single one of you they saw."

"Who survived what? Don't know what you're talking about."

"Did you mark containers for Ethan, or one of the others, to take away; to take care of?"

His gaze flicked toward her and back to the wall. His hands balled into fists on his thighs.

"I told you that your friends might talk. They might have already talked. A lot."

"I don't have friends. At Patapsco or anywhere else, lady. I don't know who you have here from Patapsco, but I'm sure that whatever they did has nothing to do with me."

"Sea Wolves," Metford said.

Jenkins flinched and his fists tightened.

Ava named off the murdered agents except for Vanessa Morales. "Someone is hunting your group. One at a time, they're being taken out for what all of you did."

He grinned again. "Then I guess I'm in the safest place in the world to avoid being taken out by some mysterious assassin."

"That sounded a lot like an admission to me. Didn't it sound that way with you, Metford?"

"It kinda did. Why would you worry about being somewhere safe if you did nothing and have no idea what we're talking about?"

When Jenkins clammed up again, he stayed that way. He sweated, and his fists were clenched hard enough to make them purple and white around the knuckles, but he never broke his silence.

Ava and Metford left him and told the guards to return him to his cell, and they told the guards to bring Stillwell back with them.

Ava went into the observation room to await Stillwell's arrival, and Metford went down the hall in search of police station coffee. One of the strongest brews known to man, in her opinion.

Metford returned with two cups and gave her one. "I don't know if you'll be able to drink it or not. The woman in there said it tasted like hot swamp scum."

Ava sniffed her cup. "It's so strong you don't even have to drink it," she said. "Couple of good whiffs of it, and I think I'll be revved up for a couple of hours." When she tipped the cup, the coffee left a dark stain on the inside of the Styrofoam cup.

The guards entered the interview room with Stillwell. They seated him and left the room.

"Showtime," Ava said. She stood and went to the door.

Stillwell was calmer than before. "You're back," he said. "I thought you were done with me for the day."

"I wish we were," Ava said. "We discovered something that I thought you might be interested in. You said you didn't know what Ethan's role was or what it entailed; that after he took possession of the girls, you didn't think about them anymore, right?"

He remained still and said nothing.

"Well, we found out what he did to at least one of them. She would have come through Patapsco a little over a year ago."

He scoffed and chuckled. That time, it sounded like a chuckle. That he was able to manifest that sound infuriated Ava. "And you think I'm going to remember one female who came through that long ago?"

"Jesus, man," Metford said. "How many do you see in a year? Seriously, how many?"

Stillwell shook his head. "A lot."

"Not the sort of thing you keep a tally on, huh?" Ava asked.

"Not really," he said in a tone that matched her humorless, sharp one.

"I bet you will remember this one," Ava said. She worked with her phone for a moment and then turned the screen to face him. "Chloe Williams. Really young when she showed up. Pretty, too. Look at it, Mr. Stillwell. Look at her picture."

He squinted at the picture and looked away quickly.

"That picture was plastered all over San Diego by her parents. They ran that same picture in the newspapers, put it on the local news broadcasts, and posted it all over social media sites."

"Looks like some of your group were holding her in a bunker that was dug out underneath an old abandoned Victorian house over on Ashburn Street," Metford said.

"And guess what?" Ava asked as she laid the phone on the table with Chloe's smiling picture facing him. "She escaped. She escaped that dungeon where she was held, where she lived for who knows how long, that hellhole of a house where she was pimped out to the men who visited for that very reason."

"For only that reason," Metford added.

"But she's out now. And I think she's the one killing off members of your Sea Wolves group at Patapsco Bay. Did she ever see your face, Mr. Stillwell?"

His head jerked up. His eyes had gone wider, and the panic stared back at Ava, satisfying a part of her that she didn't allow to roam freely. It was that part of her that might take the step across the line. The part that might exact revenge instead of seek justice.

"No. No, I don't remember seeing—"

"Lies. How is that going to help you at all? We might not have a lot of evidence yet, but we're collecting it from your house, your workplace, and the house on Ashburn right this very moment. We'll have enough to put you away for a long time, Mr. Stillwell. But, if you're looking for a lighter sentence, it might be possible."

"How?"

"By helping us save lives."

"I don't know where she went. Swear to God, that's the truth."

"No, I didn't think you did, but you might have an idea where she will go next."

He looked confused. "But I don't."

"She's killing CBP agents who facilitated her capture, transport, and wrongful incarceration for the last year. I'm sure you are on her list. You, Jenkins, and Chambers, too. But you three aren't all of her list, are you? There are more members of Sea Wolves, and she saw all of you at one time or another. Whether you turned a blind eye, or you participated in her torture, she knows. You three are safe in here. But you could tell us who else is in this group that she might go after."

"I don't—"

"He isn't interested in helping himself," Metford said, standing. "Come on. Let him keep his secrets."

"No, no, I am interested. I am," Stillwell said.

"Then give us names," Ava said, all trace of geniality disappearing from her voice. "We're not going to sit here and waste precious time dickering with you. Either you give us names, in which case we will put in a good word for you with the ADA, or you don't give us names, in which case, we will leave you to your fate."

He looked down and sighed heavily. "I don't know for sure who she would be after next. Really, I don't." He shifted and glanced at Ava before dropping his gaze again. "I do know that Jasper Halloway, Christopher Wells, and Ethan were really close."

"Jasper Halloway. That's good. Who else?"

"I think she'll be looking for me," he said in a defeated voice.

"You? I thought you didn't—"

"I know what I said. It was a lie. Is it so shocking that I would lie? Given my current circumstances, that's kind of like... a *given*, isn't it?"

"Duly noted," Ava said. "Why would she be after you? What did you do to her? And remember, coming clean, admitting your part now will look better when the case is out of our hands."

"I remember her. Chloe Williams." He jutted his chin toward the phone screen with her picture still smiling out at the world. "I'm the one who pointed out how gorgeous she was. That's what turned Ethan on to her in the first place. I don't think he would have given her much notice if I hadn't said anything."

"She was sixteen," Metford said.

"I know that now, but I didn't then."

"As if it would be better if she'd been eighteen?" Metford asked sarcastically.

"No, nothing makes what we did any better."

"Mr. Stillwell, go on with your story. My patience is wearing thin and we have other things to do."

"She was a fighter, too, and that stoked Ethan and Chambers. They thought it was hot. Didn't matter that the other guys had hurt her, threatened her, and drugged her, she still fought for her freedom. She fought until she was knocked unconscious. None of us had ever seen anything like it."

"What other guys? Who had already hurt and drugged her?"

"I was talking about the crew who grabbed her and put her in the container."

"You mean the men who abducted her in San Diego?"

He nodded. "I wish I had kept my mouth shut about her. I heard that Ethan kept her. I didn't believe it at first, but then I heard Lawson talking to Chambers one day about how he'd had the feistiest piece he'd ever had. Chambers laughed and clapped him on the back. He said he knew he'd been to visit Chloe on Ashburn Street."

"Ethan was selling her to men in that house," Ava said.

"Yeah."

"Who were some of the men?"

"I'm not sure, but like I said, Jasper Halloway was close with Ethan and Christopher Wells."

"That's all you've got for us?"

Stillwell nodded.

Ava stood. She pulled the door open and was met with a female officer who looked flustered.

"I was told to come find you," she said.

Ava held up a hand and waited for Metford to exit the room. Once the door was shut, Ava led the officer away from the door to prevent Stillwell from hearing anything.

"What's going on?"

The officer held out a piece of paper to Ava. "It's a 911 call from Deputy Commissioner of Customs and Border Patrol, Jasper Halloway. He was attacked by a female with a knife while he was lying on a lounger by his pool. The attacker got away, but he said she's hurt. Mr. Halloway said he punched her in the face and broke her nose. They fought in the yard, and he's sure her right arm is broken, too."

"Did he know the attacker?" Ava asked.

"No. He didn't say he knew her."

"Thank you."

The officer hurried away.

"731 Harborview Lane," Ava said.

She and Metford rushed to the vehicle again. Ava's heart raced. If they got there in time, they might be able to pick up Chloe's trail before she got too far. If her arm and nose were broken, the pain might slow her down.

"Jasper's a big guy, Ava," Metford said.

"I know."

"He probably hurt her bad if they fought."

"I would bet he did. Worse than he said to the 911 operator. Call the rest of the team to meet us there. We might need the help searching the neighborhood for her."

The house at 731 Harborview was a McMansion; a super-sized monstrosity of a house that stood out in stark and ugly contrast among the more reserved and much smaller New England-style homes of the elite neighborhood.

The home said a lot about its owner, and Ava knew when the property was researched, it would be revealed that Jasper Halloway had the house built.

"Where's Halloway?" Metford asked as he and Ava walked toward the police officers at the front of the house.

"He's already gone to the hospital, is my guess. He called for police and ambulance, and I'm sure he didn't call an ambulance for Chloe."

"What if it's not her?"

"It's her." Ava asked the cops for the rundown on the events.

Ashton, Dane, and Santos arrived, and Ava left Metford to give them the highlights while she walked around back to the pool. She wanted to start searching as quickly as possible.

CHAPTER THIRTY-SEVEN

IT DIDN'T TAKE BUT A FEW SECONDS TO LOCATE THE LOUNGER WHERE Halloway had been attacked. The chair had been overturned and smeared with a streak of blood. More blood had dripped onto the whitewashed concrete under the lounger. The attacker must have gotten in at least one good hit with the knife.

From the concrete, Ava followed the blood drips away from the pool and into the grass, where she lost the trail a couple of times. The second time she did, she stood and scanned the expansive yard. It was the first large yard she had seen anywhere in Baltimore.

At the end of the property, there were two trees and just beyond them, a low, white fence. Even from her distance, the bloody smear on the white pickets stood out like a neon sign. She rushed to the fence.

"Ava!" Metford yelled.

"She's crossed the fence," Ava replied without looking back. She hoisted herself easily over the fence a few feet from the blood smears.

How much harder would it have been for Chloe to get over the fence if her arm was broken?

The blood trail was easy to pick up on the other side. Chloe had been hurt badly. Maybe even stabbed, from the look of the trail.

"We're behind you," Metford said, closer.

"Keep an eye out. She went this way. She could be anywhere."

"Got it."

The soft *whumph* of three more sets of feet hitting the grass as her team crossed the fence was a comforting sound. With all of them out there looking for Chloe, it would be faster.

Circling around the first house, Ava startled and pulled her gun as a door flew open and an angry woman demanded to know who she was and what she was doing on private property.

Ava re-holstered her gun, nodded to Dane to speak to the woman, and kept tracking Chloe.

Entering the second yard, Ava got the sense that the house was either empty or rarely used. Maybe a vacation property. The grass was tall, and the chairs on the porch had been turned upside down. Something people often did along the coast to prevent winds from tossing their outdoor furniture around and damaging it, or neighboring property.

She spotted a quarter-sized spot of blood on the left side of a lattice archway decorated with climbing flowers. Stepping through the arch, Ava saw another spot on the siding of the house. It looked like someone had put their bloody hand on the siding for balance. Chloe was probably getting weak from her injuries, and possibly blood loss.

A few feet from the spot on the siding, the small door to a crawlspace was unsecured and slightly open. Cautiously, she stood behind the door and pulled it open so that the wood was between her and the crawlspace. If Chloe lashed out to defend herself, the door would offer some protection.

"Hello, are you under the house? I'm Special Agent James with the FBI. If you're under there, answer me."

The rest of the team gathered behind Ava.

"You sure she's under there?" Santos asked in a low voice.

Ava nodded and pointed at the blood on the siding. "The door was unsecured and slightly open. Just walking by in the yard, I might have missed it."

Ava called out again, but no one answered. "Chloe, are you under there? Chloe Williams. We're with the FBI. You're safe now. You can come out."

After a few seconds, Ava pulled out her flashlight. "I'm going in."

"No," Metford said immediately.

"He's right," Santos said. "That's tight quarters, and you don't know that it's Chloe."

"I agree with them," Ashton said.

"If she's had a psychological break, there's no telling what she's capable of," Dane added.

"Doesn't matter. I'm going in. I can talk to her, get her out, and get her some help. She obviously needs medical attention. We don't have time to wait for a rescue team to get here. She's lost too much blood." She dropped to her hands and knees, turned on the small LED light, and clamped it between her teeth until she got under the house.

"Ava, come back," Metford said, hovering at the opening. "Don't go in there."

She put the light in her hand and turned as much as she could in the narrow space between the foundation wall and the pillar. "Do not follow me in here. I won't have any room to move if you do. All of you stay out there. That's an order." She turned back and began moving along.

To her left, the ground rose steadily until the house was no more than a foot above it. In front of her, the earth rose and fell, making some spots tight enough that she had to go down to her elbows and stretch her legs out behind her. The disturbed dirt and occasional spots of blood in front of her let her know she had been right. She just hoped she was right about the perpetrator being Chloe.

After several feet, the crawlspace opened up into a room. Flicking the light around at the entrance, she spotted a bulkhead to the right side. The room was an unused root cellar, but a few large baskets, a few empty potato sacks, and two sets of wall shelves remained as testament to the room's intended use.

Glad to have standing room finally, Ava turned backward and dropped into the room. The shelves were merely slabs of rough wood that had been planed to similar thickness with stacked cinderblocks as spacers.

Chloe was huddled at the far end of one of the shelves.

"Chloe?" Ava asked in a low voice. "Chloe, I know you're hurt. I'm here to help you."

Had she been so institutionalized that the mostly empty dirt room had felt safe to her? Had she retreated there because that's the only thing she could relate to after what she had endured at the hands of all those men?

Ava took a step toward the girl. "Please, Chloe, let me help you. We need to get you out of here so you can get medical help."

The girl spun suddenly, lashing out with a knife. Ava leaped backward, barely dodging the blade.

"Chloe, stop. I'm not here to hurt you." She stepped back again as Chloe advanced, her teeth bared, the knife high.

"That's what you always say!" she screamed. "Never again! I'm not going with you. I'll kill you! All of you!" With every word, the knife arced downward or side to side.

The only light came from the bobbing flashlight in Ava's hand. She couldn't get a good bead on the knife with the light moving so erratically. She tossed the light aside and ducked another swipe at her face. The blade sliced the air in a shrill whistle. She might be a kid, but Chloe was not playing around with the knife. She intended harm.

Ava walked backward, watching the up, down, right, left of the blade. As her back hit a wooden support post, she jabbed with her left hand, hitting Chloe's wrist and knocking the knife out of her hand.

Without missing a beat, Chloe kicked Ava in the shin as hard as she could. Ava yelped in pain and shoved Chloe away. The injured girl stumbled backward, lost her footing in a pile of potato sacks, and fell hard.

"Chloe, stop. I'm not the enemy. I know what those men did to you, and I'm here to help you."

"Bullshit." She was on her feet quick as a cat, and ready to pounce again at the first opportunity.

"I don't want to hurt you, but I won't let you continue to attack me, either."

"Of course you want to hurt me. All of you do."

She moved toward Ava, holding her injured arm close to her body. Dried blood coated her upper lip and chin. Her eye was bruised, and her cheek was swollen. When she moved, Ava saw that her shirt was blood-soaked under the injured arm.

"Are you cut or stabbed?"

Chloe bent and picked up a large, smooth rock.

"Did he cut your arm? Your side? How bad are your injuries, Chloe?"

Chloe lunged forward, screaming wordlessly. Ava had nowhere to move out of the way. Her only option was to shove forward and take Chloe to the ground, although she feared injuring the girl further. When she felt them falling, Ava let go of Chloe and put out her hands so her full weight wouldn't smash into the girl.

Chloe didn't hold the same consideration for Ava. She brought the rock up in a full, arcing swing even as they fell. The expression of pure hatred on her face stunned Ava, and she realized too late that the rock was still in motion.

A split-second before her hands touched the earth, the rock made contact with the side of her face and knocked Ava to the side. The strength in that hit was far beyond what Chloe should have been able to muster.

Addled, Ava rolled to the side and put a hand quickly to her face to assess the severity of the damage. Chloe scrambled toward her, kicking up a cloud of dust. Running on training and instinct, Ava vaulted to her knees and then to her feet as Chloe neared. The sudden, unexpected movement threw off the girl's aim, and Ava grabbed the hand gripping the rock. Chloe tried to bite Ava's arm. It was obvious there would be no reasoning with her.

Ava yanked Chloe's arm down and spun her. After swiftly disarming her, Ava wrapped her up into a chokehold.

Someone hammered at the bulkhead from the outside. Chloe thrashed and bucked, but Ava took her to the ground and wrapped her legs over Chloe's so she couldn't kick.

"Stop! For the love of God, just stop!" Ava bellowed in the girl's ear.

The bulkhead flew open and light flooded in, temporarily blinding Ava. She squeezed her eyes shut against the sudden brilliance.

The team rushed down the steps and into the root cellar.

Realizing that she was not going to be able to escape or continue to fight all of them, Chloe strained upward and screamed. The sound was ear-splitting and went on for several seconds. When it was over, she collapsed completely limp against Ava.

"She's out," Santos said. "Unconscious. Let her go, Ava."

Ava loosened her grip. "I didn't choke her out. I was just holding her." Santos and Metford hauled the girl off Ava. Dane and Ashton dropped to their knees beside Ava and started checking her for injuries. She swatted at them. "I'm fine," she said, pushing to a sitting position. "Holding her was like trying to hold onto a tiger. Watch her injured arm. I think it's broken like Halloway said. She's bleeding from the arm or her side, too. I couldn't tell which."

"It's her side," Santos said. "Nasty deep cut there."

"Her knife is over here." Ava tried to stand, but the room spun and she ended up back on the ground.

"You're not fine," Dane said. "You're probably concussed. What did she hit you with?"

Ashton put his hand behind her neck and urged her to lie back. "You need to be still for a few minutes. There are two ambulances on the way."

Ava pointed to a rock on the floor against the wall. "The rock. She brained me with it after she tried to Anthony Perkins me with the knife." She pointed over her head in the general direction of the knife.

"This is why we didn't want you to come in here," Metford said sternly. "Should have waited for the rescue team. From the looks of you, she wasn't close to dying. She would have been fine until they got here."

"And if you had given us a little time, we might have realized the crawlspace led to the root cellar, and we could have opened the bulkhead to extract her," Ashton said in a low, even tone.

"Just make sure she gets medical treatment, but do not let her go in the ambulance alone. I'm telling you, just stay with her, and be ready for anything."

"I'll ride with her," Santos said.

"Dane, you go with her, too. One of you ride up front, the other in the back with Chloe. She starts fighting, you strap her down, cuff her, whatever it takes. She's convinced that everyone is out to hurt her."

The second ambulance arrived and the EMT wouldn't take no for an answer. Ava needed to have X-rays at the hospital, and she couldn't drive until she had been thoroughly checked by a doctor.

Too exhausted to be very mad, she grumbled, but went with them.

"We'll be right behind you," Metford said.

Ashton raised a hand before turning back to the root cellar.

Ava laid back and closed her eyes. She could feel every heartbeat in her face and head, and her shin felt as if it were swelling. Making sure Chloe was safe had been worth it. No matter what came after, at least the girl wouldn't be living in hell and torture anymore. At least she would be free of that.

CHAPTER THIRTY-EIGHT

"Coming through!" a man yelled. His voice cut through the droning constant noise of the hospital.

Ava moved to the side of the hallway and pressed herself against a rack of medical supplies. A team of nurses and doctors rushed past her calling out the vitals of the woman on the gurney.

There were beds in the hallway and pushed up around the nurses' station of the emergency department. Some patients groaned and writhed under the white covers while others lay completely still, and the only sounds came from the machines hooked up to them. Ava made her way out of the emergency department. People gave her only passing, cursory glances. The butterfly bandages over the cut on the side of her head did little to obscure the purple bruising or the swelling.

Metford and the others stood and sat in a waiting room. They gasped in unison when she entered.

"Did the doctor say it was okay for you to be up walking around?" Santos asked, hurrying to Ava's side.

"I'm fine." Ava smiled. The pain spiked in the side of her head from the movement, and she dropped the smile almost instantly.

"I remember the last time you said that," Santos stated, stretching an arm behind Ava as if afraid she might fall.

"You don't look fine," Metford said.

"Are you concussed?" Dane asked.

"No." Ava shifted her eyes to the side. That wasn't exactly the truth, but if she told them what the doctor's initial evaluation was, they would want to sideline her just like Dr. Davis had wanted to do. It had taken the better part of half an hour to convince the doctor otherwise.

"What did the doctor say?" Ashton asked.

"Not much. Which room is Chloe in?"

"Nuh-uh," Santos said. "You're slick, but not that slick. What did the doctor tell you?"

Ava took a breath. "I'm fine. Is she through this door?" She pointed to the door to the left.

Santos scowled. "You did talk to him, didn't you?"

"Yes, and it was a her. Dr. Fran Davis."

"And?" Metford asked moving in front of her, blocking her path to the door. "Did you send all of us to find Chloe because you didn't want us to hear what the doctor had to say?"

"Don't be silly." She sidestepped him and went out the door.

The team followed her.

"Don't tell us," he said. "That's fine. I'll just go by and speak to the doctor before we leave."

"Fine. If it makes you feel better, go ahead." Ava slowed at the first door on the left and peered inside. It wasn't Chloe's room. She continued on.

"It's the next one," Dane said. "The nurses were with her about five minutes before you came in."

Nodding, Ava stepped to the threshold and knocked on the open door.

Chloe acknowledged Ava and the team with a look but said nothing.

They walked inside and Ashton closed the door. He stood near it to prevent anyone from walking in unannounced.

Bruises had bloomed over Chloe's face. Some were yellowish-green while others had already turned deep blue and edged toward black. Her lip was split, her nose had been taped across the bridge, and both eyes were swollen. Her right arm was in a bright pink cast and resting in a mesh sling.

"Chloe," Ava said. "We need to get some information from you about the things that happened to you over the last year."

Chloe scoffed and turned to stare out the window. Not that it was much of a view. Pavement, parked cars, and people walking to and from the hospital's main entrance.

"We know you were abducted in San Diego over a year ago. We're trying to get ahold of your parents so they can come out and be with you."

"Won't do any good. They won't come, and I don't even blame them."

"I'm sure that's not true. They will be overjoyed to learn you are alive. They never stopped looking for you." Ava wasn't sure that was the truth, but she knew Chloe's family had done everything in their power to keep Chloe's face and information circulating through the city for several months.

"If they gave half a damn about me, I wouldn't have been on the street that day."

"So, what, did you have an argument with them? If that's it, it's in the past. Trust me, they aren't worried about whatever it was you argued over."

A tear slipped down Chloe's cheek. She didn't move to swipe it away.

"Chloe, do you know who took you? Can you give us a description?"

"You can't catch them. There are too many of them."

"What about the men who kept you in that house on Ashburn Street? Can you describe them?"

She shook her head. It was a very slight movement. More tears trekked down her cheek. Ava's heart pained for the girl trying to be so strong when, surely, all she wanted was to break down and let out all the pain.

"I'm not stupid, you know," Chloe said, still staring out the window.

"Of course not," Ava said.

"All we want to do is make those men pay," Santos said. "The men who hurt you."

Chloe surprised them all by laughing. She rolled her eyes and wiped away the tears which seemed to have instantly stopped flowing. "It wasn't just me they hurt. They hurt a lot of girls."

"All you have to do is talk to us, and we'll do everything we can to make them pay."

"I told you, I'm not stupid. I'm a murderer. You won't just overlook that like it's nothing. Doesn't matter how much I 'talk' to you. Doesn't matter how much information I give you, I'm still going to prison for killing the nasty pricks."

"You're right. We can't overlook it, but considering what you went through—"

"Would someone open my window, please?" Chloe interrupted, turning tortured, pleading eyes to them. "I want to feel as much fresh air as possible before…" She looked back to the window.

"I'm sorry, but the windows don't open, Chloe," Metford said. "It's a safety thing in most hospitals."

She laughed again. "Why not? Am I going to plunge a whole three feet to my death?" She shook her head.

"We really need you to talk to us, Chloe," Ava said. "If we don't stop these people, they are going to hurt other women, other girls just like you."

Chloe nodded and looked at each of them in turn. For just a moment, she was a normal teenager, a little rebellious and a lot scared.

"Fine. I'll talk, but just to you." She looked at Ava. "I don't want to talk about it to… to *all* of you. It's humiliating." Tears welled but didn't spill as she lowered her head.

Ava gestured to the others. "I'll meet you back in the waiting room when we're finished. It's all right." She waited for them to leave and shut the door. "Okay, they're gone. It's just us now." Ava moved closer to the bed.

"Where do I start?" The girl's voice sounded small, fragile.

"Wherever you want to start. I'll just listen, and when you're done, if I have questions, I'll ask then. Okay?" She took out her notepad and pen.

After clearing her throat, Chloe coughed lightly. "Would you do something for me first?"

"If I can." Ava set the pen and pad on the windowsill above the heater.

"Could you please get me a glass of water from the bathroom sink? I'm dried out and they didn't bring me anything to drink yet."

"Of course." Ava opened the bathroom door and looked around. "There's no cup."

"It's right here. They left a little one but nothing to put in it."

Ava picked up the foam cup from the bedside table. "It's got ice in it, at least."

"Cold water will be so good. I haven't had any in a long time."

Ava went back to the bathroom and opened the faucet to full flow. "I'll let it run a little so it doesn't taste like chlorine."

The bathroom door slammed shut and something thudded against it from the outside. Ava dropped the cup and grabbed the doorknob. She pushed, but something had been jammed against it on the other side. She pounded on the door.

"Chloe!" she yelled. "Chloe, open this door! You don't want to do this. Open the door now!" she yelled louder.

Glass shattered in the room. Ava called for the others as she put her full strength into pushing the door. When she got it open enough, she squeezed through. The bed had been pushed sideways against it and the wheels had been locked.

The glass from the shattered window lay on the floor, and a rolling stool lay to the side with two of its casters missing. Ava sprinted to the window and yelled for Chloe to stop. The girl ran heedless of pedestrians or moving vehicles. Ava radioed the others and told them Chloe was on the run, and then she leaped out the window and gave chase, her heart in her throat.

She couldn't slip away. If Chloe got away, she might never be caught again. She would do her best to disappear, Ava was sure of it.

Ava gained on the girl as they crossed the massive parking lot. Chloe was tiring quickly and her legs looked as if they were getting wobbly. Her arms began to flop awkwardly, and finally, Ava was a few steps behind.

Something shiny glinted from Chloe's right hand. Ava couldn't make it out but thought it might be a piece of broken glass that had caught in her sling and looked like she was holding something.

Chloe stumbled to a stop. Ava didn't rush up on her; she slowed to a walk, ready to break into a sprint again if the girl took off.

"Chloe?"

The girl stood straight and spun. The shiny thing was in her outstretched left hand. It wasn't a piece of glass. It was a pair of scissors. Ones she probably snagged after the nurses bandaged her side.

"Stay back. I swear on my life I'm not going to live the rest of my life in a damn cage. No way I'm going with you." The tears streamed freely as she brandished the scissors.

"Please, Chloe. I promise I can get you help. This is what I do; I help women just like you."

"And how many of them killed anyone?" She slashed the air in front of her with the scissors. "I killed *five people!*" she screamed. The sobs wracked her body, but she never lowered the scissors.

"I know, and I understand. I do."

"You understand?" She stepped forward with her teeth bared and a wild animal look in her eyes.

Ava recalled that look from earlier. Chloe the scared girl was slipping away, being replaced by the thing that only knew pain and darkness; the thing that knew only violence.

"Please, I'm begging you. Put down the scissors and just let me help you." Ava glanced around. "I might be able to get you out of this. Get you somewhere safe, but you have to trust me."

For a second, reason flashed through her eyes, but then the reason was gone. "No. I don't want to live with this. No one can help me. I'm ruined. You have no idea what they did to me. What they're doing to those other girls."

"What other girls, Chloe? Tell me about them. With your help, I can save them, but if you don't tell me what you know, I can't do anything."

The scissors lowered the tiniest bit, and Chloe looked for just a moment past Ava.

Hearing the approaching footfalls on the pavement, Ava knew the team had caught up. She took her opportunity and leaped forward, grabbing Chloe's outstretched arm.

The violent struggle that ensued was worse than the one in the root cellar. Ava managed to avoid the scissors, but she didn't avoid being headbutted in the nose and mouth. The world swam and Chloe nearly broke free.

Ava held out a hand to the team. "Stay back," she said. "I have her."

Chloe struggled and pedaled her heels against the pavement, moving them closer to the edge of the parking lot. An eight-foot-wide strip of grass separated the parking lot from the busy main road beyond.

Chloe and Ava were locked in a struggle. Metford rushed forward, but Santos blocked him.

"No, she said stay back." She put her hands on his chest. "Come on, we know she's the best at this sort of thing."

He stepped back from the women and paced with his hands on his hips. They were right. He knew they were, but Ava was injured, and as her partner, it was his duty to assist her. Ava would have called it a misogynistic fault with him, but it was there nevertheless, and it wasn't ever going to change.

The struggling duo seemed to stop fighting against one another, and Ava's eyes widened as Chloe's mouth moved. What was she saying? There was no way to hear at this distance. The traffic noise was too loud.

It looked as if Chloe was coiling. Like a snake readying to strike.

"She's going to—no!" Metford yelled, pushing past Santos and Dane. He ran toward Ava and Chloe, but it was too late.

Ava screamed loud and long. Metford reached her and physically turned her to face him as the tires screamed against the pavement.

"No!" Ava screamed. She first pressed her face into Metford's chest, still screaming, and then pushed him away and bolted toward the chaotic scene in the road.

The team was right behind her as she fell to her knees by the broken, bloody body of Chloe Williams. Amazingly, the girl was still gasping and semi-conscious.

The driver of the bus came toward them with his hands on the sides of his head. He wasn't screaming but the sound he was making was close.

"Didn't see her. She just, just, just…" He looked toward the parking lot and made that long moaning sound again.

Ashton and Dane helped him to the edge of the road.

"Somebody help!" Ava yelled. Panic rose inside her. It was not a familiar sensation, and she hated it. "Chloe, Chloe, we're going to get you help. Just hold on." Tears fell from her face and mingled with the blood coating Chloe's face. "Just hang in there, baby. We're getting help." Ava turned to Metford and screamed at him to get someone, anyone.

CHAPTER THIRTY-NINE

Ava walked out of the trauma room feeling completely drained. Metford put an arm around her for support.

"Hey," he said.

"She's gone. She died, Metford. I couldn't save her. They couldn't save her." Her breath hitched, and she wanted to give in and lean on Metford, but she couldn't allow herself that luxury. Not after what she had learned from the strongest teenager she had ever met. She gently pushed Metford away. "I'm okay. I'll be okay. We still have work to do."

"It wouldn't kill you to take a breather, you know," he said.

"No, it wouldn't kill me, and I would like nothing better right now, but there are more young women like Chloe who need me to keep going."

"Is that what she was telling you outside when you were trying to hold her back?"

Ava nodded and then shook her head. "She told me a little out there; the rest of it, she told me before she died. She wanted her last breath to be spent helping save other women and taking down Jasper Halloway. Said she failed to kill him, so he deserved the next worse thing."

"Jasper Halloway?" Metford asked.

Ava motioned for the others to follow them as they left the hospital. At the cars, she gathered the team and told them everything Chloe had told her in the trauma room.

"Halloway owns a farmhouse out in the country," she said. "We need to find that address and get out there fast. Chloe doesn't know how long the girls have been there for sure, but says they came over at the same time as she did. One tried to escape when they were being loaded into the shipping container, and their abductor shot her in the head. He threw the body in with them and sealed the container. She says members of the group took turns tending to the girls and overseeing their male visitors."

"They might have been out there for a while without anyone going to feed them," Metford said.

"Yeah. Halloway and the others likely would not have risked being caught after we turned the heat up on the investigation."

Ashton went to work immediately finding the address of the farmhouse.

Ava was wounded soul-deep at the loss of Chloe. It was such a pitiful waste of a life that could have been saved if only she would have listened. It was even worse because she had suffered so much that she thought she was ruined beyond all hope. The girl knew she'd never be able to live with the memories living in her mind, and she said as much while they were struggling in the parking lot. She had begged Ava to let her die, to kill her and say she was attacking a federal agent. Ava thought she would never be able to get Chloe's voice out of her head begging her to let her die.

"Are we going to pay Halloway a visit now?" Dane asked.

"Not yet. We have to raid that house and find those girls first. He will have them killed if he thinks we're onto him," Ava said.

Ava and the team arrived at the farmhouse within two hours of Chloe's death. The place looked deserted. The grass was high, there were no vehicles in the drive or the garage, no furniture on the porches, and the windows were bare.

The team didn't stop at the house but drove past it to the horse stables with the attached barn. They parked, confirmed that the other teams were on their way, and then circled the structure quietly and with their guns drawn.

The tall grass in the bordering field rasped as the wind soughed through carrying the fresh scent of pine from the mountain in the distance.

All the entrances had been secured with hasps and Master locks. The team called out as they circled the structure again. They called out for anyone who might be inside, and repeatedly announced that they were the FBI, and that they had come to help.

At the big double doors, Ava stopped. "They're in there. We need to break this lock."

"We don't have a warrant," Dane said.

Ava put her ear to the door and looked surprised. "Did you hear that?"

Dane leaned close and then shook her head. "What was it?"

"A woman screaming for help," Ava said. "Metford, get a hammer or something I can use to break this lock."

"I don't hear anyone screaming, Ava," Dane said.

"I heard it plain as day," Ava said.

Catching on, Santos moved forward and confirmed that she heard it, too. She hit the door with her palm and yelled, "Hold on, ma'am! We're coming to help you!"

Dane looked confused and shook her head. "I still didn't hear it."

Ashton came forward, adjusted his glasses, and put his ear to the door. "Yes. I hear that, too. Sounds like more than one to me, though." The whole time he spoke, he held Dane's gaze.

Metford returned with the doorbuster from the trunk. He made his way to the door and drew back. Ava grabbed his arm and yelled for him to stop. She motioned for the doorbuster.

"Give it to me. I'll do it. I was the one who heard the screaming first."

He looked disappointed but handed it over and backed away.

"Oh, now I get it," Dane said.

Santos shushed her. "You mean, you hear the women screaming, too, now?"

"Yeah, yeah, that's what I said, isn't it? I hear them. Sounds like a few."

Ava smiled as she lifted the doorbuster and brought it down on the lock. There was a satisfying pop and snap. The lock dropped from the hasp, and she dropped the doorbuster on the ground. It was good to know that the whole team had her back on this one.

She pushed the doors open.

There were nine women trapped in a room under the horse stables. The only access was a small trapdoor that had been covered over with dirt and hay. The Sea Wolves had fully intended on letting the women starve to death down there, and if not for Chloe, they likely would have.

The other teams showed up. Forensics, emergency medical techs, cops, and more feds. Within a half-hour, the place swarmed with uniforms.

Ava and the team went to their vehicles.

"It's time to get that arrest warrant," Ava said.

Ashton opened his tablet and turned the screen to Ava. "This just came in."

"Ethan Holt is listed as the current owner of the house on Ashburn Street," she said. "Not a surprise."

Ashton swiped the screen and pulled up something else. "This was in an hour ago."

"Well, I can't say I'm disappointed that Ethan was killed," Ava said. "He had held at least six other girls in that house before Chloe," she told the team. "Ash, find all the properties listed under the names of all CBP agents who work at Patapsco."

"On it," he said, getting into the backseat and pulling the door shut behind him.

"That'll take a while," Santos said.

"Nah. Not for Ashton. He'll probably have those records by the time we get back to the city," Ava said. "Six before Chloe, and these nine here." She scoffed in disbelief. "How many before them? How long has this been going on right under everybody's noses?"

CHAPTER FORTY

One of the most satisfying things Ava did during the entirety of the case, except saving the girls at the farmhouse, was walking up to Jasper Halloway and telling him that he was under arrest and then naming off all the abducted and abused girls, including Chloe Williams.

The man was remorseless. He didn't care what happened to the girls. He didn't care that his comrades had been murdered. All he cared was that he had been caught, and that his name was going to be dragged through the mud. His sparkling reputation would be completely ruined. He even had the audacity to blame the victims for his downfall.

The rescued women talked. They talked and talked, naming other members of Sea Wolves on the East Coast, West Coast, and even in the Gulf region. They told the team where to find evidence, where the abductors' stash houses were, and almost every bit of information produced enough evidence for more arrests.

THE FORGOTTEN GIRLS

Some were shocked to learn that there were also female members of Sea Wolves. Emily Harper had not been the only female member at Patapsco. She had been one of three at that facility. There was a total of seven women arrested from San Diego to Florida and Maryland. Ava was disgusted, but not shocked. She had seen it many times before, and after the first few times, she stopped being shocked. Women could be as ruthless and money-hungry as any man alive.

In total, there were seventy-one arrests and forty-seven rescued victims. Ava couldn't help but feel good about that. It was a swift take-down that spanned the coastlines. It happened in weeks, not months or years. Even if there were ones who got away, they posed less of a threat with their network decimated.

Two of the local Sea Wolves members from Patapsco, David Ramirez and Julia Thompson, took the coward's way out as the FBI surrounded their house. Ava couldn't feel sorry for them.

Three months later, Ava and the team had returned to Fairhaven and their regular jobs. The case was spoken about like it was a war story among the agents. Most people talked about the cold-blooded teenager who was a brutal killer without a conscience in that case. Ava didn't agree with them, and made a few enemies when she defended Chloe in those instances.

She understood why Chloe killed the CBP agents who had brutalized her for so long. She understood the girl's motivations, but she also knew Chloe was a murderer because of those horrible circumstances.

Was it really her fault that she turned out that way? Ava was torn on the answer to that. Part of her believed it wasn't Chloe's fault. It was the fault of rotten people like Ethan Holt and Jasper Halloway. The other part of her believed Chloe could have fought the urge to take out her anger in the form of revenge killings.

Being with her best friend, Molly, for so long, Ava understood that a person who was trafficked out for a prolonged amount of time, a person who suffered at the hands and whims of others, could mentally break that victim to the point that their perception of right and wrong was permanently skewed or just became nonexistent.

Metford seemed to be the only person who tried to understand Ava's dilemma about Chloe. They bonded over the subject and over many cups of coffee from various shops around Fairhaven. He was there to listen when no one else could be or would be. Just like he was there for her after Jason Ellis, even though she pushed him away, Metford was always there to offer his support.

"Am I losing my edge?" she asked over the coffee.

"You aren't losing your edge. I'd say you're still the sharpest edge on the team," Metford said. "Why would you even ask that?"

She shrugged. "Should I feel sorry for a killer?"

He thought about it for a minute. "Chloe was more than that. First and foremost, she was just a kid. She was sixteen when they grabbed her and thrust her into that vicious life full of pitiless people who used and abused her whenever and however they wanted. Before she was a killer, she was just a regular kid. She didn't want to become a serial killer. It's not like she grew up fantasizing about murdering people. I guess you'd call her a result of her environment. You still saw that regular kid. You connected with that part of her; wanted to save that part."

"I tried. I keep going over what I could have done differently and wondering if it would have made a difference."

"I was there. Remember? Nothing short of shooting her would have stopped her."

The pain pierced her heart again, as it was wont to do at the most unpredictable times. "I couldn't save her."

"You can't save everyone, Ava. It's just not possible. But look at how many you did save. Fifty-six young women have you to thank for their rescue from those monsters. That's a lot of lives saved. If you're going to dwell on something, dwell on that."

She finished her coffee and dropped it into the trash bin by the bench as they passed by. "I didn't save them."

"The ones you didn't physically save, you orchestrated their rescue. Same thing in my book."

"No. I didn't save any of them. Chloe did that for the girls in the horse stable, and they, in turn, saved the other forty-seven along the coasts. I was just the mouthpiece passing along information they gave me."

"And that's all right, isn't it?" He smiled as they neared the offices again.

"Yeah. It is, actually. I'm okay with it."

And she was.

EPILOGUE

Helping Hands was the closest shelter to Ava's home. She volunteered there, and though her participation was sporadic due to her work schedule, her efforts seemed to be appreciated by staff and those in need. It was a fulfilling way to spend her days and evenings instead of sitting around at the house dwelling on how bad the world had gotten lately. She had taken up the motto of becoming the change she wanted in the world. Even the smallest kindness, the tiniest sacrifice contributed to the good of the entire world.

While working at the shelter, she heard horror stories from women, and would instantly be tempted to explain how they could have made themselves safer, less of a target for rapists, abusers, traffickers, and just jealous lovers, but she held back. She didn't want the women to ever think she was discounting their pain, their fear, or their efforts.

It was during one of those encounters when she had an epiphany. She could help to educate women about how to be safer and avoid situations that could lead to abduction or trafficking. She could teach them about situational awareness, and give them pointers on self-defense, and legal tactical weapons that anyone could carry.

She worked with many people to get the education center up and running, as a branch of Hope Horizons Foundation, a larger non-profit that educated girls and boys in elementary school and advocated for victims' rights in trafficking cases. When The Hope Education Center was finally realized, she started inviting people she knew to help with the courses and to speak at the center. It wasn't anything nearly as large or far-reaching as Aunt Kay's charities, but it made an impact in Fairhaven. Ava was fine with keeping it local for the time being.

Molly wanted to help. She agreed to share her story and what she had learned through her ordeal and even after while she was recovering from the physical aspects. Ava could not have been happier.

Before long, between her job, volunteering at the shelter, and overseeing most of the events and classes at her education center, Ava didn't have time to dwell on all the bad things in the world. She spent most of her spare time thinking how she could make the world a better place.

Her snake plant grew until she had to get a bigger planter for it. She was getting back to the sense of contentment that had been absent in her life since Jason, and the plant had apparently picked up on it. She ended up with two more snake plants. At some point, she wanted to branch out and try her luck with flowering plants.

After having time to consider why she was feeling contented again, and why that feeling had been gone for so long, she decided it was because, deep down, she needed to be doing something more to make a difference in women's lives *before* they were victims. Until Chloe, all Ava had done was come in after the fact and try to put the pieces back together again, offering to get women financial, medical, and emotional help after they had been victimized.

It was a totally different feeling to help them *not* become a victim in the first place. Empowering women gave her another sense of purpose and achievement, and she was sure it made the women more confident and secure in their own lives.

With The Hope Education Center up and running, everything seemed to be falling into place. It was a whole new world of opportunities, and Ava wanted to embrace it with open arms.

While she rearranged her office at the center for the third time that week, she answered her phone. She instantly recognized the voice. She hadn't heard it in months, and to be honest, the case had slipped from priority to back-burner in the months since Chloe died.

"Detective Reinhold?" she asked.

"You hadn't forgotten about me, had you?"

"No, no, I hadn't forgotten about you. It's just been a while. What's up?" Her heart sank. The only reason he called was if there was a development in the art murders case.

"There's been progress on the art murders."

Was that going to be a case that haunted her forever? One that chased her down the halls of time, screaming and wailing about her failure to solve it?

Looking around the office, she shook her head. Not if she could help it, it wouldn't.

AUTHOR'S NOTE

Dear Reader,

Thank you so much for joining me on this journey and for reading *The Forgotten Girls!* After finishing this book, I needed a full day to unwind. Because, wow, this one was intense. When I need to decompress, I turn to two of my favorite hobbies: baking and crocheting. I am never far from a hook and yarn, and in fact, my favorite place to write is in my crochet room. There's something about creating intricate stitches or the scent of something sweet baking that helps reset my mind after diving deep into a case like this one. Recently, in my Facebook group *Coffee and Cases with A.J. Rivers*, I shared my hobbies and got to hear about some of my readers' favorite ways to relax. If you haven't had a chance to stop by, I hope you do and share—what's your go-to way to unwind?

Speaking of unwinding, Ava won't be getting that luxury anytime soon. Her next case in The Hidden Vendetta pulls her straight into a deadly game of cat and mouse when a seemingly random diner shooting turns out to be anything but. What looks like a robbery gone wrong quickly unravels into something far more sinister—a tangled web of hidden identities, a powerful arms dealer with a vendetta, and a past that refuses to stay buried. As Ava follows the trail of deception, she finds herself in the crosshairs of a ruthless enemy willing to kill anyone who gets in their way.

Your support and feedback mean the world to me. I love hearing what you adored, what caught you off guard, or even what kept you guessing—it all helps me grow as a writer and keeps me on my toes! If you enjoyed this latest installment, I'd be incredibly grateful if you could take a moment to leave a review. Your thoughts not only inspire me but also help fellow readers discover Ava's adventures.

Thank you for your support and for joining me on this journey. Ava and the team are counting on you, and I can't wait to see where our adventures take us next.

Yours,
A.J. Rivers

P.S. If for some reason you didn't like this book or found typos or other errors, please let me know personally. I do my best to read and respond to every email at mailto:aj@riversthrillers.com

P.P.S. If you would like to stay up-to-date with me and my latest releases I invite you to visit my Linktree page at *www.linktr.ee/a.j.rivers* to subscribe to my newsletter and receive a free copy of my book, Edge of the Woods. You can also follow me on my social media accounts for behind-the-scenes glimpses and sneak peeks of my upcoming projects, or even sign up for text notifications. I can't wait to connect with you!

ALSO BY
A.J. RIVERS
Emma Griffin FBI Mysteries

Season One

Book One—The Girl in Cabin 13*
Book Two—The Girl Who Vanished*
Book Three—The Girl in the Manor*
Book Four—The Girl Next Door*
Book Five—The Girl and the Deadly Express*
Book Six—The Girl and the Hunt*
Book Seven—The Girl and the Deadly End*

Season Two

Book Eight—The Girl in Dangerous Waters*
Book Nine—The Girl and Secret Society*
Book Ten—The Girl and the Field of Bones*
Book Eleven—The Girl and the Black Christmas*
Book Twelve—The Girl and the Cursed Lake*
Book Thirteen—The Girl and The Unlucky 13*
Book Fourteen—The Girl and the Dragon's Island*

Season Three

Book Fifteen—The Girl in the Woods*
Book Sixteen —The Girl and the Midnight Murder*
Book Seventeen— The Girl and the Silent Night*
Book Eighteen — The Girl and the Last Sleepover*
Book Nineteen — The Girl and the 7 Deadly Sins*
Book Twenty — The Girl in Apartment 9*
Book Twenty-One — The Girl and the Twisted End*

Emma Griffin FBI Mysteries Retro - Limited Series
(Read as standalone or before Emma Griffin book 22)

Book One— The Girl in the Mist*
Book Two — The Girl on Hallow's Eve*

Book Three— *The Girl and the Christmas Past**
Book Four— *The Girl and the Winter Bones**
Book Five— *The Girl on the Retreat**

Season Four
Book Twenty-Two — *The Girl and the Deadly Secrets**
Book Twenty-Three — *The Girl on the Road**
Book Twenty-Four — *The Girl and the Unexpected Gifts**
Book Twenty-Five — *The Girl and the Secret Passage**
Book Twenty-Six — *The Girl and the Bride**
Book Twenty-Seven— *The Girl in Her Cabin**
Book Twenty-Eight— *The Girl Who Remembers**

Season Five
Book Twenty-Nine — *The Girl in the Dark**
Book Thirty — *The Girl and the Lies**
Book Thirty-One — *The Girl and the Inmate**
Book Thirty-Two — *The Girl and the Garden of Bones**
Book Thirty-Three — *The Girl on the Run*

Ava James FBI Mysteries

Book One—*The Woman at the Masked Gala**
Book Two—*Ava James and the Forgotten Bones**
Book Three —*The Couple Next Door**
Book Four — *The Cabin on Willow Lake**
Book Five — *The Lake House**
Book Six — *The Ghost of Christmas**
Book Seven — *The Rescue**
Book Eight — *Murder in the Moonlight**
Book Nine — *Behind the Mask**
Book Ten — *The Invitation**
Book Eleven — *The Girl in Hawaii**
Book Twelve — *The Woman in the Window**
Book Thirteen — *The Good Doctor**
Book Fourteen — *The Housewife Killer**
Book Fifteen — *The Librarian**
Book Sixteen — *The Art of Murder**

Book Seventeen — Secrets in the Acadia
Book Eighteen — The Forgotten Girls

Dean Steele FBI Mysteries

Book One—The Woman in the Woods*
Book Two — The Last Survivors
Book Three — No Escape
Book Four — The Garden of Secrets
Book Five — The Killer Among Us
Book Six —The Convict
Book Seven —The Last Promise
Book Eight —Death by Midnight
Book Nine — The Woman in the Attic
Book Ten — Playing with Fire
Book Eleven — Murder in Twilight Cove
Book Twelve — Under the Mask
Book Thirteen — Hidden Intentions

A Detective Riley Quinn Pine Brooke Mystery

Book One —The Girls in Pine Brooke
Book Two — Murder in the Pines
Book Three — Strangers in the Pines
Book Four — Shadows in the Pines

ALSO BY

A.J. RIVERS & THOMAS YORK

Bella Walker FBI Mystery Series

Book One—The Girl in Paradise*
Book Two—Murder on the Sea*
Book Three —The Last Aloha*

Other Standalone Novels

Gone Woman
* Also available in audio

Made in the USA
Middletown, DE
10 April 2025